Also by Barbara E. Saefke

Remember the Words
Belonging After All

The Jake and Peggy Series
Justice in Omaha

Justice in Omaha

The Jake and Peggy Series

Barbara E. Saefke

Order this book online at www.trafford.com
or email orders@trafford.com

Most Trafford titles are also available at major online book retailers.

Printed in the United States of America.

ISBN: 978-1-4669-7197-4 (sc)
ISBN: 978-1-4669-7210-0 (hc)
ISBN: 978-1-4669-7196-7 (e)

Library of Congress Control Number: 2012923136

Trafford rev. 12/05/2012

 www.trafford.com

North America & international
toll-free: 1 888 232 4444 (USA & Canada)
phone: 250 383 6864 • fax: 812 355 4082

Dedicated to my sister and brother,
Peggy and John

ACKNOWLEDGMENTS

Thank you to the Coffee House Writer's Guild for your support and encouragement.

Thank you to Shirley Sinderson, a special friend and cheerleader.

Thank you to Corinna Neff, my niece, who took pictures around Omaha and found the right one for this cover, the Omaha Courthouse. Thank you for your great photos.

Jessica Haider, thank you for being on the cover of my book.

Thank you to Ben Saefke for taking Corinna's pictures and merging them with Peggy and Jake to create the cover of Justice in Omaha, and for being on the cover.

In matters of truth and justice,
there is no difference between large and small problems,
for issues concerning the treatment of people
are all the same.

—Albert Einstein

CHAPTER ONE

J AKE FARMS WAS instructed to make sure a shady judge in Minneapolis was no longer able to let guilty people off and sentence innocent people to jail. Jake's contact said he wanted him stopped from presiding on the rape trial of Senator Ames' son, and didn't care how Jake did it.

Jake devised a plan, and now he was sitting in the living room of Judge Howard Klein pretending he was a college student at the University of Minnesota, and wanted to interview him about the justice system. Then Jake planned on bringing up the trial in hopes to get information from the judge. Jake was uncertain what would happen after that.

Klein, being the arrogant judge that he was, was wondering why it took so long for someone to realize he was a good judge; and only now, after being on the bench for so long, was someone finally realizing it.

&OCR

Norman, as he was called, was a hired hit man. His contact was anonymous, and Norman didn't particularly care. He was contacted about a job. He did the job, and was paid. That's all he cared about, the money.

Norman was instructed to injure a shady judge in Minneapolis so he could not return to work. In the past, Norman just did away with them.

That way he didn't have to hear them scream, and there was never the possibility of the victim identifying him. For him, it was a business; so he dressed as if he were going to a corporate job, a dark pin-striped suit, white shirt, and a fashionable tie. He even carried a briefcase.

Six blocks away from the judge's home, the cabdriver dropped Norman off, and then he walked the rest of the way. It was dusk, and he noticed the light was on in the den, just as his contact told him it would be. Confident, he rang the doorbell and waited. After several minutes the porch light went on, and a man in his late fifties opened the door.

ꝏႩ

"Excuse me, Jake. I'd better answer the door. My wife probably forgot her key again." Klein went into the foyer and opened the door. He never thought to look through the security hole in the door to see who was knocking.

The visitor didn't say anything, but the look on his face had the judge stepping back into the foyer, but it was too late. The bullet grazed his temple and he fell to the floor. Norman quietly shut the door.

Jake saw everything. The gunman apparently was too cocky to realize someone else could be in the house. He stayed where he was, stunned at what happened. He hadn't encountered this Norman person before, but Jake's contact had warned him about Norman several times.

Jake had never seen Norman's work. He would get into town either before or after the killing, never seeing it, being there, experiencing it.

Jake heard a groan and wiped his face with his hand to clear his head, then went to the judge. He thought of helping him into the chair in the foyer, but realized he had to leave. He wiped his prints off everything he thought he touched. Luckily, he'd declined a beverage earlier. Jake saw the phone, picked it up with a cloth napkin and placed the phone on the floor next to the judge's face, then punched in 911 with the napkin covering his finger.

There was so much blood. Jake took his tablet and pen and decided to go out the back door. He knew he should've stayed to give an account of what happened and to identify the shooter, but reality was the last thing that played on his senses. The urge to flee was so strong he could think of little else.

Jake went out the back door and ran to his car down the block.

ໜ໐ଔ

Norman was now in the bathroom at the Minneapolis—Saint Paul International Airport. In the locked stall, he opened his briefcase and straddled it across the toilet seat. He pulled his jeans and T-shirt from a vacuum-sealed bag. With his slim frame, the suit he was wearing was easily rolled up, fitting nicely in his briefcase. He took out the gun, wiped it down to erase his fingerprints, and wrapped it in a monogrammed towel from the hotel he stayed in last year: Hilton, Los Angeles. He took out a bag with the same hotel name on it and placed the wrapped gun inside.

Before leaving the stall, he mussed his hair with his hands. With all the hairspray he used to hold it down, he took on the look of a punk rocker. He made sure no one was watching, and before he left the bathroom, he dumped the bag in the trash, then went through security.

So far, the disposal of the gun was fail proof. He could get a gun in the poor neighborhoods of any city he visited. Since he raised his price, he didn't get as many jobs as he once did. He thought at a higher price the jobs would stop, but as long as there weren't as many, he was happy. He didn't drink and hang out at bars, and didn't brag to friends about what he did for a living, so there was no chance of getting caught.

The flight attendant offered him a beverage, but he declined. Now was his time to sleep and forget all about what he did to a crooked judge in Minnesota, to forget the pain on the judge's face, and the way his hands held his head before he fell to the ground.

He knew exactly where to shoot to create damage, and a long recovery once the victim was out of intensive care. The judge was to oversee a trial in two days, but the Honorable Howard Klein would be in ICU for several weeks knocking on death's door, and they would get a judge to replace him. But Norman didn't care. He did his part and was paid handsomely for it.

Norman landed in Chicago, hailed a taxi to the train station, purchased a ticket, and waited an hour before boarding for home. He liked the hustle and bustle of the airport, and if he wanted to get a good cup of coffee, he could. However, he enjoyed not having to go through security, taking off his shoes, and emptying his pockets. There was something invasive about that, he thought. He sat back in his seat and closed his eyes. When he arrived home, he was hoping to have a relaxing weekend without traveling.

೮೦೮೪

The ambulance was racing to Fairview Riverside Hospital as an all-points bulletin aired on CNN. *The Honorable Howard Klein was shot in his South Minneapolis home just after dusk this evening. The judge was able to get to the phone and call 911 just before he passed out. Monday morning he was to preside over a long-awaited trial. The courts will decide if they want to continue without him or to wait for the judge's recovery.*

The police want people to be on the lookout for a man in his forties, with meticulously styled hair, glasses, and a birthmark on his left temple.

೮೦೮೪

"Dammit, Ed, with Howard out of commission, we'll lose the case." He poured himself a bourbon. "The senator's kid will be locked up for a long time. I can't think of another judge that would get him off."

"With a jury, there's not much the judge can do anyway," said Ed.

"Howard was prepared to say the prosecution's evidence was inadmissible because it was obtained unlawfully."

"Why do you care about this kid so much? He's slime. He raped a minor and stole money from a safe in the parents' bedroom."

"The senator will be humiliated when his son is found guilty. He's a good man. His son is giving him a bad name."

"I'll ask again. Why do you care?"

Roy just looked at Ed Dawson like he'd said something in a foreign language. He remembered the day the judge came to his home and said he needed help in acquitting the senator's son. Roy didn't want anything to do with it. He and his wife had just talked about the incident and how they both thought it was a tragedy. But now he was offered money to help in the scam, and he couldn't turn it down. If he was ever found out, he knew his wife would leave him. But if she didn't, they would move away and start a new life.

"No reason," he replied. "I wonder how Howard is doing. I'm heading to the hospital. Do you want to come?"

"Hell, no! He's altered other cases before, and I hate to say he deserved what he got, but maybe this is an omen he should seriously consider paying attention to and retire."

∞ℤ℃

"There's no change. He's still asleep," Mrs. Klein told Roy. "You have to find out who did this," she sobbed.

Roy Jackson didn't know what to do. Whenever he and his wife had been to the judge's house, Mary Klein had been a pillar of strength, never letting her guard down and, never letting on she suspected her husband was a joke to the justice system. Now she sat there wiping her eyes.

"Have you been in to see him?"

"I went in briefly, but I couldn't bear to look at him. He's so pale, and all the tubes hooked up to him, I'd rather sit out here."

Yes, that was Mary. If you didn't dress well and look good, she wouldn't give you the time of day. It even held true for her own husband after he'd been shot. Roy didn't know of a single person who looked good after something so tragic happened. "Is there anything I can do for you?"

She pointed toward Howard's room. "Just find whoever did this."

∞ℤ℃

"Senator, you don't look well. Is there anything I can do? A glass of water? Something to eat?"

"No." He rubbed the back of his neck. Senator Gerald Ames just wanted to be alone. If he sent his housekeeper home, she would ask more questions. "I'm okay. I just need to get some work done." He got off the couch, turned off the television, and walked to his desk two feet away. "You could fix me a sandwich for later."

"Yes, sir, I'll bring it to you in an hour."

"Perfect. Thank you, Edna."

Edna had worked for him for over twenty years. She knew his son, his ex-wife, and the woman he'd been dating off and on for the past year. Edna knew everything, but one of the things she didn't know was that his son was no angel.

The senator knew the truth, though. Right after the divorce five years ago, Luke started getting into trouble. Now it escalated to rape, and Ames was embarrassed beyond belief. He thought by paying Howard to get Luke off, the community would think he was innocent. It was a case of mistaken identity. But now, his only hope lay in ICU, going in and out of consciousness.

Senator Ames turned on the television and surfed the channels until he found news about the shooting. Not much had changed. The judge was still in critical condition, and there were no leads on the shooter. The decision about the trial was still up in the air, but they had an inclination that it might be Judge Ann Benton presiding.

If a woman judge was assigned the case, Ames was sure his son would do jail time. He couldn't have that happen. His son needed to get off so he could put this whole incident behind him. He wanted to visit Howard in the hospital, but he knew the press would be all over the story, and he didn't want to call attention to himself, or his son.

ⅈ⅋

Jake Farms had his own contact, but it seemed Norman was getting the same information. Jake tried to get justice without anyone getting killed, and until recently, he had never met Norman. There may have been a purpose for killing in Norman's mind, if there is a justified purpose why people were killed.

One guy was a police officer who was dealing drugs and beating his wife and children. He threatened his wife by telling her he would take the children away and she would never see them again if she ever told on him, all while having a mistress clear across town.

Jake went to the town where the wife lived after Norman killed her husband. Jake stepped in and made sure she and the victims had enough money in case they wanted to move, or to make their life, or the lives of their children better. Money did not solve the disgrace, Jake knew, but he felt he was helping in a capacity he wasn't able to before.

One man was a serial killer and the son of a police chief who was protecting him. Several people were dead, yet the community was unable to bring him to justice with his father protecting him, until Norman killed him.

A female governor was stealing funds, but the one thing she was doing that was very disturbing, she was running a prostitution ring with minors, promising them a better life. The girls would leave home and live on the streets. Not much of a promising life for impressionable young girls, especially when, after a few months, they were never seen again. His contact told Jake she was selling the young impressionable girls and shipping them to different states, but Norman killed her.

Jake was lucky enough to confide in the governor as Jake posed as a shady pimp and wanted to buy some girls. Jake was able to help five teenage girls find a safe place to live and have spending money.

⁊☧

In the morning Jake decided to write down every detail that happened at Judge Klein's home: When he arrived for the interview, the one and only question he had time to ask him, when there was a knock on the door, what Norman looked like, the judge on the floor, and the phone call to 911. He wrote it all down until he had ten pages written. Then he put it away and retrieved the newspaper from the front step, briefly looked through it, and then took a shower. Living in a small town, there wasn't much news except who had a baby, who died, who retired, who got engaged or married, who graduated, and lots of sports. With his backpack, he took his blue Schwinn bike out of the garage and rode to the library a mile away.

Since everyone knew everybody in town, the library didn't require a log-on for their computers. The librarian of forty years would know if you didn't live in town and wouldn't allow you to use the computer. Jake typed Judge Howard Klein into Google, and several entries appeared. One entry caught his attention. The public wondered why he didn't recues himself from the case where Klein's nephew worked for the Foundation

Company which was brought to court on charges of crooked business dealings. It was brought to the attention of the Court of Appeals and declared a mistrial. They took into consideration how egregious it was, even though Klein claimed he didn't know his nephew was working for the company, and his nephew had been suspended.

Another story was about Klein letting a drug dealer go free because of evidence he declared inadmissible. *Judge Klein has been accused of throwing out evidence to make the perpetrator go free*, stated the article.

The next one he clicked on was entered earlier this morning. *Judge Klein is still in serious condition, and the controversial case of the Minnesota senator's son will be in court as scheduled on Monday morning, with a different judge presiding over the case. Senator Gerald Ames is disappointed that they aren't postponing it until Klein gets back to work.* It sounded to Jake like the senator and the judge were planning something shady to prove the son's innocence.

Jake was surprised he was only wounded after seeing all the blood. Next, he put in the name of the senator's son and found a list of crimes he had been charged with in the past. He was always found innocent. It might be a coincidence, but in each case, Klein presided. Jake closed the Internet and looked in the library catalog for some books. He wrote down the numbers, retrieved the books from the shelf, and checked out.

"Jake, aren't you done with that garden yet? It seems these are the only two books left you haven't checked out of the twenty the library owns on gardens."

He laughed. "I planted some flowers last week and so far so good, but I want to put in one of those ponds that I can put goldfish in." He put the books in his backpack.

"They should have those at the hardware store. I don't think you'll be able to get it home on your bike. Let me know when you want to pick it up and I'll send Arnie with his pickup truck."

"You're too good to me, Adeline. I'll let you know."

ଓଟ୍ଗ

Jake parked his bike in the garage and walked around to the backyard. He had rocks outlining where he wanted his pond and a few rocks where he wanted to build a deck sometime in the future. He had to make sure not to spend too much cash at once so people wouldn't talk about where he got the money. That was another problem. He needed to figure out what to do with his money. He donated money to organizations, but felt it wasn't enough. As far as Adeline knew, Jake had his own computer business, but no one knew he didn't have a computer.

Jake was deciding whether or not to give up helping victims. He was helping innocent people, but what Norman was doing was getting to him, especially after he witnessed Judge Klein's shooting. Could he walk away from the people who needed help? He would call his contact one last time and tell him he no longer wanted to work for him. Then he would cancel his answering service. After a while he might just get a phone and a computer. Most people in town had a cell phone and a laptop.

There was a light breeze which gave some relief from the sun. The pink impatiens he'd planted were next to where the pond was outlined. Jake took the lawn chair from the garage and set it up by the rock-outlined pond and promised himself he would come out and enjoy the day after he ate lunch.

CHAPTER TWO

"IT DOESN'T MAKE sense. How could the judge open the door, get shot, walk to the living room, walk back, fall on the floor in the foyer, and not be able to talk after he dialed 911. *And* not leave a blood trail." He looked at his partner. "Not only that, but he was passed out when the paramedics got there. The paramedic said he may have been able to walk or crawl to the phone, but to go back was pushing it."

"And there was no blood anywhere except right where the judge lay when he was shot. Of course with the usual splatters. The lab can determine how close the shooter was to the judge when he shot him, but it still doesn't explain the phone call."

"Do you think his shooter dialed for him and laid the phone next to the judge before he left?"

"Seems far-fetched, but after being on the force for thirty years, I've seen a lot, and not that much surprises me anymore."

⋙⋘

Mary Klein refused to go back into her husband's hospital room. He didn't seem to be getting better. She thought of the past years when their three sons grew up and left home and never kept in contact with their own parents. If they all became lawyers, their father would pay for their tuition, but they had to maintain a 4.0 average. He said none of them would be good lawyers because they'd never applied themselves in high school. There were more put-downs along the way. Mary listened to the verbal abuse and didn't say anything. She enjoyed her husband's money, and if she said anything against him, he would get rid of her, too, like he got rid of anything and everything he no longer had use for.

Mary was devastated when the boys left home right after high school graduation and pursued their education as far away from their parents as they could. She suspected her husband was crooked, but she couldn't prove it. From the things she'd heard, he took bribes from anyone who would pay big money. She realized now that losing her sons was far worse than the money her husband obtained illegally; the prestige was superficial. She felt it every time she went with her husband to social functions. People were whispering behind his back, but she refused to see anything wrong.

Mary knew her sons would not visit their father in the hospital, and they wouldn't call to find out what had happened. So she wouldn't call them either, at least not about their father. She took her purse and left the waiting room. Thirty minutes later she was home with the media waiting for her. She pushed her way through with teary eyes, unlocked the front door and slammed it shut behind her. She leaned against it, crying, not because of her husband, but because of what she did to her sons. She would find them and try to make things right.

The phone rang and she let it go to voice mail.

෨෬

Jake canceled the answering service. He didn't want any more calls. No more calls wanting justice to be served. He was sick to his stomach of what Norman was doing. Jake didn't want to ever run into him again.

He called Adeline and told her he was ready to have Arnie pick up his pond at the hardware store. Jake was happy with his decision to quit. He wanted a family and maybe someday would get a car. But for now, he was content with his landscaping project.

Arnie honked, and Jake ran out and hopped in the truck. "After we pick up the pond, Adeline wants you to come for supper. She made her famous tater tot hot dish."

CHAPTER THREE

THE MORNING THE trial was to begin, Senator Ames visited with his son, Luke, in jail. He didn't want to do it, but thought the public needed to see him show compassion to his son. He was led into a small room where his son was waiting.

"Dad, are you going to get me off?"

Not even a hello. "You've probably heard Howard is in the hospital and Judge Ann Benton is going to preside."

"So! Bribe her! It can't be that difficult. Just offer her more than you did Howard."

What have I done? If I didn't get Luke off on his first offense, he might never have gone on to rape an innocent girl. "It's not that easy."

"Sure it is." Luke got up. "The trial is at nine. You have an hour to fix it so I can get out of here." He knocked on the door and the guard came and took him away.

The senator got in his car and headed to the courthouse with little time to spare.

&OCR&

It took the better part of the afternoon for Jake and Arnie to put in the pond, and once it was finished, they went to the pet store and bought some goldfish.

"The pond looks good, and the little buggers look happy in their new home." Arnie watched the fish swim back and forth. "Adeline would love to see what we did today. Mind if I bring her over sometime?"

"That would be great. I'll invite her over for lunch next week." He looked up at Arnie. "You can come too, of course."

"Sure, set it up and I'll make sure Adeline is on time. It's hard to get her away from that library, you know."

Jake knew all too well. Adeline told him she never planned to retire, even though Arnie was pressuring her lately to quit her job and travel. "Thanks for your help. I'll see you next week."

The news came on the truck radio. "Can I listen to this first?" asked Jake.

Judge Howard Klein is still in critical condition; however, the doctors believe he will pull through to a full recovery. Today starts the trial for Senator Ames' son, Luke Ames. The senator was seen at the jail visiting his son this morning. No one is sure what went on, but he left quickly and sped down the highway toward the courthouse. It's debatable whether Luke Ames will be acquitted or sent to jail for a very long time.

℠℣

The trial was to begin at nine o'clock, and it was now nine fifteen. There were no signs of Judge Benton, and the prosecutor was getting nervous. The senator watched Luke as he smiled and laughed with his lawyer. *He could at least put on a show of remorse,* thought Gerald Ames of his own son. He was ready to leave the courtroom when the bailiff walked in and announced court would be rescheduled at one o'clock that afternoon.

The smile broadened on Luke's face, and the parents of the girl who was raped were crying as they left the courtroom. A twinge of guilt shot through Gerald's whole being, and he had to sit back down. *When does a parent just walk away?* It was a question he'd asked himself a lot lately.

Once he got home, Ames noticed the blinking light on the answering machine. He didn't want to talk to anybody. He turned on the news to see if there was anything about the trial. *The trial has been rescheduled for later this afternoon. It seems Judge Ann Benton didn't show up for court. At this time, we do not have a report on what has happened. We'll keep you updated throughout the day.*

"Senator, are you all right?"

He looked up. "Oh! Edna, take the rest of the day off," he said to his housekeeper. "I won't need you today," said Gerald in a dazed voice.

"I want to go to the trial this afternoon if that's okay with you."

He shook his head and said in a firm voice, "No, Edna, just go home."

Never had the senator talked to her like that. She took her purse off the counter and stormed out the door. This should certainly be one of the times he would need her, she thought, when his son might be convicted of a crime he didn't commit. She would go back tomorrow just to check on him.

CHAPTER FOUR

JAKE WAS AT the library reading about the trial in Minneapolis. *The long-awaited trial of Senator Ames' son, Luke, was postponed until this afternoon. Judge Ann Benton was not able to get to court this morning. This site will be updated by the hour.*

He wondered what had happened. What he really wanted to do was go to Minneapolis and sit in on the trial. It had piqued his interest, and now that the judge didn't show, it was even more intriguing. He knew Norman was the cause. Jake still had to come to terms with the fact that he was the prime witness. The only witness.

Jake was having lunch with Arnie and Adeline and would mention to them he was going to do some traveling. He didn't have to be secretive this time. He would tell them he was going to Minneapolis.

After lunch he would go to the library to make flight and hotel arrangements, and reserve a rental car. He was hoping he could attend the trial and find out just what the senator's son was like: watch his body movements, did he smile a lot, did he seem remorseful. Would the jury find him guilty?

ഇ൰ങ

As he unpacked, he thought that he'd probably be staying awhile because he wasn't sure how long the trial would take. On the news he heard that the trial was delayed until tomorrow morning. No reason of why, or if anything happened to the judge. He hoped to find out.

He took his wallet and his key card off the table and walked to the courthouse on Sixth. Then kept walking in hopes there was a place he could have breakfast, then noticed Peter's Grill on the corner of Eight Street across from St. Olaf's Catholic Church.

He loved the ambiance of Peter's Grill, large booths and a counter in the middle where people sat. The waitress was at his booth with a tall glass of water before he had a chance to look at the menu.

೮೦೦೮

Jake got to the courthouse early on Tuesday morning. He hung out on the main floor and people watched from the bench by the escalator. Through the glass doors he saw a young woman sitting in the courtyard, taking notes. He wasn't sure if she was describing her surroundings or just making a grocery list.

She had long dark straight hair, wore a navy blue suit and comfortable shoes. *Nice legs*, he thought. Then he chided himself for thinking that way. He hadn't noticed such a nice-looking woman in a long time. He didn't get out much.

Jake watched her as she pulled a newspaper out of the leather bag sitting on the ground next to her. He glanced at the clock on the wall. Twenty more minutes and the trial was to begin. He wondered if it really would take place or if he was just wasting his time. It was on a whim that he decided to come to Minneapolis, and he hoped it proved to be worth it.

Jake still didn't know why he had such a desire to be at the trial. He thought maybe it had to do with being a witness. He would figure it out later. Right now, he was where he thought he needed to be.

He sat in the back of the courtroom and pulled out a notebook and pen. Jake wanted to take notes and compare them to what the media had to say on the ten o'clock news that evening.

The mystery woman entered the courtroom. She smiled at him, then sat a row up from Jake. *She's even prettier up close. I want to get to know her,* he thought. She pulled out a shopping catalog. There were turned down pages, and as she went through it, she turned some of the pages back up, as if she wasn't interested in that item anymore. He looked up when he heard the gavel pounding.

She slipped the magazine back in her bag and took out paper and pencil and started writing immediately. They stood when the judge entered the room. Jake was glad that nothing had happened to the presiding judge. Norman had started the chain of events by sending Judge Klein to the hospital. A twinge of guilt shot through his stomach. *Aren't I just as guilty as Norman?* Jake asked himself.

After the opening arguments the judge announced a recess until one in the afternoon. As Luke was being taken away by the guard, he looked toward a man Jake assumed was his dad, and did a thumbs up followed by a wide grin. Jake was disgusted by his behavior and hoped justice would be served.

He looked at the woman sitting in front of him. She took her bag, slung it over her shoulder, and started to leave when Jake said, "Have you eaten breakfast yet?"

Startled, she looked at him. *Not as startled as I am when I heard words coming out of my mouth that I had no intention of saying,* he thought. "No, I haven't," she said.

"The only place I've been to is Peter's Grill about five blocks away if you are up for a walk."

"Sure, I'd love to walk."

"Oh, my name is Jake."

"Mine is Peggy."

They left the courthouse and headed south to Peter's Grill. Peggy was a fast walker, and Jake had to concentrate to keep up to her. "What are you doing at the trial," asked Peggy.

"It sounded interesting, and I wanted to find out firsthand what the outcome would be."

"Me, too." She realized she was walking too fast and slowed down. "I'm a news junkie, and if a case really interests me, I travel and sit in on the trial."

"This is my first one. So, do you think the senator's son is guilty?"

"Of course he's guilty. He wants his father to use his status to get him off, but I think his crime is too horrible this time for his father to make a difference."

"I thought his father did away with Judge Benton, and that's why she didn't show up for court." He looked over at her. "But that's not the case since she showed up today."

"She had an asthma attack and couldn't make it the first day."

Of all the things going through Jake's mind that could've happened to her, it turns out it was something as simple as a medical issue. "How did you know that?" asked Jake.

"I was outside the courtroom that first day when Luke's lawyer came out and I overheard him telling someone what had happened." She looked at Jake. "Luke was mad because he thought his dad had something to do with it. He didn't say nice things to his lawyer."

It was a domino effect, Jake thought. Norman may have brought people to justice by eliminating them, but Jake knew those people had friends and family who loved them and would miss them after they were gone.

Now seeing the other side of what happened, Jake was feeling guiltier about not reporting what he saw. Would the police think Jake did it and just wanted to blame someone else? Could Jake be absolutely certain that he wouldn't be found guilty? People were accused of all sorts of crimes and found guilty on just circumstantial evidence.

For now, he decided not to think about it, but it was something Jake was going to do. Report what he saw. He just didn't know when.

ᔜᘓ

Jake liked the breakfast he had the day before and ordered the same thing. "Peggy, what are you going to have?"

"A burger with fries. I might even have dessert. You never know how long the trial will last this afternoon."

Jake was amazed at her appetite. He wasn't that familiar with how women ate or what they liked. His mom didn't eat that much he remembered, but she liked ice cream on special occasions. Adeline, back home would sometimes skip butter and sour cream on her baked potato.

"Jake, do you work?" She looked into his eyes. "Where do you live?"

Ah, that was a good question. Jake didn't know how to answer that. He did work, but he didn't know how to explain it to people. He wasn't sure how to answer without making up too big of a story, or too big of a lie, so decided to start with where he lived.

"I live in Iowa, and the town is small enough where I don't need a car. I spend a lot of time at the library, and I'm undertaking a landscaping project that I don't know anything about." He paused then asked Peggy the same questions. "Where do you live and work?"

"I *was* working as a secretary at a real estate agency. The agents were all men, and they expected me to get their coffee and order flowers for their wives. One guy even asked me to go buy his wife an anniversary card, forge his signature, and send it in the mail." She took a sip of water. "I bought the card, signed another agent's name in the agency, and sent it to her. I then went back to the office, packed up my desk, and left without a word."

"Then what happened?" asked Jake.

"I got a call the next day from my boss wondering where I was. I told him I was done catering to his personal whims and that I quit."

More and more, Jake liked Peggy, her spunk, her appetite. Or was it he didn't socialize and Peggy was a breath of fresh air? He planned on spending more time with her throughout the trial and getting her phone number after the trial was over. This was one woman he definitely wanted to see again.

ဆာလ

Julie Grange, mother of the girl who was raped, was on the stand. Her pale skin, tired eyes, and droopy shoulders sent a message loud and clear to the audience that she'd been through hell. While answering questions, she looked right at Luke and directed her disdain toward him.

"How long had your daughter known Luke Ames?

"She met him at the library while studying for her final exam. That was a week before he raped her."

"Objection."

"Did he ever come to your house?"

"Just once, when he raped my daughter."

"Objection. Speculation."

Luke had a smile on his face and crossed his arms over his chest.

Tears formed in Julie's eyes, but she told herself she wouldn't cry. She had to get through this and send Luke Ames to jail. She didn't care if he was the senator's son. He was going to pay.

"Did you ever meet Luke Ames?"

"When he came to the house, my daughter introduced him to me."

"What was your impression of him at the time?"

"Objection, Your Honor."

"Stick to the facts, Counselor, not speculation."

"What happened after you were introduced?"

"I had to go to a church meeting, and I left shortly afterward. Now I wish I never would've left the house." She dabbed her eyes with a tissue and continued, "He talked about his dad being a great senator and how much he was doing for the taxpayers and hoped he got reelected."

Senator Gerald Ames grimaced and felt sick to his stomach. He wanted to leave the courtroom, get on a plane, and never come back. *What went wrong with Luke?* he asked himself. *Was it the divorce?*

"Then what happened?"

"When I got back home, I yelled out for Cassie, and when she didn't answer, I went to her bedroom. That's when I found her lying on the floor with cuts on her face and her clothes ripped. I checked to see if she was okay, then I called the ambulance."

"Was Cassie able to say anything?"

"Yes, she said that Luke Ames had raped her, but Luke told her not to call the police because his dad, the senator, would make sure she suffered for it."

Nauseated, Senator Ames got out of his chair, moved slowly out of the courtroom, went down the long corridor as he hung onto the wall, and walked to his car. Once he felt able to drive, he turned out of the parking ramp, drove down the street, and entered the 394 entrance ramp, then kept driving. It was dark when he realized that he didn't know where he was going. He exited at the next off-ramp, found a hotel, and checked in for the night. He stripped off his clothes, took too many pills, crawled into bed, and fell into a deep sleep.

CHAPTER FIVE

JULIE'S TESTIMONY WAS over, and the judge adjourned for the day. Jake didn't want to go to the hotel so early. He enjoyed being with Peggy and yet, he didn't want to wear out his welcome. Being unsure about his relationship with her, he decided to just say goodbye and hoped he would see her tomorrow. But before he could get the words out, Peggy spoke.

"Let's go out for supper." She stood. "Or I'll cook if you don't mind coming to my place."

"I would rather go out to eat somewhere downtown if you don't mind. I'll get lost on the way back from your place."

She was silent a moment, contemplating where they could eat, then said, "Let's go to The Times Bar and Cafe. They have good food.

"Do we drive or walk?"

"I'll drive to your hotel, then we can walk."

ဆုဌ

In the morning, both Jake and Peggy heard the same newscast. *The owner of Motel 6 went to Senator Ames' hotel room early this morning. The senator told the clerk the night before he wanted a wake-up call, and if he didn't answer his phone, he was to come and knock on his door. When he didn't answer, he used the hotel card key and opened the door. Senator Ames was found dead, apparently from an overdose.*

The guard at the jail told Luke about his dad's death. Luke Ames was quoted as saying, "Good, he never did anything for me anyway."

Trial will be postponed until tomorrow.

୫୦୧୫

"That's terrible." Jake took a gulp of the hotel coffee. "What did the senator do that made his son hate him so much?" asked Jake when he called Peggy.

"He probably just loved him and wanted the best for him, and Luke felt that wasn't enough. He wanted his dad to support him in his misdeeds, and when that didn't happen, he decided to hate him," said Peggy.

"You're probably right. We have the day off. What would you like to do?"

"So you don't have to come all the way to Coon Rapids, we could meet halfway. I have to do some landscaping this afternoon, so maybe we can fit that in, too."

"Just let me know where, and I'll be there."

"Take the street in front of the hotel and turn right on Third. Go a couple of blocks and take a left on University. Follow that until you come to a Perkins, which will be around ten miles. We'll start with breakfast and figure out what we want to do after that."

"I'll head out now." He disconnected from Peggy and dialed another number.

"Adeline, this is Jake."

"Jake, your fish are still alive. They even *look* bigger. Maybe I'm feeding them too much." She laughed.

Jake told her he was having a good time, relaxing and enjoying his vacation. Then he asked her if she would take a picture of his pond and send it to his e-mail address. After giving her the information, she said she would go after work tomorrow and take the picture. "I'll probably let Sue upload it to your e-mail for me. She knows computers better than I do."

"Thanks. Gotta go, Adeline. You're a dear. I'll call again. Bye for now."

CHAPTER SIX

"THERE IS A man that has to be brought to Justice. It came to my attention that he is abusing small children." He looked at the other man. "That is the worst crime."

"Why don't you call your contact?"

He slammed his fist on the table and said, "Because I can't find him!"

"I thought you had his number."

The heavyset man stood. "I have his number. I called all day yesterday." He paced the room. "I called this morning, and the recording said the box was full and could take no more new messages."

"Keep calling. He's bound to take his messages before you need the job done."

"No, dammit!" He looked at his longtime friend. "This afternoon, the recording said that the number was disconnected."

"Can't you look up his address on the Internet?"

As he paced, he debated whether he should tell his friend how careful or how stupid he'd been. He'd purposefully never got his last name, address, or home phone so there would never be a connection. He just assumed he would always be there. In the past, he left a message on his answering service, and eventually, it was done as planned. He decided to confess. "I don't know his name." He sat down. "I don't know anything about him, but I'll tell you one thing, I'll find him." He ran his fingers through his hair. "And when I do, I don't know what I'll do . . ."

His friend gave him a worried look. He had been so diligent in bringing heinous criminals to justice. He was dedicated in protecting the world from these people. He was in control, except for now when he could no longer find his contact. He sat down, touched his friend's hand, and said in a consoling voice, "I'm here for you. I'll help in any way I can."

ଛୠଔଷ

Peggy and Jake had a big breakfast. Jake enjoyed getting ideas from the landscaping she was helping people with and seeing her work. She definitely was doing something she loved, and it showed.

He didn't know what life was like outside of Iowa unless he was working, but that was different. He flew in and flew out of anywhere he was needed. Never once did he take a nice long vacation. A mental note was added to Jake's growing list of things to do. But the one thing he really had to do was report that he saw Norman. The sooner, the better.

ଛୠଔଷ

Judge Klein is fully awake. The honorable judge turned up the volume. "Since I'm fully awake, then where the hell is my wife?" *The case he was supposed to try will start again Monday of next week, giving time for the family members to grieve the loss of Senator Ames. Luke, his son, showed no remorse and was actually heard saying, "What a coward," in his jail cell. The Senator's former wife is distraught over the ordeal and was not available for comment.*

"Yes, what a coward," boomed the judge. His nurse was at the front desk, and she needed to give the judge his medication but hesitated because he was unbearable. She liked him a whole lot better when he was unconscious.

She noticed his wife hadn't been to the hospital for three days and wondered if she finally got sick of him, too.

She heard him yelling at the TV and decided to get it over with. She took several deep breaths, threw her shoulders back, and walked toward his room.

 ଊଓଷ

They were back in court, and Jake and Peggy noticed Luke wasn't smiling anymore. He didn't talk to his lawyer, smile at the jury, or make comments to anyone in the courtroom. The people in the courtroom knew Luke's new attitude had nothing to do with his father dying. It had more to do with the fact he got himself into this mess and there was absolutely no one who cared if he was found guilty. Even the senator's housekeeper, who once thought Luke was innocent, now knew he was guilty, and the lawyer for the defense was tired of the whole thing and just wanted it to be over.

"I have no more witnesses, Your Honor." Luke looked at him, then whispered, "What do you mean? You're supposed to be defending me."

"I've done all I can. Called everyone I can to testify." He looked away, then turned back. "You have a crime-filled past. Who else did you want me to call? Your probation officer?"

"The prosecution rests as well, Your Honor."

"We'll reconvene after lunch for closing statements. We'll meet back here at one o'clock."

 ଊଓଊ

Jake and Peggy walked to the Marriot food court, brought Subways back, and sat outside at the courthouse. "I think they'll find him guilty," said Peggy.

"You don't think they'll take pity on him because of his dad?" asked Jake.

Peggy hit him on the arm. "Are you crazy? They better not." Jake couldn't help but laugh. She took a bite out of her sandwich, then asked, "What will you do after the trial?"

Jake finished chewing. "I'll probably head back home."

"Then what will you do?"

"I want to start on my new garden." He looked at her and asked, "What are you going to do?"

"Probably try and find a full-time job with benefits. I'm not sure what I want to do, so it'll be hard."

"Go into landscaping full-time. You're very good at it. Take pictures of the gardens you've worked on and put them in your portfolio. Anyone looking at them couldn't help but hire you."

"I never thought of that. Hey, that's a very good idea. It will be like I'm playing every day and getting paid for it."

They finished eating, then headed back to the courtroom.

⁡⁡⁡

The prosecutor was brief. "Luke Ames was at the house with the woman in her own bedroom when he raped her." He leaned over the railing, looked at each one of the jurors, and continued his closing remarks. "If they let Ames go, given his record of committing a crime and being let go, he will think that he can treat women any way he wants and do it again and again." He sat down.

The defense was just as brief. "Please, I urge you to think of the trauma my client is under because of his father's suicide. Find him innocent and he'll go out and follow in his father's footsteps and be an exemplary citizen in the community."

The judge dismissed the jury.

"So how do we know when they have reached a verdict?" asked Jake.

"I don't think it will take long, so if we hang out here, we should be able to hear someone talking about it." Peggy looked at Jake and realized she didn't want the jury to reach a fast verdict. She wanted to spend more time with him. Maybe she could convince him to spend a couple more days. "Let's go outside for a while though. It's so beautiful out."

They walked around the block a few times, mostly in silence. They each were thinking how they could spend more time together. Jake wanted Peggy to come to his home and help him with his garden, but knew she wanted to find a job. He decided to ask her anyway.

"I know you want to find a job, but I'd love it if you'd come to Iowa and help me with my garden."

"Yeah, I need to find a job." Peggy laughed, then touched his shoulder. "I've never been to Iowa before."

"You'll like it." He quickly took inventory of his house. Was it clean and picked up, when was the last time the guest room had clean sheets, where would he get a car so they could go sightseeing or even go to the landscaping store. Maybe inviting her wasn't such a good idea after all. With no car, he couldn't possibly have her stay at his house. She might get bored or want to go out, and where would they go in Boone, Iowa?

"That will be nice, Jake. No one has ever invited me to their house before."

"I can't believe that. Surely, you've dated a lot."

Embarrassed, she said, "No, not really. I've been too interested in other things to think about dating, and no guy ever took an interest in what I was interested in."

"Well, I'm interested."

After an hour, they went back inside the courthouse. They saw the lawyers come in and head back to the courtroom. Jake and Peggy followed. Some people had just stayed in the courtroom waiting. The jury was brought in. The written verdict was taken from the head juror, given to the judge, then it was given back to the head juror.

"Please, read the verdict," said the judge.

Luke had a big smile on his face, knowing the jury would find him innocent. No way would he follow in his father's footsteps, or become a good citizen. He enjoyed being in control too much for that. Next time, he would watch what he said and did, and not get caught next time.

The juror cleared his throat, the piece of paper held tightly in his hand, his voice shaky as he said, "Your Honor, we find the defendant . . . guilty."

Immediately, the grin left Luke's face, his mouth dropped in shock, and he glared at his lawyer. The bailiff came and handcuffed him. Luke was screaming about injustice as he was escorted out of the courtroom. But justice had been done. Now the family of the victim would wait for the sentencing which would happen in two weeks.

CHAPTER SEVEN

"ARE YOU GOING to wait in Minnesota for the sentencing?" asked Peggy, anticipating the answer to be no.

"I thought I'd go home." He looked at her. "I can read what the sentencing is on the Internet." He couldn't take his eyes off her. "Or, you can call me and tell me."

"I'll call you for sure. We've been in this together. It's the least I can do."

"When I get back to the hotel, I'll call the airlines."

"Why don't you wait a few days? I'll show you the sights." She took his arm. "There's more to Minnesota than nurseries to buy plants."

"I enjoyed that part the most. We could go back, and I'd never get sick of it."

I can't believe Jake likes the same things I do! She loved the nurseries, too, and could never get enough. She would ask him to go to one more place and see if he likes that, too.

As they walked to Peggy's car in the ramp, she asked, "Would you like to go to an apple orchard? I can make a great apple pie."

He was silent, then took her hand, and stopped walking. She faced him. "I'm not exactly sure why you asked me that." Peggy thought she had said something wrong and hoped he wasn't upset. "I was thinking the same thing and would love to go to an apple orchard." He took her by the shoulders. "Let's make sure we have enough cinnamon ice cream for the pie."

She looked into his blue eyes. "We'll have to go to the store and get some. I've never had cinnamon ice cream before. It must be good."

He dropped his hands from her shoulders, and they started walking again. "It's very good. Adeline had it once, and I loved it. It's only noon. We have the rest of the afternoon. I can always call the airlines later."

"There is one by Stillwater. We have to buy a pumpkin, too." She opened the car door and looked across at him. "Let's pick up some steaks. You grill and I'll bake."

Jake followed Peggy home in his car and made sure he wrote down every direction so he could find his way back to the hotel.

ଚଠ

That afternoon, they walked around the orchard and bought apples. Peggy picked out a pumpkin—one that was lopsided, but she said she liked those the best. They stopped at the store and picked up fixings for supper and cinnamon ice cream.

"I can't wait to get home. I'm starving." Jake slipped when he said home, but Peggy didn't say anything, and he wasn't going to point out the error. He really enjoyed Peggy's company. As far as decorating her apartment, she stuck to the basics, nothing more. But unlike Jake, Peggy had a computer, cell phone, and a car.

ଚଠ

They were sitting on the couch. "I'm so full. I'm glad we saved the pie for later." Peggy took his hand and stood. He did the same. "Let's go for a walk, we'll feel better." She wasn't sure if she really wanted to go for a walk, or if it was to make him forget he had to call the airlines.

ଚଠ

"Okay, I'll ask you one more time. Why didn't you get his personal information? Do you even know his first name?"

"It's Jake, and I don't know why I didn't get his information. He was reliable. I didn't need anything more than his first name."

"Don't you have a contact at the phone company? That lady you used to date, what was her name?"

"Nell. I forgot about her. After several months, she said she didn't have time to date. She was promoted and was working most of the time. Maybe she'd like to go for a drink tonight."

耹❧

"The walk felt good. Now I'm ready for pie and ice cream," said Jake.

They went to the kitchen. Peggy sliced large pieces, and Jake put a scoop of ice cream on each piece of pie. They sat at the table and savored every bite.

"I'd better get back to the hotel," said Jake. "I'll call the airlines in the morning. I really enjoyed the day." He thought about kissing her, but said good night instead.

I wished he would've kissed me, thought Peggy.

Peggy didn't date much, and what she called the 'weirdos' she attracted wanted to get her in bed on the first date. Jake was different. They found things they both like and have had a good time doing them. *I guess I can wait. It will certainly be worth waiting for*, she hoped.

Peggy put on a pair of shorts and T-shirt and crawled into bed. It was a long day, and she was exhausted, but she couldn't sleep. Jake was on her mind. She wanted to call and wake him to talk about flowers, gardens, anything.

The ring of her phone startled her. "Peggy, are you awake?" asked Jake. "I can't sleep."

"Neither can I," admitted Peggy.

They talked for an hour and decided they should try and get some sleep. He told Peggy he was able to get a flight late the next evening. Peggy was dreading his going back to Iowa. She wanted to go with him, and spend more time with him.

耹❧

Jake drove back to Peggy's apartment in the morning, and they combined breakfast and lunch and had another piece of pie with cinnamon ice cream. Before long, it was time for Jake to go to the airport. Peggy didn't remember ever feeling this way about a man before, if at all, but she did know she wanted to see Jake, and hoped it wouldn't be too long before they saw each other again.

"What are you smiling about, Peg?"

"Nothing really."

He took her in his arms and kissed her, long and slow. She grabbed the front of his shirt with both hands to hold him there. He put his hands on her face, and his kiss became more intense. He pulled away. "Peggy, I have to go. I'll call you tomorrow."

"Don't forget. I'll be waiting. Have a safe trip." She felt like she couldn't say enough to him, but had to let him go to catch his plane. "Goodbye, Jake."

CHAPTER EIGHT

Peggy smiled every time she thought of Jake's kiss. Her apartment felt empty, and she didn't know how long it would be before she saw Jake again, but hoped it would be soon. She kept busy by calling some of her clients to ask if they needed anything, and when darkness fell, she realized she was very hungry and very tired.

೫౦೦౩

"Have you found him yet?"

"I didn't ask Nell to look into the answering machine service. I thought I would wait until our second date."

"Time is running out. We need this done before he harms others."

He stood, paced the room, then turned to his friend, "I had to send the money to post office boxes when the job was done." He dug through his desk drawer and pulled out a piece of paper. "Here it is!" He looked at the list of cities and post office boxes listed. "He used a different last name every time. Chances are he rented the answering service in a false name, too."

"We'll never find out if you don't ask Nell to research it for you."

"Tonight, I'll just have to call her and ask her out again. Then maybe by the next date, I'll have enough nerve to ask her to do the research for me."

₧₨

Jake was feeling lonely on the plane. He had had reservations about going to Minneapolis, but now, he was glad he went. It felt good to just travel for a purpose other than bringing someone to justice, and in the process, he met a lovely lady. He would have to be honest with her if the relationship was to continue. Honest about what he did and honest about what he saw. Jake decided to work on alerting the Minneapolis police to what he saw in the judge's house, but he had to think of a really good plan first.

He pulled a piece of paper and a pencil from his backpack and wrote down how he would tell Peggy about his career, so to speak. When the plane landed in Iowa, he had written four pages. He stuffed them in his backpack and left the plane.

He went outside the airport where Arnie and Adeline were already waiting for him. Arnie had his big truck, and Jake slid in the backseat and buckled up.

"How was your trip, Jake?" asked Adeline. "We missed you." She looked back at him. "People at the library were getting worried. They hadn't seen you in over a week.

It felt good to be home and to know that people cared about him. But it was even nicer to have a lovely lady care about him, too. He would get home, start drawing the garden he wanted, and then get the plants the next day. He wanted to build a walkway to the pond, with flowers on both sides. He would plant an array of different colors like one of the gardens Peggy worked on. She told him she liked lots of colors, and he liked Peggy.

When Adeline invited him over for supper, he was going to say no, but realized that he didn't have any food at home, so he said, "Yes," perhaps a little too eagerly.

"Adeline sure missed you," said Arnie. "I think she missed taking care of you. We went to your house every night after work to feed your fish. I swear they grew since you were home last."

They had a nice dinner, and Adeline noticed Jake was having a hard time staying awake, so Arnie took him home. His house was cool, so he pulled on a sweatshirt.

He dug his cell phone out of his pocket and dialed. "Hi, Peggy. I don't know how many more minutes I have, so I'm not sure how long we'll be able to talk."

"What a wonderful surprise. I just came in from outside. I had another piece of pie. I couldn't resist with your cinnamon ice cream." Peggy told him how to check his minutes on the phone, and he realized he had five hours left. "That's a lot of time!"

"It sure is!" agreed Jake.

He told her about eating at Adeline's, and said her dessert wasn't as good as Peggy's apple pie. Peggy told Jake she was going to make one of her clients a walkway with different colored flowers around it.

"No way!" said Jake. "I'll read what I have written." He took the paper off the table. "Make a walkway with different colored flowers planted around it. Different colors because Peggy likes lots of color."

"Hey, that's nice."

They talked for an hour and didn't mention the next time they would see each other, but decided they would talk every night on the phone. Jake decided he either needed a home phone where the minutes didn't matter when she called him, or his own cell phone for long distant calls to Peggy, or maybe both.

What he did next surprised even him. Something he didn't think was all that important, but now he had a desire to know, a desire to make things better for him and, someday, Peggy, too.

He went to the garage, took down a screwdriver and a flashlight, and put them in two stacked five-gallon buckets, then walked quickly back into the house. He started under the sink in the bathroom. He took out the cleaning supplies, loosened the screws, removed the plate, reached into the wall, and pulled out a fistful of money. Once that hiding place was empty, he secured the plate with screws, put back the supplies, and moved on to the next hiding place. He took out the dirty clothes in the wooden hamper and pried the bottom panel out. Once that money was in the bucket, the bottom panel replaced, and the clothes back in the hamper, he moved on.

The guest bedroom closet had nothing in it, but once a piece of the paneling was pried loose, he took his screwdriver, removed a plate, and there was a big area that held a lot of his money. That money, too, was all put into a bucket.

The living room was next. By the front door he unscrewed the switch plate, removed the fake plug-in, and reached inside and pulled out more money. Once that was placed in the bucket and the switch plate put back, he went to the next hiding place.

He pulled a chair to the kitchen cabinet, climbed on the chair and stood on the counter, opened the cupboard above the sink, took some bowls out and set them on the counter. He pried a panel out of the top of the cupboard, and money spilled out all over the kitchen counters. Jake quickly got down and picked up all the money. Realizing there was no more room in the bucket, he quickly took another one and placed the money inside. The panel and dishes were put back, and the chair was moved back to the table. Jake had one more place to go, the basement. He knew most of his money was in the basement, but now he wanted to put it all in one place. He wanted to know how much he had.

Jake felt there was a future with Peggy, and he wanted to be able to provide for her. He had to know if he had enough.

The sound upstairs startled him. He hid the buckets of money under the stairs and went up to answer the door. *No one comes this late at night, and I already saw Adeline and Arnie.* Jake had a fleeting thought it might be Peggy, but that quickly passed when he saw flashing lights in his driveway and a policeman at his door. In his mind, he saw the judge being shot. *I knew this would happen. They would find me, think I worked with Norman, arrest me, and throw away the key.* All he could think of was Peggy, and how he let her down. How he let himself down. *And now the money is easy to find. I just put it all in one place. They'll think I got paid for helping shoot the judge.* But they wouldn't find the bulk of it because it was still hidden.

Jake broke into a sweat and reached for the door to let the officer in, but his hand wouldn't move, couldn't move. He wiped his dripping forehead with the sleeve of his other arm. The knock came again, and he jumped. He willed his hand to open the door, and when the door was open, he said a very weak, "Hello."

"Are you Jake Barns?"

His legs went weak, and he grabbed the door to steady himself. Barns was one of the many false names he used in the post office boxes to collect his money. No one knew where he lived, he never told his contact his real name, and no one should have tracked him down here. Jake felt like throwing up. His whole body was clammy and weak and if he didn't sit down soon, he would fall to the floor. That in itself, he thought, would make the police think he was guilty. They would think he killed the people that Norman had killed if they see all the money Jake had.

"Sir, are you all right?"

"I don't feel good. I would like to sit down." The officer came inside. After he sat, Jake asked, "Why are you here?' He asked so he could get this torture over with, so he could know he was going to be led away in handcuffs, so he knew his life was over, his life was over with Peggy, with Adeline, and with Arnie. He asked again, "Why are you here? Why are the lights blinking out there?"

The officer laughed. "My partner likes to flash the lights all the time, makes him feel important."

Not funny, thought Jake.

"I probably should've told you right from the start. Adeline reported your bike stolen when you were away, and my partner and I were just here to return it. We found it in the alley behind Myra's Bakery."

Jake knew Myra would borrow his bike, something only the two of them knew. The garage was always unlocked, and she was welcome to ride it whenever she needed to. She did deliveries at her bakery, and when her husband needed the car, Myra would use Jake's bike because it had a big basket on the front.

Jake let out a big sigh of relief. *But that doesn't answer the question of why he asked for Jake Barns.* "You don't have the right last name. It's Farms."

The officer looked at his notebook. "You're right. I don't know why I said Barns." *To give me a heart attack*, thought Jake.

"I'll put the bike in the garage if that's okay?"

"Yeah, go ahead, and thanks for finding it."

"Sure. I hope you feel better. You look better." The officer left the house and helped his partner put Jake's bike in the garage. They stopped and looked at the fish pond, then got in the squad car with lights flashing and drove away.

It was amazing how quickly he felt better. He locked the door and went back downstairs, only he wasn't in the mood to pursue his treasure hunt anymore. His life flashing before him got him out of the mood very quickly. Jake went back upstairs and decided he really needed to talk to Peggy. Even though he was not ready to give her all the details, he needed to hear her voice.

He checked the time and thought she might be in bed already, but it was a chance he was willing to take. She answered on the first ring. "Jake?"

"I hope I didn't wake you."

"No, I was awake. I was actually thinking about you."

He smiled, and realized that he felt so much better. If he hung up now, the smile might just be permanent. "I needed to hear your voice."

"Me, too."

He walked into the living room, sat in the recliner, and reclined all the way back. "I think we should meet again real soon. I don't have that many minutes on my phone, not enough to talk to you all night. And besides, if we saw each other, I wouldn't have to worry about minutes."

Peggy smiled. "That's true." She sat in her recliner and reclined all the way back. "Besides, I should probably do some more traveling before I get a new job." She laughed.

"I don't want to keep you. I just wanted to hear your voice."

"I'm glad you called. Goodnight, Jake."

They stayed in their chairs, pulled a blanket over themselves, and fell asleep with a smile on their faces, Peggy in Minnesota, and Jake in Iowa. Yet they felt as one, even so far away. They slept well and woke up the next day with the same smile.

CHAPTER NINE

Jake woke refreshed. He lifted himself from his chair and the cell phone dropped out of his lap. He picked it up, shut the cover, and laid it on the kitchen table. He decided to finish what he'd started last night and lumbered down the stairs. With screwdriver, flashlight, and bucket, he went to the furnace room.

He wedged himself behind the furnace into an empty space. He pried a panel from the wall. When that was off, he tapped on the wall with the handle of the screwdriver. When he found the hollow space, he pried off another section and then used his screwdriver to take off the plate. The space was much larger when the money was emptied from the wall.

With the buckets, he sat in the small room without windows in the basement and sorted the bills into piles. He couldn't believe all the money he had. Jake knew it was time to make another anonymous donation. He would find out what interested Peggy and make a donation to her favorite charity.

It took Jake two hours to get the bills sorted, counted, written down, and added up. Some had to be unfolded, and he wanted all the faces on the bills facing the same way.

The one hundred dollar bills alone when counted numbered three thousand bills. There were half that many twenties, three hundred tens, no fives and ones. *Unbelievable!* He decided he needed to open a checking account. Instead of the small town where he lived, he decided he would wait until Arnie took his monthly trip into Des Moines and go with him to the bank. In the meantime, he needed to get the money back in hiding. He didn't want so many different places. He just wanted one. He went back behind the furnace, took off the panel, and hollowed out the wall even more, then stacked the cash from top to bottom until it all fit. He found a larger plate, screwed it in place, then put back the panel to cover the plate.

Jake fried eggs and potatoes, sprinkled on shredded cheese, and put sour cream on top. He could eat that every day for breakfast and never get tired of it. He put the dishes in the dishwasher when he finished eating and decided to stop in and see Myra in case she needed his bike.

It was late in the afternoon before he finally got home. Myra needed his bike, so he walked uptown and visited the phone store where he bought a cell phone and a one-year plan. He asked the sales clerk to please show him everything about how to use the phone. On his walk home, he took out his rental phone from his pocket and called Peggy, but she didn't answer. He left a message to call him back.

Back at Myra's Bakery, he picked out a doughnut of his choice which was for the use of the bike. "Jake, I love that bike of yours. Where did you get that big basket?"

"I made it. It's big enough for groceries, books, whatever you want."

"I should ask my husband for a bike for my birthday. Would you make me a basket, too?"

"Of course, just let me know when you get your bike. I'd better get home." Not sure why he said that, because really, he didn't have to get home, except for one thing, to get his cell phone set up.

Once he got home, he put on sweats and took out his new phone, cords, and instructions and put it all on the kitchen table. He read the instructions and set up the ring, a message, and added Peggy's number to his address book. He could take pictures, text, and get on the Internet. He had bought a disc so he could download the pictures he took to a computer, which he didn't have, but he knew Peggy had one. He was excited about his new purchase and now only wished he had someone here he could share it with.

The other phone rang, and he quickly took it off the table and answered. "Peggy! Thanks for calling back."

Jake told Peggy all about his phone and all the cool features, then realized she probably already knew all that stuff, but she sounded just as excited as he was. But he told her he wanted to use all the minutes on the rental first. By the end of the night, that was done.

⚛⚛

The next day for Jake was filled with long rides on his bike and taking pictures of flowers and trees in the lush parks. He had his backpack and lunch in his bike basket. Jake found a shaded area, sat on the grass, and ate his sandwich. He was craving some apple pie, or was it Peggy he was craving?

He laid back and stretched out on the grass. The sun was shining, it was warm, and he thought the day was perfect, except that Peggy wasn't there. He dug out his cell phone from his pocket and dialed her number.

They talked for an hour and then Jake headed home. Peggy had been in her garden when he called. She had heard that Luke would be sentenced the next week and asked Jake if he would come back for the sentencing.

Jake had a much better idea. Since he could just go on the Internet, or on his new phone and find out the sentencing, he invited Peggy to come to Iowa. She readily accepted. She would fly out in two days. He would have to ask Arnie to go pick her up. Knowing Adeline, she would want to come too, so she would be the first to meet his new friend.

⚛⚛

Jake spent the next two days cleaning, washing sheets, and scrubbing the floors. He had not done a thorough cleaning in a long time and it felt good. Only this time, it was for a reason, not just to tidy up the place, but he was actually having a guest.

He went to the store, bought lots of food, and noticed they were selling candles next door at the craft store. With everything loaded in his basket, he pedaled home with a smile on his face.

The day before Peggy arrived was dedicated to cooking, something Jake didn't do often. He dug out Adeline's recipes and put them on the counter. He started with the meat loaf recipe. When that was finished, he moved on to the lasagna, stuffed chicken, and a cheesecake. He thought the cheesecake would last a few days, so he only made one dessert. With the other recipes, there would also be leftovers.

Jake knew they would be dining with Adeline and Arnie, too. He just hoped Adeline made something other than what he made. The aromas in the house from his cooking smelled wonderful, he thought.

Peggy would be staying for two weeks. He was so excited that when he was done cooking, he went for a bike ride so he would be exhausted and could sleep.

ುುಲ

As expected, Adeline came along to pick up Peggy. Luckily, Arnie said he would drop off Jake at the baggage entrance, and he and Adeline would wait in the ramp. Jake was not sure how he would react to seeing Peggy since he missed her so much. He paced in front of the baggage claim area where the Minneapolis travelers were supposed to pick up luggage.

Jake was so nervous, and he wasn't sure why. Peggy and he got along so well, and they had talked to each other on the phone every night. It should be okay, he thought, but his insides were telling a different story.

He jumped when he felt someone grab his shoulder. "Jake," she said in a soft voice. Jake turned, pulled her to him, and kissed her, long and hard.

"Peggy, how wonderful to see you." She had on jeans, boots, and a T-shirt that read, I Love Iowa. Jake laughed and pointed to her shirt. "You've never been here."

"Doesn't matter. You're here, so I love Iowa."

Jake nestled his nose in her hair, and she smelled like musk which reminded him of the earth. He held her tight, then realized that Arnie was waiting for them. "My friends are waiting for us, so we'd better hurry."

Peggy just had a carry-on, so they headed to where Arnie and Adeline were parked. He opened the car door for her, and they got in the backseat of Adeline's Buick, buckled up, and got situated with Peggy's carry-on between them.

Jake did the introductions, and then they were on their way home. It seemed Adeline would have a sore neck by the time they got back, with her turning around so often with questions for Peggy. When Adeline asked Peggy to come for dinner, Jake was a little disappointed because he wanted her all to himself the first night and was surprised by Peggy's answer.

"Wow, that is so nice. But if you don't mind, I would just like to get to Jake's and settle in. But hey, I would love to come tomorrow if it's okay with everyone." She said it so sincerely that Adeline was not offended, and was actually looking forward to the next day when she could fuss all over again for Jake and his new lady friend.

CHAPTER TEN

"I LOVE YOUR home," said Peggy. "Show me everything."

He had already showed her the pond, and she loved the goldfish. He didn't feed them that morning so Peggy could do it. He went into the garage and handed her the food. She loved watching them come to the surface to gobble the food.

"The fish are awesome. I'll have to put a pond in my yard."

Next was the tour of his house. He took her to her room first. It was in the opposite side of the house from his. She loved the simplicity of it and immediately unpacked her bag and put her clothes in the empty blue dresser. Jake painted it blue after sanding off the old finish. He wanted some color in the room and painted it to match the bedspread. A project Arnie suggested and colors Adeline chose.

"I'll be right back. I'm going to put dinner in the oven." Jake put the meatloaf with two baked potatoes wrapped in foil in the oven and set the timer for sixty minutes. *Enough time*, he thought, *to give Peggy her surprise.*

He finished with the tour, showed her where everything was, and then took her to the basement. "It's finished, but I haven't put anything down here. I'm not good at decorating." The table with two chairs, where he counted his money not so long ago, was in the middle of the empty space.

"Neither am I, but you don't want too much either."

He took her hand, went up the stairs, then outside. "I have a surprise for you in the garage."

"More fish food?" She smiled, and he went weak.

"No, something even better," said Jake.

He turned on the light, and they walked into the double-car garage. The back wall held tools of various sizes and shapes hanging on it, and there was nothing else in the garage, except for Jake's bike and Peggy's surprise.

He went over to the corner, and from behind his own bike, he pushed out a brand new blue bike for Peggy. The same color as his. He made her a basket but wanted to ask her first if she wanted it. "This is your bike. I don't have a car, so I thought we could ride around town and I'll give you the big tour tomorrow."

Peggy went over to the bike, got on, and pedaled around the spacious garage. "I love it." She kept riding around, then stopped in front of Jake. "Can I have a basket like yours? I could put that to good use."

Jake went over, got the basket from the workbench, and attached it for her. She got on again and rode around the garage. "This is so cool, Jake. Thank you."

Jake got on his bike and followed her around the garage. As silly as it seemed, they both were enjoying themselves. After a while Jake said he'd better go in and check on dinner. Peggy was right behind him.

Peggy set the table, poured milk, sat, and waited for Jake to take the food out of the oven. "This is my first attempt at cooking. I used Adeline's recipes so the meatloaf should be good." And it was. They ate in silence, trying to comprehend that they were indeed with each other and so far having a good time.

"We'll have the cheesecake later. If you want, you can go sit down and I'll clean up."

"What are we doing tomorrow?" asked Peggy.

"I thought we could ride our bikes over to the library and say hi to Adeline. She'll probably give us a time to come over for supper. Then let's go to the park. It's about four miles away. We'll take a lunch and hang out and enjoy the sun if it's out."

"While you're cleaning up, I'll make sandwiches for tomorrow." Peggy took the meatloaf and cut it into slices. Jake took out the bread, mayonnaise, and ketchup. "What do you want on your sandwich?"

"I like ketchup."

She made one with ketchup and one with mayonnaise. She found the sandwich bags and took the chips from the top of the refrigerator. After bagging the sandwiches and chips, she took two apples out of his fruit bowl on the cupboard, then took two oranges.

Peggy put the wrapped sandwiches in the fridge and the rest on the counter. She was envisioning the wonderful basket on her bike. "Jake, do you have a blanket we can bring?"

"There's one in the living room on my recliner."

Peggy brought the blanket to the kitchen, folded it, and laid it over one of the chairs. "What else do we need?" she asked.

He went over to her. "I'll tell you what we need. We need to kiss."

Peggy smiled at him. Jake put his arms around her and kissed her. They were the same height, so it was easy to kiss her. Besides, her lips were so willing. He snuggled into her neck and realized that if he continued, he might not be able to stop himself.

"Ah, now I think we need to stop kissing each other," whispered Jake.

Peggy nodded. She didn't want things to move too fast. She wanted to get to know Jake before she allowed anything serious to happen. For now, she was enjoying his company and knew tonight she would be able to sleep knowing they were together.

"Let's go see the fish. I think they need to be checked on." Peggy laughed and went outside. "Do our bikes have lights on them?"

"Yep, they do. Sometimes at night when I'm craving M&M's, I head over to the store and pick some up."

"Let's go to the store now. I want to ride my new bike."

The store was six blocks away, and when they arrived, Jake showed her the bike rack on the side where they parked their bikes.

Once in the hardware store, Jake said, "Hi, Roger, I want you to meet my friend, Peggy."

"Hi, Peggy, nice to meet you." He shook her hand. "I didn't know you had any friends Jake, except Adeline, but no one as pretty as Peggy."

Jake blushed. "I agree. She is pretty."

"What can I do for you? Don't tell me you are craving M&M's again."

"No, this time, I am," said Peggy. "As soon as he mentioned M&M's, I wanted some."

Jake and Peggy hung around the store eating their candy and talking to Roger while he was closing up for the night. The money was counted and put in the safe in the back. He stocked some of the shelves, and when he put on his baseball cap, the phone rang. "Yes, dear, I'm on my way home. Guess what, you'll never guess." He looked at Jake. "Okay, I'll tell you. Jake has a lady friend. They're both here right now keeping me company. Sure, I'll tell him. Bye, honey, I'll be right home."

Roger hung up the phone. "Gail says to say hi, Jake, and wants to meet your friend. She's been acting so strange lately that I doubt . . . never mind." He took out his key. He looked at Peggy. "How long are you staying?"

"For two weeks. With hospitality like this, I might never go home."

"Any friend of Jake's is a friend of ours."

They left the store and said their goodbyes while Roger bolted the door.

���

They slept well knowing that the other was just down the hall and not across state lines. Peggy was thinking about her bike and thought it was one of the nicest presents anyone had ever given her. She couldn't wait to ride to the park and eat lunch.

Peggy looked for a coffeepot but couldn't find one. She pulled eggs, bread, butter, and bacon out of the fridge and started cooking breakfast. Jake was watching her. He thought she looked good in the morning. "Hey, Baby," he said with a laugh.

She turned. "Hey, yourself." His hair was sticking up in front, and although it wasn't his normal style, Peggy thought he looked good with spiky hair. "I couldn't find a coffeepot."

"I knew there was something I forgot." He couldn't take his eyes off her. "I'll go get some. Roger sells coffee at the store until noon every day. Do you like flavored cream?"

"I love flavored cream."

He dressed and went to the garage. The wooden device he took off the work bench had four holes carved in it and sat snuggly into the basket. Now he just had to make sure he didn't tip his bike.

∞∞∞

When Jake came in the house with steaming coffee, Peggy put bread in the toaster. She had the table set with eggs and bacon already on the plates. She took her coffee and took a deep breath. "This smells wonderful. Thanks, Jake."

It was so good to have her in his house. He was worried about her coming, about her bike, about not having a car, but she didn't care about any of it. And most of all, he could tell she loved her bike, and that made him happy. *She* made him happy.

They ate breakfast while plotting the day. Peggy put their dishes in the dishwasher. "Do you want me to start this or wait until we get back?"

"I usually wait until I'm here the whole time." He moved to the sink, put his arm around her, lifted her face to his, and kissed her. "We'd better get going. I could stay here and do this all day."

"We'll have to save that for another day." Peggy would have been fine with it being today, but she didn't want to fall too fast, too soon. He kissed her one last time.

"If we remember, let's pick up a coffeepot. Roger sells them at the store. Well, I guess there is not much he doesn't sell."

∞∞∞

Peggy and Jake stopped at the library to see Adeline. They parked their bikes outside. "No need to lock up the bikes. There's not much crime here." He took her hand and led her to the front desk where Adeline was sitting.

Adeline came around the desk and gave Peggy a hug. "It was so good to meet you last night. I hope you were able to get some rest."

"Yes, I fell right to sleep. We just got done with breakfast, and we're heading to the park."

"I heard Jake got you a present. I didn't think he knew you that well to be buying a ring, but Arnie set me straight." She took Peggy's hand. "How do you like your new bike?"

"I love it. Jake put a basket on it, just like the one he has."

"I better not keep you. I don't want you to miss seeing the beautiful Ledges Park we have here in Boone. The best you'll find for miles around." She patted Jake's arm. "Let's have dinner around five tonight. Will that work for both of you?"

"Yes, that works, Adeline," said Peggy.

Jake smiled as he watched the two of them talk back and forth. He was thinking more and more about his idea of staying home with Peggy and kissing her all day.

"Jake. Jake." Peggy was smiling at him. "Did you want to go?"

He shook his head, still thinking about kissing Peggy. "Ah, yeah, I'm ready."

CHAPTER ELEVEN

"LEDGES STATE PARK is about twelve hundred acres, Peggy. The sandstone ledges are beautiful. There are lots of hiking paths, and you can see the spectacular sites of Pea's Creek Canyon.

"I think it officially became one of Iowa's first state parks in 1924." Peggy and Jake biked to where the ninety-one mile route started and decided to put aside several days sometime in the future to bike it. They would hang out at the library first and research it before they took on that adventure.

Jake showed her the arch stone bridge. They got off their bikes and walked across the bridge. Jake took a lot of pictures, and he made sure Peggy was in every one of them. They found a place to spread the blanket and eat lunch. Not far away was a family on their blankets. There were three children. The baby was content after eating his baby food, and now with his bottle.

They both watched the family for several minutes, then Jake broke the silence. "I've always thought having children would be nice."

"I would like to have children, but I thought I'd be having them sooner." She looked at him. "Do you want girls or boys, or both?"

Jake smiled. He'd never had this conversation with anyone before. "I want both."

"Me too," said Peggy. "But I think I need a job first so I have enough money."

She also thought she should get married first. Peggy thought she would never get married, but she always wanted children. Now maybe, just maybe, things would change with Jake.

Jake figured he had enough money for all the children they wanted. He needed to tell Peggy about the money, what he did before they met.

They ate their lunch and cuddled next to each other on the blanket and fell asleep. It was a sunny day, and they weren't sure if the warmth of the sun or the warmth of their bodies made them content.

Peggy woke up and stretched while Jake was watching her. "Come here, lady." He patted the space next to him. She rolled over and snuggled into his body. "That's better."

"What time is it? We're not going to be late for dinner, are we?"

Jake didn't want to look at his watch. He didn't want to go to Adeline's. He just wanted to stay on the blanket with Peggy, but he looked only because she wanted to know. "We have an hour."

"We should go, but I'd love to just stay here with you."

"Do you always have to say out loud what I'm thinking?" He rubbed her back.

"I guess so, but I didn't think I was doing that."

He continued to rub her back, but eventually, they packed their things and headed for Adelines.

⁂

Peggy helped in the kitchen, and the men took up their places in the garage in front of the workbench. Adeline was happy she would have companionship tonight. Maybe she could teach Peggy how to knit, or sew. Teach her something as if she were her own daughter, since Adeline never had any children.

When Arnie and Jake were done in the garage, they started the grill; and once the steaks were done, they headed into the house. Adeline had oven fries, green beans, and the salad Peggy made, already on the table.

"What are you working on this time out in the garage?" asked Adeline. "Have you showed Jake how to use that new saw of yours?"

"No, I'll show him some other time."

"Arnie showed me how to make wooden cylinders to make kaleidoscopes. It sure looked hard, but it's quite easy." He took a long drink of water.

"Good old Arnie really gets into his work," said Adeline. "We went for a ride last week, and Arnie here pulls over and plucks off a few feathers from a dead bird. He said they'd be good in the kaleidoscopes."

Peggy laughed. "I can't wait to see what the feather looks like. It must be fascinating."

"Mighty fine dinner, Adeline," said Arnie. Jake silently thanked her for not making any of the recipes he had made for Peggy.

"Peggy and I will do the dishes," said Adeline. "Then we'll serve dessert."

Peggy was glad she was included, as if she were part of the family. She would much rather be in the garage learning how to make something, but Adeline was a nice lady, and she enjoyed her company.

"After we do the dishes, I need some help with the computer I got from the library. We just had new ones installed, and I was allowed to take one of the old ones home. Arnie doesn't know anything, and I just know how to look for books." She squirted soap in the water. "I could use a crash course."

While they were doing the dishes, Peggy asked her a lot of questions. "What would you like to do on the computer? Do you have an Internet connection? Do you have an account at the library where you can look up books at home? Some Adeline could answer. Others she couldn't. Like what she wanted to be able to do, Peggy gave her the basics and made sure she wrote down the instructions so she didn't forget anything.

It was a long night, but both Peggy and Jake enjoyed themselves. Adeline was able to turn on the computer, get on the Internet, and look up knitting sites where she could find patterns and print them out. Arnie finished showing Jake how to put together the kaleidoscope. It was dark when they left, and Jake was glad the bikes had lights.

Jake unlocked the door and turned on the light. Peggy shut the door behind her. He took the cheesecake from the fridge. "I can't believe Adeline didn't have dessert. She always has dessert."

"I noticed there was something that looked like Oreo cookies and pudding in her refrigerator."

"Seriously! I love that stuff. She must've forgotten."

Peggy took out two plates and forks, then cut the cheesecake. They took their plates into the living room. Jake told her to sit in the recliner, and he sat on the couch next to her. The furniture was brown, different colors of brown. There were blinds covering the big picture window which were cream colored. Jake wasn't much on interior design. He just liked comfortable and easy.

The phone rang. It was Adeline. She apologized to Jake for forgetting to serve his favorite dessert. Promised she would never do something as silly as that again.

"What should we do tomorrow?" asked Peggy. "I had so much fun today. I never thought that riding a bike would be so cool. With my car at home, I usually drive everywhere, but now I'll think about biking or even walking."

"First, I think we should sleep in, then . . . oh no! We forgot to feed the fish today."

"Just sit and I'll go out and feed them."

"I really should go with you so you don't get lost. You know, being your first time in Iowa." He grinned at her.

She laughed. "Okay, hurry up."

They watched as the fish ate the food and then decided the fish should have names. They couldn't think of five names and decided to add it to their to-do list for tomorrow.

Dishes were added to the dishwasher, they kissed each other good night, and went to their rooms. Peggy had a mental to-do list for tomorrow. One thing, she was going to call Adeline for her Oreo cookie pudding recipe, and check up with her on how she's doing with her computer. Remember to feed and name the fish were also on her list. She smiled as she mentally put kissing Jake on her list.

Jake was so happy that Peggy was there with him. He wanted to do something special tomorrow, something special every day. But where he lived, there wasn't that much to do. *I wonder if Arnie would want to go into Des Moines. Or maybe,* he thought, *they could take the bus and stay overnight.* It sounded like a great idea to him. *Oh, and kiss Peggy* was put on his list.

∞CR

While Jake was at the hardware store getting coffee, he decided to just buy a coffeepot. He picked up filters and coffee and wondered if he could put it all in his basket. When it wouldn't all fit, he called Peggy.

"Hey, Peg, I'm at Roger's buying a coffeepot and can't carry everything. Can you ride over and help me?"

"Sure, I'll be right there."

Now that Jake had help, he was also able to carry flavored cream. As soon as the coffeepot was unpacked, Peggy made coffee. It smelled so good Jake couldn't believe he never owned a coffeemaker. They had a leisurely morning drinking coffee, sitting in lawn chairs next to the pond.

"Let's not do anything today," suggested Peggy.

"I like that idea. Do you like to take naps?"

Peggy answered, "No, not really, unless they're three-hour naps."

Jake laughed. "We'll have to plan that for today then." Jake wished he could take a nap with her instead of sleeping in separate beds. He would work on that.

"Okay, we have to name the fish. You go first," said Peggy.

"Let's name the blue one Mickey."

"Okay, the yellow one is Mable," said Peggy.

"Let's name the striped one, Spice."

Peggy pointed to the golden one. "Do you like the name Goldie?" laughed Peggy.

"Yeah, that's a good name. Okay, one left, the greenish one."

"We'll have to name it Irish, then."

Peggy and Jake sat back in their chairs and laughed. "Okay, mentally cross that off our list," said Jake.

"Should we eat?"

"I'll go put in the lasagna." Jake got out of his chair. "It will take about an hour." Jake walked into the house, turned on the oven, took out the lasagna from the refrigerator, and put it on the stove. While he waited for the oven to preheat, he watched Peggy through the window.

She was pointing at the fish and calling them by name. Jake smiled. *I wonder if I met Peggy earlier, would I have still been in a situation that I needed to call 911 after a serial killer wounded a judge in Minneapolis?* He didn't want to think about it, yet he had to think about it. He had to tell her, and the sooner he did, the sooner he would find out if Peggy would want what he did as part of her life. Maybe after their three-hour nap, he would take her downstairs and tell her.

⊱⊰

They had a leisurely lunch, and once the kitchen was cleaned, Jake announced it was time for their marathon nap. He took Peggy's hand and pulled her into his bedroom. He lay down and told her to join him. "This is going to be awkward," he admitted, "but I don't want to nap alone."

Peggy snuggled in beside him. Her hair was against his face, and he took a deep breath and breathed her in. *This will be a lot more awkward than I imagined,* he thought.

This feels so good, thought Peggy. *I don't think I'll be able to sleep at all.* They felt content with each other, and knowing they would still be together when they woke up, it eased the sexual tension between them, but it didn't disappear.

⊱⊰

Jake had been awake for a few minutes when he realized it was dark out, which meant they took more than a three-hour nap. He put his arms tighter around Peggy and snuggled his nose in her hair. "Peggy, Peggy," he whispered, "time to get up, my dear Peggy." He kissed her hair, then her face. "Time to get up and make your man some more coffee."

He could feel Peggy giggling, then he heard her addicting laughter, and he laughed with her. She turned in his arms and kissed him on his face, then his lips. She felt the sexual tension surface and knew she should get up.

Jake wanted to make love to her, but first he wanted to tell her what he did for a living which led to the incident in Minneapolis. He wanted to call the Minneapolis police. The urge was strong, yet he didn't. Jake knew he had to straighten that out.

Jake knew it would be difficult. He didn't want to be associated with the murder, and yet the longer he waited, the harder it would be. He closed his eyes and held her closer. He wanted Peggy to be a part of his life, and if she chose to stay there with him, he would be a happy man.

CHAPTER TWELVE

"N ELL, YOU LOOK lovely tonight."

"Thank you. You don't usually hand out compliments so freely. Is there something you want?"

"I used to be that way. I want our relationship to continue, and besides, I've changed." *Now I'll have to wait before I ask her to trace phone records for me. I thought the compliment was a stretch. Now I'll have to wait longer, and I'm not a patient man. Damn that Jake, or whoever he is. I'll track you down with or without Nell's help.*

"I'm glad to hear it. Just what are you doing with yourself these days?"

৪১৩

Jake was warming up the lasagna in the microwave, while Peggy was making more coffee. "Nice coffeepot, Jake." She looked at him. "It even has a timer. I'll set it up tonight, and we'll wake up to the aroma of coffee."

"Peggy, after we have dinner I want, or I need to talk to you."

She went to him. "You sound so sad. I hope you're all right."

"I need to talk to you." The uncertainty of how she would react tore at his insides. He certainly didn't feel like eating, but he went through the motions anyway.

She brought the poured coffee to the table, sat, and noticed a sadness on his face. "Jake, are you sure you want to eat?"

He forced a smile. "You're right. I don't feel like eating."

"Follow me." She followed him down the stairs.

Jake took the screwdriver and the flashlight and led her behind the furnace. He thought it would be better just to show her the money and then explain it. But there was no good way, he was sure, to reveal the incident in Minneapolis.

The plate was off, and he held his breath. "Look, Peggy." She looked at the money stacked in several piles. "This is what I have to tell you about." She counted seven piles, and the money in each pile was stacked about twelve inches high.

"This is giving me the creeps, Jake. What's going on?"

He put the plate back and the two panels. They sat at the table downstairs. It was a dark room with no windows, and dark paneling on the walls. The walls needed to be painted lighter, and now he wished he'd done it already. He was feeling overwhelmed, and he didn't know how to start.

Peggy took his hand off the table and held it. "I don't know what you are going to tell me, but I know it's uncomfortable. Just tell me."

Right this minute, Peggy was his world; and she would soon be a part of his life if she chose to accept him, a coward that couldn't face the authorities to report details of a shooting. Jake decided to just tell her.

He paced for a few minutes and tried to compose himself, but it wasn't working. So he just sat and started the confession he'd planned since he met her.

"Peggy," he began, taking her hand, "the money, all that money, is payment for bringing justice to victims of crimes." He was silent a moment. "The money would be delivered to a PO box that would be set up ahead of time. I would do what needed to be done, get the money, and come home.

"The crimes could be any number of things. The last several times though, a man called Norman got there ahead of me and murdered the criminal. I still got paid, but I didn't do much to bring him or her to justice.

"I had a fear that someone would link me to Norman because we always seemed to be in the same town or city at the same time."

"If you weren't near the shooting how could they possibly link you?"

"They might have thought we were partners. Norman did the dirty work. I was the brains behind it." Jake laughed. "It's not funny."

"You are too kind to want to murder anyone."

"There's more." He played with her fingers, then stopped, realizing he needed to continue. "Norman and I never saw each other. He probably didn't know I existed, but I knew about him from my contact.

"I was interviewing Judge Klein, pretending to be a University of Minnesota student. I asked about his cases and was about to ask him about Luke Ames' case when the doorbell rang.

"He went to answer it, and there was some talking. I wanted to hear what was being said in case I could use it against him. I walked over to the entryway and saw a man with a gun. The judge backed up and cried, 'No, no, you can't shoot me.' I heard the gun and saw blood splatter everywhere. The judge fell back and landed on the floor." He held up his hand when Peggy was about to say something.

"Let me finish, Peg. When Norman left, I panicked. I grabbed my stuff. I looked around the room where we were doing the interview to make sure I didn't leave anything.

"I took a napkin, lifted the phone receiver, punched in 911 with the napkin, laid the phone by the judge's body, and left. I'm sure the police thought it strange the judge had the phone with no blood on it."

"They may have thought Norman did it," said Peggy.

"True, but I need to talk to the police about it. I just don't know how."

They talked for over an hour, and when they thought of every possible scenario, they stood and held each other. The intimacy of holding Peggy, knowing she accepted him and what he had done, made him teary eyed.

Jake's phone rang. He dug it out of his pocket, knowing only two people had his phone number, one was Peggy and the other Adeline. "Hello." He wiped his sleeve over his face. "Let me ask her. Just a minute."

"Adeline wants to know if you'll visit her at the library tomorrow. She has a computer question to ask you." He closed his eyes waiting, thinking she'd want to go back home and not deal with anything right now.

"Tell her I'll call her tomorrow."

Jake touched her face and whispered, "Thank you."

When they finally went to bed, Peggy and Jake slept in the same bed. He held her close. They were both still thinking of how to resolve Jake coming forward and telling what he knew.

℠℠

Peggy called Adeline in the morning as she drank her first cup of coffee, then she rode her bike to the library. Adeline was cheerful and happy that Peggy came. She did notice Peggy was distracted with something and hoped she and Jake didn't have a disagreement.

When the computer problem was resolved, Peggy rode back to Jake's and had another cup of coffee.

"Tonight, when we get back from the Cole's, let's go over my options again, Peggy. I want to put this behind me."

℠℠

Adeline was doing quite well with the computer, and the knitting lesson was basic enough that Peggy could catch on quickly. Once she did, she loved it. "Where in town can I buy yarn and needles?"

"Come with me," said Adeline. Peggy followed her to a spare bedroom away from the kitchen. She pulled open the drawers on the wooden-carved dresser and showed Peggy skeins of yarn that were never touched. "I've always had a project in mind. Some I finished. Most I didn't. Pick out what you like and we'll find you some needles."

"This is wonderful." Peggy opened the drawers, took the colors she wanted, and put them on the dresser. There was a drawer with all kinds, shapes, and sizes of knitting needles. Adeline picked out a basic beginner pair and put them next to Peggy's yarn on the dresser.

Then Adeline asked a question Peggy didn't expect. "Is Jake all right? He looks sad, and his eyes are so red. I'm worried about him"

"We took a long nap this afternoon, but I think he's okay."

"Good. I don't know what I'd do if anything happens to that kid. He's like a son to us. He's actually the nicest kid I've ever met at the library. One day, I was stocking the shelves with books. I was on a step stool, and Jake came by, helped me down, and stocked the shelves himself. I was so happy he came along because heights make me dizzy, but I needed to do my job. Ever since then, we've developed a wonderful friendship; and whenever I need to stock the high shelves, he does it for me."

"He *is* a nice guy, and I like him very much. All this is so new to me. I never dated, and when I met Jake, I knew right away he was a great guy."

"I'm so glad you two got together. Jake needed someone in his life besides us old codgers." Adeline laughed. "Let's bag up this yarn and go see what the boys are doing."

ᏸᎧᎃ

Peggy had the yarn out of the bag and on the couch. She walked into her bedroom and pulled out her laptop and went back to the living room. Jake watched her. Once it was booted up, she browsed knitting sites, looking for free patterns.

Jake sat next to her. "What are you looking for?"

"Patterns for slippers. I thought I'd make us matching slippers. Or scarves, whatever is easier, so probably it will be scarves."

"Peggy," said Jake, "are you okay?"

She looked into his blue eyes, the ones Adeline mentioned were red and sad. "I'm trying to be. I thought knitting would take my mind off what you told me. I guess it's my way to cope with things."

"I'm so glad you didn't pack up and leave. I thought you'd scream at me and leave for good, and here you are, still in my home." He took her hand. "I don't deserve it. I don't deserve you."

"I'm not so sure I *can* stay, but right now, I know I can't leave."

He kissed her hand. "Thank you so much." Tears splashed on her hand and she wiped them from his eyes.

She smiled at him, a smile that gave him hope. She wasn't leaving now, but he knew she might choose to leave tomorrow. Right now, he wasn't sure of anything, but he did know it was right to tell Peggy what he saw, and what he didn't do about it. He smiled back, and knew right now, this minute, she was with him, and he would enjoy every minute of it.

"What are we doing tomorrow?" asked Peggy.

"We could take a bus to Des Moines. I might have to talk to Arnie first. He likes driving in, and if he finds out we went without him, he might not be too happy."

"I like Adeline and Arnie. They are so nice. I got the recipe of your favorite dessert." She pulled it out of her pocket and unfolded it. "We'll have to go to the store and get the ingredients."

"Yum! Let's do that first thing in the morning."

"Jake," she took a minute, "what was it like to see Judge Klein get shot?"

He looked at his hands, thought for a few minutes, then explained as best he could. "If he had just fallen to the floor and groaned, I don't think I would've panicked, but when the blood was all over the place, his bloody head and his hands bloody from touching his head, I panicked. It was as if I couldn't breathe. The house was closing in on me, and I wasn't thinking rationally."

It was after midnight when they finished talking. It was more of the healing process for Jake to say it out loud to an understanding person. It was his past, and he planned on keeping it there. But now he realized it was more important to heal and move on than to bury it where it could surface and consume him. Peggy was very understanding, and she asked a lot of questions. She held his hand through it all, and for that, no matter what happened between them, he would always be grateful.

"I'll figure this out, and when I make my decision to report what I saw, I would like you by my side."

"I'll be right there with you," said Peggy and kissed him on the lips. "I'll be there."

They decided to make a list of things they wanted to pick up for tomorrow, whether they went to Des Moines or just to the local grocery store. Peggy was looking in some of the drawers in the kitchen to find some paper when she came across copies of cashier's checks from the First Bank of Des Moines. One was made out to the Cancer Foundation for twenty thousand dollars, the Children's Foundation for the same amount, the Humane Society for the same amount, and there were several more.

"Did you find that pad of paper?" He went over to her and saw the copies.

"I think your heart is in the right place. It wasn't the money because you apparently don't spend much of it on yourself. It was a way to get justice." She put the copies back in the drawer and took out paper and pencil. "I have an idea. I'll tell you in the morning. I have to formulate it in my mind first."

"The idea better start with making me coffee in the morning."

"Of course, the only way to start the day!"

They made their list and decided to call Arnie in the morning to ask if he wanted to make the trip into Des Moines sometime this week. Peggy set up the coffeepot so they would have fresh coffee when they woke up. Jake wanted her to sleep with him, just like she did before, but he wasn't sure she would want to, and he didn't want to ask. The last thing he could handle right now was rejection.

Chapter Thirteen

In the morning, Peggy took her coffee, went outside, and fed the fish. It had been a long day yesterday, full of distractions, and she forgot their daily feeding. She sat in the lawn chair and watched the fish swim around as she sipped her coffee. She figured out her plan during the night, but she just had to find a way to tell Jake. He might want to leave this whole thing in the past and forget all about it, but it was one way to get justice, possibly faster than Jake was doing in the past.

She smelled bacon, went inside, refilled her cup, and sat at the table. "Good morning, Jake." He turned and smiled at her. It seemed she always looked good no matter what. She didn't wear makeup, and there was a natural glow to her skin. Her straight long dark brown hair never looked tangled. Her plaid pajama pants and T-shirt were the same things he wore when he went to bed. They had so much in common.

"Morning. I called Arnie, and he said he'll drive to Des Moines tomorrow. He said Adeline wanted to come, too. Arnie said she wants to show you the yarn shop. So today we have the day to ourselves."

"She is such a nice lady. I can't wait to go to the yarn shop. Maybe I can pick up some interesting patterns."

"Yeah, slippers, right?"

"I'll start with that. I'll probably knit you a sweater, then maybe some boxer shorts." She laughed. "Let's go for a bike ride today and have a picnic."

"I was thinking I might have to take another nap today. I didn't sleep much last night."

"We'll just ride after our naps, and then we'll have dinner on the road. That diner down the street from the library looks interesting."

"They have great barbeque sandwiches, and they have tables outside in the back."

"Perfect." Peggy raised her arms and stretched, then yawned. "Must be nap time soon."

ঙCষ

Peggy told Jake she wasn't going to sleep with him for their nap. Her body still wasn't trusting, but her heart knew he would never hurt her. Jake accepted her reasoning and told himself it was not a rejection. It still hurt, but one thing was sure, she was still there, and right now that's all that mattered to him.

They didn't pack a lunch and had a nice bike ride at Ledges Park. The air was cool, and the leaves had changed colors. The sun was bright, which made it a nice day for a ride. Peggy could feel her legs get stronger the more she rode her bike. She thought bike riding was easier than when she and her sister took up jogging. They stopped at the restaurant down from the library.

"These sandwiches are wonderful," said Peggy as she took another bite. "I think we should get the recipe or take several home for tomorrow."

"I'll go in and ask if they give out their recipes." He smiled at her as he stood. "I'll be right back, either with a recipe or twenty more sandwiches." He laughed as he went inside.

Peggy brought paper and a pen in her bike basket. She wanted to propose her plan to Jake, but didn't want to do it at the house. For some reason, she thought if they talked about it away from home, they might see a different perspective.

Peggy watched Jake carry a bag full of sandwiches and set them on the table. "No recipe?" asked Peggy, disappointed.

Jake took the recipe out of his pocket and handed it to her. She read out loud, "Beef, bottle of barbeque sauce, buns, mix beef and sauce together, put on bun." Peggy could hardly finish reading because she was laughing so hard. "Is this for real?"

He pulled out another recipe for the sauce. "This is for real. I decided to buy more in case we didn't feel like cooking later." He looked at the pad of paper that was now on the table. "What's the paper for."

"I have a plan, Jake." Peggy explained her plan, the need to reconnect with his contact, and the time that it would take to bring these people to justice. "We shouldn't be the judge of these people, so we'll do research with the information the contact gives, and decide from there our plan of action."

Jake was interested in any plan that would save lives and still fight the insidious crime that was done against innocent lives. The way he was doing it was slow, and Norman always got there before he could finish with his plan.

"For now, I'll just let you think about it." She dug into the bag and took out a sandwich, took a big bite, and looked at Jake. "There is still a lot we don't know about each other. You don't even know if I have any sisters or brothers, or where my parents live, or even if I have parents."

"And you don't know those things about me either," said Jake. Seeing how Peggy was enjoying her food, he took out a second sandwich and ate while there was silence. The silence was comfortable between them. He looked at her outline and studied it. "The plan could work," said Jake, "but I don't know if I'm ready to go through with it."

"I'm here until next week. We don't have to decide now. I want to enjoy every minute with you, Jake." She kissed him on the cheek and smiled. "Then I want to let Penny, my sister, live in my apartment until my lease is up, and I come and live here. I really like the small town, riding bikes to almost everywhere, and now that I've met Adeline and Arnie, I'd have to see them all the time.

"I didn't mean to invite myself into your life. I realize now that I'm forcing myself on you, wanting to live with you and setting up our own plan for justice." She put her sandwich down.

He turned her face toward him. "Peggy," he said, looking into her deep brown eyes, "I want you in my life, and don't think differently. I would love to have you here with me all the time, but I want you to be ready first. I don't want to force you to do anything."

"I'm glad you feel that way, Jake." She finished her sandwich, threw away the empty wrapper, then put her tablet and pen in her basket. Peggy was trying to sort out her feelings, and the more she tried, the more she realized one thing. She still liked the man who came into her life in Minneapolis, and she wanted to be a part of his life. Whether they carried out her justice plan or not, loving Jake would be the most exciting thing she'd ever done.

"Let's go to the grocery store and get the stuff for sandwiches," said Jake. "Hey, and let's invite Arnie and Adeline over for barbeque after we get home from Des Moines."

"Perfect idea," said Peggy.

ℬℭ

Arnie and Adeline brought the Buick to pick them up in the morning. They were instructed not to eat breakfast as they would be eating on the way to Des Moines. Peggy and Jake had small backpacks, Jake's held ten thousand in cash, and Peggy had five thousand. They were going to open an account in Des Moines.

At breakfast, Adeline was telling everyone the schedule, what they were going to see, where they would shop, and that Arnie and Jake would have to find something to do while Peggy and she went to the yarn shop.

ℬℭ

Arnie dropped the women in front of the blue awning at Knitted Together. Peggy was excited to learn more about knitting and to actually make something. The knitting store, Peggy thought, was awesome. There were shelves with yarn, and tables with people sitting around, knitting different projects. Part of the room had plush couches and seasoned knitters were knitting sweaters, and some were knitting socks.

Adeline introduced Peggy to the owner. Adeline, when she was younger and drove, took a lot of the classes and taught a few classes herself. Now she was excited to be able to show Peggy what a wonderful shop it was.

One lady was giving beginning lessons, and Peggy sat in on the session. When she was done, she wandered around the store and looked at the kits that were for sale.

Adeline waved at her from across the room. Peggy went over, and Adeline showed her the slippers kit she picked up. "This is really easy. Is that the right color of yarn?"

"No, I was thinking blue." They picked out navy blue for Jake's slippers and light blue for Peggy's. Adeline bought the kit, and Peggy paid for the yarn. Two hours later, when they went outside, Arnie and Jake were waiting for them.

"Okay, we'll head over to Wells Fargo, and you two can do your banking." Adeline and Arnie waited in the parking lot for them.

Before they left home, they decided to open just one account. Peggy remembered from her sister being a teller that there would be a Currency Transaction Report that would have to be filled out for any transactions made to a financial institution over ten thousand dollars. Jake was hesitant at first but decided in the end to have Peggy together on his account.

The banker asked personal information of them both, wrote up the papers, and escorted them to a teller window. The banker shook hands with Jake and Peggy and told them to enjoy the rest of their day in Des Moines.

Peggy filled out the deposit slip, but the teller was watching Jake as he pulled out the money from both backpacks. "There is fifteen thousand," Jake told the teller, "but I know you'll recount it."

The teller put the money in the counting machine, and her total was fifteen thousand as well. She marked it off the deposit slip, put her initials, then wrote that the full amount was paid in hundreds. She took the pen that detected counterfeit bills and check the bills. When she was satisfied there were no fake bills, she brought the money to the vault. When the teller returned, she handed Jake the receipt.

The system automatically entered the information for the Currency Transaction Report, but there was one question that was needed for the form to be complete. "Sir, what is your occupation?"

Jake quickly replied that he fixed computers. The teller turned to Peggy and asked her the same. Unemployed was her response. Thirty minutes after entering Wells Fargo, they headed out to the parking lot to find Arnie and Adeline sitting on a bench in the grassy area by the plush garden.

They smiled and waved when they saw Peggy and Jake leave the building. "Did everything work out all right?" asked Adeline. She wasn't sure what had happened in the bank but hoped if Peggy opened an account that meant she was moving to Iowa. But it was none of her business, so she bit her tongue and didn't ask what her plans were. She would love to have Peggy here where she could pamper her and teach her things. She sent up a silent prayer in hopes that it was true. Peggy was staying.

🐒🌓

The sandwiches were a big hit. Adeline had never eaten at that restaurant even though it was so close to the library. "I don't need to go there, I can come here and eat for free." They all laughed, and when they were done eating, Jake set up lawn chairs by the pond.

Peggy pointed to the fish one by one and told Adeline their names. Jake and Arnie were already talking about their next project. "I'll show you how to make a deck. Where do you want it?"

Jake and Arnie walked to the front of the house, then to the back. They decided that the best place would be in the back where they could look at the wooded area at the end of Jake's property. After doing some measuring, they were going to head to the hardware store. Arnie was a person who thought of an idea and then had to complete it right away. He would probably work on the deck first thing in the morning and would still be at it at midnight if it wasn't completed. Then he realized he had the Buick and not the truck.

"We'll have to wait until tomorrow to pick up the lumber," said Arnie.

"That's fine with me," said Jake, but wasn't too pleased that Arnie would want to get started when the lumber yard opens at seven in the morning. "Why don't we go inside and have some cheesecake?" Jake held the door open. "Adeline's recipe of course."

"Then I'll have some. You can't beat Adeline's recipes, especially her cheesecake," said Arnie.

After they had dessert, Adeline helped Peggy get started on her slippers. She was happy that Peggy caught on to the pattern so quickly, and was confident that the next time they met, Peggy would have both pairs done.

ಬಿಲ್ಲ

Jake was outside with Arnie building the deck, and Peggy had just finished Jake's slippers. She thought they looked good for her first attempt at knitting. She took a long hot shower, dressed, and drank her second cup of coffee.

Peggy put the slippers in a bag and went outside to check on the guys and their progress. "Things are going good. So far, nothing has gone wrong," said Arnie. "We'll only be working through the night." He winked at Jake.

"I hope that was a joke," said Jake, already sore from the hammering.

"I'm going to the library to show Adeline Jake's slippers." She pulled them out of the bag, and Jake looked them over.

"These are great, Peggy." He kissed her, then realized Arnie was there, and pulled away.

"Adeline will be proud of you," said Arnie.

ಬಿಲ್ಲ

As expected, the deck was finished that night. Jake and Peggy ate dinner at the table Jake and Arnie found at a garage sale. "I love this deck," said Peggy.

"Arnie is good at what he does. I don't think there is anything he can't do, and he's teaching me everything." Jake looked at Peggy. "I love you being here. I didn't realize how lonely it was around here before you came. I guess it was what I was used to, and now I'm used to you being here."

"I thought I would be homesick. I've never been away from home this long, but I feel like I belong here. You've made it so easy to fit in."

"Tonight we should talk about our lives apart from each other. What we like, our dreams, our family, our friends," suggested Jake.

"Good idea."

"Let's clean the kitchen, make coffee, and settle in the living room."

"I hope you didn't mind me making barbeque sandwiches again?" asked Peggy. "I'll try and find something different for tomorrow."

"I think I could eat them every day. I have a recipe box in the cupboard with all of Adeline's recipes."

"Super!"

They were settled in the living room, Peggy in the recliner, Jake in a chair across from her. "Let's see," said Jake, "where to start." He took a gulp of his coffee. "I'm an only child. My mom and dad are still alive. They live in Missouri." *I think.* "They didn't like the winters in Minnesota. We lived there the last years I was in school. I did research on places to live when I left home and wanted to find a small place where it was quiet. That's why I don't have a computer or phone.

"Except now, I have a cell phone." He smiled at her and pulled out his phone. "I need to call my girl, you know. Otherwise, I would use the pay phone in front of Roger's store.

"I think I was a pretty good kid," said Jake. "I finished high school, but didn't want to go to college. I didn't have any friends really to speak of, so when I moved, I really didn't leave anyone behind. My folks know where I live, but they don't write or anything. I should contact them." He stared into space. "Yeah, that would be a good idea to contact them. I'd like to see them, too, but I'd have to wait to see when they are traveling to plan the trip.

"I didn't really have any dreams, or want to get rich, but now I have plans. I want to get married and have children, and continue my friendship with Adeline and Arnie. I want to eventually put my past behind me and move on." He moved to the couch next to the recliner Peggy was sitting in and looked at her. "I want you in my life."

"I want that, too," said Peggy.

Peggy asked questions about Jake's childhood, more about his parents. When she had all her questions answered, she started with her story.

"I have a sister, Penny. I think I mentioned her before, and we are really close. I told her I was coming to stay with a guy I had just met, and she was really nervous about it. I haven't called her since I got here because I didn't want her asking a whole bunch of questions, but I'll call her in the morning.

"My parents live in Coon Rapids, several miles from me. My sister, Penny, lives with them until she can find a job and move out. She's younger than me, but people say we look alike. I'm not so sure about that.

"I was a loner in school. I studied all the time. After high school, I went to the University of Minnesota. I graduated with a degree in business, minor in computer science. I was on the Dean's List. I thought I would eventually get married, and have children, but thought I should date first." Jake laughed.

"What do you like to do besides garden?" asked Jake.

"I like being on the computer and researching everything I can think of. It keeps me up-to-date on things. I like reading the Minneapolis Star Tribune on line, too. I usually skim the headlines, and if anything sounds interesting, I'll read it."

"You haven't been on your computer at all since you got here, except to research knitting."

"I don't miss it either. I guess I was just filling the void of not having anyone around."

"I usually do the same thing at the library. Research in the morning, then go home and hang out. Sometimes I'll go bike riding in the park and wander around. Not much else, except I went to Minneapolis. I wanted to find out about the trial and Judge Klein. Lucky for me, I met you."

"Lucky for me, too."

☙

Judge Klein was getting out of the hospital today, and he was crabbier than ever. It may have had something to do with the note he received the day before from his wife.

Howard,

> *I will not be coming to the hospital anymore. I've decided to leave you. You will shake your fist and yell that I will be cut off from all funds and never be able to see you again. But that's exactly why I'm leaving. To never see you again.*

You pushed our sons away, and I let you because I wanted your money. I realized I lost a lot more than money can buy, the love and respect of our children. You won't have me around to manipulate, so I'm not so sure what you'll do with your time because you lived for that. I've moved to a nice townhouse in St. Paul. I bought it with the hush money you kept throwing at me to tell everyone that our sons were always stopping over and calling when they weren't. Now I will tell the story of how you pushed our sons away, and yes, I'll admit to some extent it was my fault for not standing up to you.

When I dropped off the note at the hospital, the staff begged me to take you home, so you would stop yelling at them for no reason. I told them that's what you do best.

Oh, and I have a meeting next week with your friend at the paper, only he wants to interview me, *this time.*

Goodbye forever,
Mary

CHAPTER FOURTEEN

"NELL AND I had a great time. I couldn't ask for the information I needed because at one point during our date, she said she couldn't believe that I didn't rekindle our relationship because I wanted something."

"I understand *that*! Women are so touchy. So will you ask her at all, or leave it alone for a while?"

"I've really enjoyed her company, and would like to get more serious. So for now, I'm not asking her for anything."

"Probably a good idea."

"I just wish I'd gotten more information from this Jake person. I want the guy in Omaha brought to justice, but now I don't think it will happen. I guess it doesn't matter when it happens, but without a contact, it won't happen anytime soon."

ഇരുക

"I didn't even know your last name was Bailey until we opened an account."

"I don't remember ever hearing your last name either until then. But I remembered your first name, what you looked like, and your love for all the things that I loved. That part really amazed me, how much we have in common." She took a sip from her cup. "How we can get by with so little, especially you. I've never known anyone who doesn't have a computer or television."

"Peggy, I want to make love to you."

Startled by the sudden change of subject, Peggy let out a nervous giggle. She had thought of that many times herself, but she didn't know if she was ready just yet. Jake pulled her to her feet and held her close. "I want to make love to you, but we just started to know each other. He kissed her hair, then her ear, then pulled her face into his and kissed her. Slowly. Sweetly. Passionately.

He put his hands on her shoulders. "I want you, but I'm willing to wait. Then when we really get to know each other and accept each others lives, past and present, I would like the honor of making love to you."

"I would like that, too, Jake, but what do we do in the meantime?"

He smiled at her. "You'll have to teach me how to knit."

Peggy laughed. "I'll have Adeline teach you."

"No, I think you can teach me just fine."

"Maybe I'll teach you how to roll the yarn into balls. It will keep your hands busy."

"I think I'll have to roll a lot of balls of yarn for that to happen." Jake brought her close again. "What do you want to do tomorrow?"

"More of this."

"Then it will be a mighty fine day." He gave her an Eskimo kiss, which made her giggle.

෩෬

The next morning, the first thing Peggy did was pour herself a cup of coffee. *I love that timer. Roll out of bed, drink fresh coffee.* She had her computer and Wi-Fi plugged in on the kitchen table. She researched the trial in Minneapolis, and the article she read told of the jury's verdict.

"Jake," she yelled, "come read this."

Luke Ames was sentenced this morning to thirty years in prison. Ames didn't have the usual smirk on his face. He looked pale and drawn while waiting for his fate.

Judge Howard Klein left the hospital this morning. His wife was not at his side as she was the first few days of his hospital stay. A source close to Mrs. Klein says she's left him and is filing for divorce.

Although the judge has been discharged, he will require twenty-four-hour care for at least two weeks. Hospice will provide in-home care for him.

"Luke got justice, I think," said Peggy.

Jake was quiet, thinking about what he had seen and not reported it. The images of the judge doubling over in pain, returned. He rubbed his head and poured coffee, as if the caffeine was going to make him feel better. He filled Peggy's cup and sat back down.

"I think I need to lie down, Peg."

Peggy looked at him, and noticed how pale he was. She touched his face, and it was clammy. "Sure, let's go lie down." She took his hand and led him to the bedroom.

"Going to bed will probably make it worse," said Jake. "Let's go for a bike ride instead." They got dressed and took off down the rode on their bikes.

Peggy followed Jake. He was pedaling fast toward the park, going at a fast pace along the trails, and soon he was on the other side of the park and kept going. Peggy was able to keep up and was wondering how he was doing. She knew he had to work it out on his own, but she would be there when he needed her.

∞CB

Brad Hensley was trying to set up an appointment with Daniel Johnson, the director and founder of *Be There for the Children*. He had heard of the great things Johnson had done to protect children, and wanted to meet him in person. Johnson had been instrumental in building a shelter and had started programs for abused kids. He also wanted to make sure no child would be victims of pornography, to be used, abused, and then cast aside to fend for themselves once they were too old for anyone in the pornography world to care about them.

Johnson set up the foundation because he had six children of his own, and wanted his children to be safe. With his new organization, thousands would benefit. He also urged spouses of abusers to turn them in before they traumatized their children beyond repair.

Brad Hensley wanted to personally thank Johnson for all his hard and diligent work on this much-needed issue. He thought he would fly into Omaha to personally thank him, take him to dinner, and find out how he could get this program started in his home state of Florida.

⁏⁐

Nell pulled up the covers over her shoulders. "Did you know you talk in your sleep?"

"No, I didn't know that," said John.

"You talk a lot about justice, and usually the one person you talk about was arrested or shot." She turned to face him. "It's been past cases, and it's as if you arranged it," said Nell, laughing.

He felt the heat rising to his face. Nell had never told him he talked in his sleep, and it seems she has figured out what he does. Not good if he was to continue on with his personal *Bring to Justice* campaign. Nell did not know of the millions of dollars he had inherited from his parents, nor would he ever tell her. One way to put the money to good use was to find injustice in the world and make it right, but he didn't want anyone to find out about it.

His parents donated a lot of money to worthy causes, and in the end, they were persecuted by the justice system. John has tried to come to terms with it, but he was still struggling with it.

There was a man in Omaha that he wanted stopped before he abused any more children. This time, the perpetrator was actually fighting against the one thing the perpetrator believed in. *He had to be stopped, would be stopped*, thought John, whether he found Jake or not.

John pulled Nell into him. "I'll work on not talking in my sleep, but now that we're awake, let's make love again."

⁏⁐

Jake put on the breaks, dropped his bike to the ground, and sat on the grass. Peggy soon joined him. He reached for her and pulled her into him and started to shake. She held tight, and after a few minutes, she felt his pain surge through her. The intensity of it tore Peggy's heart.

He pulled away from her and whispered, "I need you in my life, Peggy. I see Judge Klein's bloody image in my mind all the time. It's time I did something about it."

She sniffed and wiped her eyes on her sleeves. "I'll always be here for you. Just let me know what you want me to do."

Jake pulled her close, and tears came freely, not just for his past, but now for the happiness of his future. His future with a wonderful woman. When he thought about it, his past was what brought Peggy to him, and now they could build a life together. He knew it would be a long time before he didn't think about what happened to the judge, and hoped he could start the healing process after he reported what he saw. Peggy kissed him on the cheek, and with that, it was confirmed, thought Jake, she would stay in his life and help him.

CHAPTER FIFTEEN

NOTHING WAS PLANNED for the next few days. Jake and Peggy stayed close to home. Peggy knitted another pair of slippers, then decided to knit Arnie and Adeline a pair. Jake sat mostly on the deck reading. Adeline had her list of *must reads*, and Jake was getting a good start on her list. Most were fiction by local authors. She even listed some Minnesota authors for Peggy. Mostly though, Jake liked the *how-to* books, and found one on building a fire pit. He wanted one far enough from the deck so it wouldn't be a fire hazard, and yet close enough so it could be enjoyed.

When Jake was ready to attempt the project, he invited Arnie over for lunch. Peggy made hamburgers and baked fries, and made the Oreo cookie pudding dessert and made the adjustment to Adeline's note on her recipe card of what Arnie liked best. She packed leftovers and put them in the fridge so Arnie could take them to Adeline, when he was finished for the day with the fire pit project.

Jake and Arnie went to the hardware store, and Peggy was left alone. She called her mom to tell her how she was doing. The only thing she had mentioned to her was that she was traveling to Iowa to see a friend.

Now she could tell her the friend was a guy, and that it all turned out well. Her mom had a lot of questions. "When are you coming home? Are you sure you're okay?"

Peggy told her she learned how to knit, and her mom said she wanted a pair of slippers, and said not to knit any for her dad because he never wore slippers in his life.

Peggy promised to bring Jake for a visit in the near future, but right now, she was having a lot of fun. "I can't believe he doesn't have a car, and you are riding bikes as your only means of transportation." There was a moment of silence. "That must mean he doesn't have any money. Peggy, you can do better than that. Find someone with a stable job so he can support you and a family."

If she only saw what Peggy saw in Jake's basement, she would know he had enough money to provide for her *and* a family. "He does fine, Mom. I'll call you in a couple of days. Love you."

Peggy went outside in the sun by the fish pond, and soon she fell asleep. Arnie's truck woke her when he pulled into the driveway. She stretched and yawned a couple of times, then joined them at the back of the truck. Peggy took a couple of bricks and dropped them in their chalk circle on the grass.

In no time the fire pit was built and the guys were building a fire. Peggy was on the deck knitting and watching them. "Hey, Peggy, call Adeline and see if she wants to come over for a campfire," said Jake.

"Yes, I would love to," was Adeline's response. "I thought those boys were up to something when Arnie said he was going to Jake's for lunch. Since it's not that far, I'll just drive over."

"She's coming," Peggy relayed the message to the guys. "She's driving over."

"I'll have to drive her home," said Arnie, "if it's after dark. Will it be okay if I leave her car in your garage until morning?"

"I think it will be too crowded with our bicycles in there," said Jake, trying not to laugh.

Arnie put his arm around Jake's shoulders. "You need a car. Your woman's not going to put up with biking when she's eight months pregnant."

They all laughed. It seemed so natural when Arnie said pregnant, and yes, Peggy wondered if she could still ride a bike if she was pregnant. A subject for much later, she decided.

Five minutes later, Adeline pulled in and walked over with a baking pan. "Peggy, go put this in the oven. I made a homemade pot pie this morning, and we can eat out here on the deck if you want. It will take about an hour to heat up. Peggy went inside and Adeline sat on the deck. She saw Peggy's knitting and examined the slippers. When she came back, Adeline asked, "You have four pairs of slippers, is that in case you and Jake wear them out?"

"Those blue striped ones belong to you and Arnie." Peggy watched Adeline smile. "Something you can wear around the library." Peggy laughed.

With a smile, she said, "That library doesn't have good ventilation, and my feet get so cold. I think wearing slippers is a good idea."

"It might be because your feet don't have the circulation they once did." Arnie chuckled.

Adeline laughed. "You're probably right.

They ate dinner on the deck, and although the pot pie recipe was new, it was made Adeline style, perfectly wonderful. When the dishes were cleared away and brought into the house, the four of them sat and enjoyed the fire. After several minutes of silence, Arnie asked, "Are you two getting married anytime soon?"

What Jake thought may be an uncomfortable question for Peggy, he found very timely. "I have to ask her first, and we thought we'd take the rest of our time together to get to know each other better."

"So you have been thinking about marriage?" inquired Adeline.

"As soon as he found out I could knit, he asks at least five times a day," mused Peggy.

Adeline laughed. "Arnie married me because I could cook."

"She was the best cook this side of the Mississippi. My dad said I'd be a fool to pass up such a good deal."

It seemed they could not offend each other, and it was obvious they were still in love the way they took care of each other. Arnie kept busy puttering around the house and helping Jake, and Adeline loved working at the library. She said all the time that it wasn't work if you were doing something you loved.

Jake would love to ask Peggy to marry him, but he didn't have a ring, and he didn't know if it was too soon to ask. He could always ask to see if she would want to first. Then they could take their time before their wedding. He smiled and decided he would think about marrying Peggy tonight before he went to sleep.

The Buick was parked in the garage, and Arnie and Adeline drove away. Peggy fed the fish, then they both went in the house. Peggy told Jake about her mom wanting to meet him, and Jake thought it was a good idea. "I could fly back home with you and meet her."

"That would be nice," said Peggy.

"We have another week here, so you have plenty of time to warn your parents." "I won't have to warn them, that's for sure, silly you."

Jake took the Oreo dessert from the fridge and dished up two bowls full of pudding. "This is so good, Peggy. I think I'll have to ask you to marry me because you're such a good cook."

"And I'll get a job in the library!" Peggy laughed, and so did Jake.

"Come here, you," Jake said to Peggy. "I want to thank you again for being there for me at the park."

Peggy walked to him. Jake took her bowl, set it on the counter, and held her close. "I think I love you, Peggy. I don't want to move too fast, but I did want to tell you that." She held him tight.

"After Minneapolis, I didn't want to do any of it anymore, but I still think about these people that will get by with their lies, their physical and sexual abuse, their arrogant and deceitful behavior.

"I want to look at your plan, Peggy." He took a bite of pudding from her bowl. "I want you to go through the whole thing with me. I want to keep helping this guy, but I want to truly feel good about helping and not wondering about Norman."

Jake fed her a bite, then she walked to her room and brought her notebook back to the kitchen table. Jake had read her mind and was making coffee.

When coffee was poured, Jake and Peggy sat at the table and went through Peggy's *justice plan*. They planned everything out, and Jake took notes of the things they needed to do the next day. Peggy booted up her computer and did research on resources they might need.

Around two, they left all the paperwork on the table and went to their separate rooms. They were excited, and exhausted. Jake padded to

Peggy's room and crawled in bed with her and pulled her close. "Don't be alarmed. I just need to hold you for a while."

෩෬

Nell got up and took a long hot shower. It was good to have John back in her life. *He is a nice man,* Nell thought. But she had been the one to call it off the last time and was sure he would never come back, but she was wrong.

John had a fitful night talking about a Daniel Johnson and children. She tried waking him, but he kept tossing and turning and saying this man's name. She was tempted to turn on the television and wait for the, "We will interrupt your daily program with earth-shattering news . . ." but she didn't. In case she was right, and someone was dead, wounded, or arrested, she didn't think she could handle that right now.

"Nell, baby, I'm heading for the office." He moved the shower curtain until he saw her naked body. He leaned in and kissed her. "I'll see you after work. Think of where you want to eat dinner." He wanted to say he loved her, but he winked and left.

Chapter Sixteen

Peggy and Jake were busy from the first moment they got out of bed. Jake loved waking up with Peggy in his arms. He slept straight through until morning. No nightmares, no thoughts of what Peggy might be doing in her room, or thoughts of the world. He knew he was safe in her bed, with his arms wrapped around her.

Jake now had all the paperwork from the post office box, his check receipts from his charity donations, and receipts from plane tickets. He knew that if he was ever caught with this information, it would prove beyond a shadow of a doubt that he was where Norman was, and would be found guilty.

Peggy had a great idea. Tonight would be the healing ceremony, where the past was burned in the fire, and the future was toasted with wine and good food. They would get the groundwork done on their justice plan, and by evening, they would celebrate.

Jake set up a new answering service and then went to the library and used the pay phone to call his contact. He left a brief message with the new phone number, hung up, and rode back home. He could get messages from the answering service with his cell phone, but he would continue to make calls to his contact on a pay phone.

Jake marinated steaks and put them in the fridge, along with the wine. They had a full morning and decided to take their ritual nap. They raced to Peggy's room and got under the covers. Jake pulled her close, and when they were done laughing, they were quiet. Sleeping so close to each other was getting harder and harder for them to resist temptation.

80C3

"What do you want? You said you had to see me right away."

John stood up and paced. He smiled just thinking about the message he received that morning. He wanted to tell his good friend, Max, right away.

"This morning I got a phone message from Jake. He said, in so many words he was back in business." He stood in front of Max. "Can you believe he contacted me?"

"You look very happy about it."

"Just one problem, and that's with Nell."

"I thought you two were doing okay."

John sat down behind his desk. "She said I talk in my sleep, and in the morning, the names I mentioned were reported on the news as dead."

"I didn't know you talked in your sleep. You just snore loud on our fishing weekends."

"This isn't funny, Max." He looked away. "I think I'm in love with her. I'm not ready to tell her about what I do on the side."

"You'll have to do it sooner or later," said Max.

John hung his head. "Maybe I don't want to do this after all." He looked at Max.

"I should just call Jake back and tell him *no more*."

Now it was Max who paced. "It's up to you. Try it for a while, and if you want to quit, then *you* terminate the relationship."

Max sat down, and there was silence for a few minutes. John thought of Nell, thought of how it would be to get married and leave his need to make the world right, behind him. Nell was still young enough to have children, and they could grow old together.

"Just days ago I wanted to find Jake so badly I couldn't sleep nights. Now that Nell and I are back together, I'm having second thoughts. I'll have to think about it. I'm supposed to take Nell out tonight. I'm afraid if I spend the night, I'll do more talking in my sleep, and I can't afford for that to happen. And that damn Norman. I want him out of the picture."

"Go. Take her out, sleep with her, then find out what you talk about tonight. Maybe if you know, you can program your mind to think better thoughts."

"What are you? A freaking hypnotist?"

Max laughed. "Nope. I'm just trying to help. Now can I go back to work?"

ଚ୦ଔଓ

Two days before Peggy was to go back to Minnesota, the call came.

Daniel Johnson lives in Omaha. You'll find him hanging around his newly founded Be There for the Children shelter. He opened it to protect children, however, it's debatable whether he abuses all six of his own children. He hangs around the shelter to see how many more relationships he can have with the children there. He is an injustice to children. Stop him and the world will not cry because of it.

Peggy and Jake made a list of what they needed to do. They told Arnie and Adeline that Peggy had lengthened her stay, and they decided that tomorrow they were going to travel by car to Nebraska. They were up most of the night making arrangements. In the morning, Arnie and Adeline took them to a car rental place in Des Moines.

"You two have a good time. We'll miss you while you're gone, and don't worry, we'll feed your fish and keep an eye on the place." They gave each other hugs, and Peggy and Jake went into the rental office.

Jake set the GPS to the hotel address where they were staying in Papillion, close to Omaha. They decided to go there because it was just outside of Omaha. It was a quaint hotel and had the amenities they needed.

Peggy made the first of many calls after they unpacked. "Hi, my husband and I would like to take a tour of the shelter. I called yesterday to set it up." There was silence. "Maybe I didn't talk to you. It was about a donation."

"Oh, yes, I remember now." The woman on the other end shuffled papers, then said, "You are scheduled for five this afternoon. I hope you don't mind that it's so late. Daniel Johnson would also like to be here when you arrive, and it was the only time he had available."

"That's wonderful. What does the good Daniel Johnson do during the day?"

"He teaches at the elementary school and then coaches basketball after school. He does so much good for the children that he hardly has time for anything else."

"My husband and I will see you at five."

While they waited the hours before their appointment, they headed to a department store in town. Jake thought they needed wedding rings to make it believable that they were married. They picked out basic gold bands. When they got back to the hotel, Jake poured wine, and they put on their wedding bands.

"This is only temporary, Peggy, until we make it official."

She twisted her ring around and thought about how fast everything was happening. One thing she could say for sure was that no matter what, she was happy. Peggy looked at Jake and went into his arms. "I think I'm falling in love with you."

"I think that's just wonderful." He picked her up and twirled her around.

"Let's toast to our engagement." They touched their glasses and drank the wine.

"Now it's time to get ready, my dear wife. You can have the bathroom first."

"Why thank you, my dear husband." Peggy giggled, gathered her clothes, and went to the bathroom to take a shower.

∞∞∞

"I'm Joyce Armstrong. Please come back to the lounge area." Joyce was thin, had her dishwater blonde hair pulled back, and wore a knee-length black skirt with a red blouse.

Jake had on a navy blue suit, white shirt, and tie. Peggy had curled her long hair, pulled it back, clipped it, and put on makeup which she rarely did. She wore a black suit with a white blouse. She thought heels were a worthless thing for a woman to wear, so she had bought a pair of comfortable black shoes.

Joyce thought they looked too young to take an interest in giving donations, but everyone who wanted to give money was welcomed. Daniel was late as usual. She was getting sick of covering for him and thought of starting the tour without him, when he came through the door.

Daniel shook hands with Peggy and Jake and made excuses why he was late. "Should we start the tour?" asked Joyce.

Daniel looked at Joyce, and she knew she would hear about it the next day. Daniel Johnson liked to run things his *own* way. They walked past several administrative offices, then walked back to the shelter area. There were several large rooms, and each room had ten beds with a small dresser next to each bed. There was some closet space, but not much.

"With the large rooms, families can be together, and they also have a support system with other families who come in."

"What if the mother is the abuser?" asked Peggy. "Where would the fathers sleep?"

Daniel had never been asked that question before. He figured just men indulged in such pleasure. "We would make adjustments in the sleeping arrangements. However, it has never happened yet."

"If we give you a donation, what would our money go toward?" When Daniel wasn't answering, he looked at Joyce.

Joyce was instructed to say there is a fund for each child for counseling and rehabilitation, but she knew Daniel took most of it. While she was standing there struggling with what to say, she mentally asked herself, *"And why are you working here when nothing happens the way it should?"*

Sick of waiting for Joyce to answer, Daniel looked at Peggy. "Um . . . we give a portion to the children so the parents can get them counseling and into a rehabilitation program." He nervously looked at Joyce. "For the upkeep of the building, and we pay our employees good money to keep the shelter running."

Joyce thought minimum wages were not *good* money, and she was the only employee. She only did it because her father had abused her when she was small, and she knew she could relate to the children. She felt, too, that she could talk to the mothers in a way they would understand not only why it happened, but how their behavior is the most important thing for the child right now.

The next room had several children with their mother. Peggy felt she was invading their privacy, as if they were put on display, and she was there to gawk at them. A little boy pointed at her, then came padding over and wrapped his arms around Peggy's legs. Peggy rubbed the top of his head and asked, "What's your name?"

He looked up at her with his innocent blue eyes. "My mom calls me sweetie. What's your name?"

"My name is Peggy." He looked at her and noticed the big scary man behind her and took off screaming.

"Mommy, mommy, there's the big scary man." The little boy cried with such suffering it brought tears to Peggy's eyes.

Joyce sent in an aide to comfort the family. She wasn't totally oblivious to what the outburst was all about, and hoped their guests sensed something was wrong as well. Joyce wanted to go to the authorities and give them all the information she had about the supposedly honored Daniel Johnson, but she knew deep down she would not be believed. She had to find another way but didn't know how to go about it.

Sensing how upset Peggy was, Jake called an end to the tour.

"I have to go home anyway, so it's good to end the tour," said Daniel. "Joyce will show you out." He hurried down the hall and out the door.

"Joyce, please join us for dinner." Peggy didn't know if Joyce had to check in with her family first, though, or if she had a family.

"I would love to." Joyce hadn't gone out for dinner in such a long time, so she welcomed the invitation. She needed to unwind, and Jake and Peggy seemed like a nice couple she would like to get to know.

Jake and Peggy followed Joyce to the restaurant several miles away. It was a quaint restaurant with just enough background noise where they could have a private conversation with Joyce.

Jake cleared the air by telling the waitress to put everything on his check. They ordered, and in no time it seemed, they had their food. Peggy asked Joyce a few questions about the shelter, and Joyce offered a few suggestions of her own that would make the shelter even better.

Peggy surprised Joyce by asking, "What happened with the little boy? He was so upset after seeing Daniel."

Joyce had tried to gauge what kind of people this young couple was. They were sincere. They wanted to donate money. But was that all they wanted to do? Usually, people just mailed in their money or wired it to the shelter. They were young, and she sensed they were very much in love. But . . . her thoughts trailed off. She decided to just wait and see where this night would take her. Maybe she would get lucky and find out a lot more about this couple and see if they could be trusted with her secret about the shelter.

So Joyce answered, "I can only speculate."

Peggy put her hand on Joyce's. "Please let us know what you suspect happened."

After that one question, that one little question, food was forgotten, and three people sat and talked and proposed a plan.

ॐ

John decided to sleep at home after he relayed his message to Jake. He didn't want Nell to concern herself with his problems. He didn't realize he talked in his sleep until he woke up several times, flailing his arms and legs and saying things he didn't understand. So he decided that even though he missed Nell, he had made the right decision.

The first thing he did in the morning when his feet hit the ground was turn on the television. In the past, Norman usually stepped in, and before Jake started his plan, the perpetrator was eliminated by that evening or first thing the next day.

This morning, he expected it to be done by Norman, but hoped his contact would take care of the situation instead. But when there was no news, he had to calm down. He knew justice wasn't in an instant, not like Norman liked to get justice. John took a couple of deep breaths.

The phone startled him. He grabbed it ready to yell at someone, no matter who it was. "Hi, John, did you sleep well?"

Okay, so maybe I won't yell at Nell. "Hi." He'd slept lousy, was crabby from no sleep, and would really like to see her later. "No! I didn't sleep well." He calmed himself. "Why don't you come here? I might even cook." Cooking calmed him, distracted him. Yes, he would cook. "Bring the wine. See you around five."

He paced after he hung up, his usual activity of late. He decided he'd better get out of the house or he'd be glued to the television. John took a hot shower, dressed, and drove to the grocery store.

CHAPTER SEVENTEEN

T HE SUN WAS rising in Omaha, but Peggy and Jake were awake and up long before that. They were across the street, sitting at McDonald's, eating their breakfast. The notebook with today's plans was spread out on the table.

As part of the plan, Joyce was to keep her eyes and ears open and to report to Jake as often as she could if things changed. Joyce would have a busy day. She knew a family was coming in to the shelter. She always did the paperwork the day after they had settled in, so they would feel welcomed upon their arrival, not just rushed through the system.

Besides, Joyce thought, she would do it her way as often as she could. Daniel wanted things done right when they arrived because he didn't want to miss out on funding. Done right meant his way. Every time he told her how to do it, she muttered under her breath, "Bastard, you don't care about the children, you care about the money."

The morning went by fast, and when Joyce met Jake and Peggy for lunch, she was exhausted. She walked over to Peggy and Jake sitting in a booth at the restaurant they met the night before. Seeing them revived her and reminded her why she was here and that she needed to help protect every child in the shelter.

Peggy wrote down bank accounts, passwords, and account numbers that Daniel Johnson had, either through the shelter or personally. Joyce had copies of statements, canceled checks, deposit ticket copies, and receipts for Johnson's personal and the shelter's accounts. She did his personal banking on occasion, but donations were handled strictly by Daniel Johnson himself.

Jake was asking more questions about Johnson's schedule, where he went, what he did. Did he have any favorite coffee shops, restaurants that he frequented, friends?

"One thing he does without fail is go to Starbucks on Main Street every morning around seven." She ordered coffee when the waitress came. "At night, before he goes home, he stops in at city hall and talks to the mayor for around thirty minutes."

Jake wrote it all down: addresses, places, the mayor's name, everything he thought would be helpful. The three of them had several pots of coffee before Joyce had to get back to the shelter. Peggy and Jake stayed and wrote out their strategy.

‘’‘’

Brad Hensley called the shelter in hopes of talking to Daniel Johnson. He would be in town in the next couple of days and wanted to look at the shelter and find out how it was run. But most of all, to talk with the man who made it all possible: Daniel Johnson.

"Hello, Children's Shelter, how may I help you?"

"Is Daniel Johnson there?"

"He doesn't come in unless he has an appointment." *Unless there are boys that* "What would you like to talk to him about?" *Oh my god!* It finally came to Joyce that her boss, the man everyone adored, was actually—she couldn't think or speak it. But she knew she was right and would call Jake and Peggy as soon as she hung up from this Brad person.

"I would like to meet him. I'll be in town tomorrow until Friday and would like to talk to him about starting a shelter in Florida."

It was hard for Joyce to think. She just wanted to talk with the younger couple that came to deliver justice. She had thought mostly that Daniel was taking the shelter's money and was blinded by the fact that he started the shelter for a reason, for a selfish reason. She just prayed his own children were safe. She let out a sigh. He had six sons.

"Mr. Johnson works during the day but could meet you here tomorrow at the shelter around five. Will that work for you, sir?"

"Perfect."

"Will you have a place to stay when you get here?"

"I haven't gotten that far yet. I just wanted to make sure I had an appointment first."

Joyce had an idea, dug through her purse, and pulled out the card Jake gave her. She read off the name of the hotel and told Mr. Hensley there were restaurants and coffee shops in the area. When he hung up the phone, Joyce immediately called Jake. When she was finished with that call, she called Daniel and set up the meeting.

ಹೊಡ

Peggy worked on her computer and tried to tap into Johnson's banking accounts, but she was too new to computer hacking to be of any good. She did have an idea though, and called the bank where he kept his personal accounts. With all his information, passwords, and account numbers, Peggy was able to get the deposits he'd made for the last six months.

She compared them to the check copies of donations. Every time there was a check cashed, he would make a deposit within twenty-four hours. Only twice the donations actually went into the shelter account. Peggy figured he needed something to run the place.

Peggy found out that he also had a safe deposit box and wondered how she could get into the box without being suspected she was not his wife. She quickly googled Mrs. Johnson's name and found photos of her with her husband around the time the shelter was to open. She and Peggy looked nothing alike. *But with a blonde shoulder-length wig, I might be able to pull it off. Of course I need a key, too.* Maybe Joyce could help her get the key.

Joyce told Peggy she would check out his desk. He never locked his drawers because he thought he was always above reproach. Joyce hoped there was a key.

ಹೊಡ

Jake heard the card key in the door and watched while Peggy came in, but it wasn't Peggy. This woman had blonde hair and prominent crow's feet around her eyes. Jake stood and was ready to find out just what this woman was doing with their hotel card key when she smiled. "Peggy?"

She twirled around. "What do you think?" She put down her folder and pulled out the picture she got off the Internet and held it up. "Do you think I can fool anyone?"

"You fooled me." He looked at the picture. "How did you get that wig to look just like Mrs. Johnson's hair?"

"I brought the picture with me to the wig store and told the lady I wanted it styled just like in the picture."

He took her by the shoulders. "You look older somehow. What else did you do?"

"They call them wrinkles." Peggy looked at her watch. "I'll have time to go to the bank. I picked up the safe deposit box key from Joyce." Peggy went to Jake and put her arms around him. "I'm so nervous. I'm afraid I'll mess things up."

"You'll do fine." He held her close. "Do you want me to give you a ride to the bank?"

"I'd better do this myself, although, I would love a ride." She put the key in her pocket and took her new purse off the bed, the one she couldn't believe she'd ever use again, but it looked similar to the one Mrs. Johnson had in one of her pictures.

೮೦೦೮

"Hi, I would like to get into my safe deposit box," said Peggy when she walked up to the teller.

"Sure, follow me," said the teller. Her name tag read Brittany.

Brittany had Peggy sign the card filed in the vault. Peggy turned over the card in hopes she would see Mrs. Johnson's signature so Peggy's signature would at least be close, and there it was on the front of the card. She didn't study it too long because she didn't want to call attention to herself.

Peggy signed and put the same loop in Johnson. She handed back the card with the signature and date. Brittany didn't even look at it. She took down the universal vault key and helped Peggy open her box. Then she was left alone in a tiny room to look at the contents.

It was apparent Johnson's wife was not allowed in the box. There were pictures and cash. She looked through the pictures, and her heart stopped beating, then the tears came. It was a head shot of the little boy at the shelter who screamed when he saw Daniel Johnson.

She took some deep breaths, then slowly looked at all the pictures. They were of small boys. They must have been from the shelter because, thankfully, they were clothed. Peggy went through the pictures, then set them aside along with the cash. There were two business cards sitting on the bottom. One was a porn shop. The other was a photographer. She took the business cards and put them in her bag. She arranged the pictures on the small ledge and took pictures with her cell phone. Then she set the pictures and the money back, and locked the box with Brittany's help.

⬥⬥⬥

"Why are you so crabby? I thought we would have a nice dinner, and all you can do is scowl. If we hadn't already ordered, I'd strongly suggest we leave."

"Nell, I'm sorry. I've had a lot on my mind lately." John took her hand. "Please forgive me. I know I was going to cook. I was distracted . . ."

"I'll try and forgive you, but you really have been a bear."

"Like I said, Sweetheart, I'll work on it." Maybe he needed to take Nell home with him and have sex. Maybe it would clear his head. He really needed answers from his contact. He already had the money at Jake's post office box, and the job wasn't even done yet. *If I could only get my hands on Jake.*

"Now what's the matter, John?"

Why couldn't he tell her what was on his mind? Would she understand why he paid out all that money to get justice in another state? Depending on what happened after dinner, he would call Max and ask him to get information on Jake. John already knew the answer: Max would just tell him to ask Nell to do the research. He was so confused he couldn't think straight.

The waiter brought the food to their table, and John immediately asked it be put in take-out boxes and gave the waiter his credit card. Nell looked confused, but didn't say anything. They left in a hurry and John drove fast to his house. He put the food on the counter, took her hand, and led her to the bedroom. "No making love this time. I need to have raw, lustful sex. Hopefully that will take care of this mood I'm in."

Nell smiled. "I'll do my best."

∞∞

"No, no one asked to see my ID. I guess I looked enough like Mrs. Johnson, so no one doubted me." She took off the wig and scratched her head. "It's hot under there." Peggy put the wig back in the box and asked, "Did you hear from Joyce?"

"Yes, she called." Jake told her about the man coming to find out how he can start his own shelter in Florida. "She also told me something disturbing." He motioned to one of the comfy chairs by the bed, and he sat in the other one. "She thinks Johnson is molesting the boys in the shelter, and maybe even his own sons."

Peggy pulled out the two business cards she found in the safe deposit box and handed them to Jake. "There was also a picture of the boy that screamed when Daniel walked in the room." She pulled out her cell phone and showed Jake.

"Oh God!" He stood. "We'd better get this over with before he has a chance to hurt anyone else."

"Mr. Hensley's visit will give us an advantage. The evidence we plant will be found during Mr. Hensley's stay." Jake sat. "But first, we're going to visit the addresses on these business cards and find out if they know Johnson, and in what capacity."

∞∞

Jake and Peggy went to the photographer first. In the waiting area were high school-aged kids. Peggy went to the desk and asked if they could see the photographer, Justin Styles. He was in but didn't have time to meet with anyone without an appointment right at the moment.

"Tell him Daniel Johnson sent us." Jake stared at Peggy and wondered why she mentioned his name.

The receptionist stood immediately and walked to the back room. When she came back, she had a man with her. "Please come with me," he said.

They went into a small office, shut the door, and motioned to them to sit down.

"Why did Daniel mention my name to you?"

Jake looked at Peggy, because he was still shocked by how fast they were able to see this guy, and hopefully, Peggy was able to explain it to him.

"He mentioned what a good photographer you were . . ."

"Get to the point! I'm a very busy man and I'm very good at what I do, and the only reason Johnson would mention my name . . . just get to the point."

"He wanted us to check in with you to set up a shoot." Now it was Peggy's turn to look at Jake. "We . . . he wonders if you can bring the kids this time because right now no one is at the shelter and he wants to use the shelter as a studio."

"Is he willing to pay the price? Ten thousand up front. Of course he'll make a lot more off the material when he sells it. Did he tell you about George?"

"Yes, he did. He gave us his business card." Peggy took it out to prove that they had the card.

"Okay, good, because he'll take the pictures from my camera and put them on a disc, ready for sale." He looked at his appointment book. "The only time I can fit everything in is tomorrow night between five and six. It will be a rush, but who cares? It's not like anyone has to know how to act."

They all shook hands which made Peggy sick, knowing what they just arranged. Jake and she left the building, got into the car, and sat in silence. Thirty minutes had passed when Jake started the car and drove to the hotel. Peggy called Joyce to fill her in.

Jake looked over Johnson's bank records again, comparing bank records with donations, and personal records of the Johnsons. They talked a little more and decided Peggy would go back to the bank and take out ten thousand in cash, if she could pull it off. That way when they look at Johnson's records they'll see the withdrawal for the same amount that was deposited into Styles's account and will hopefully make the connection. The records won't show who made the deposit.

"Try and go to the same teller. She should remember you from today and might not ask for ID."

"Back on with the wig."

"I like you in the wig." *I like you all the time!* He thought.

"Let's go have supper and get to bed early. I think tomorrow is going to be a big day. Everything should come together."

Peggy took off the skirt she wore to the bank, pulled on a pair of jeans and tennis shoes, and tied her hair back. "I'm ready. First though I think I should get a hug from my husband."

"Ah! I would love to hold my lovely wife."

CHAPTER EIGHTEEN

"Jake, get up."

It was still dark and he tried to think where they had to go today that required him to be up so early. When he couldn't think of one good reason to get up before sunrise, he groaned.

"Jake, I'm scared."

That got his attention, and he rolled over and sat up. "Peg, what's the matter?"

She sat down on his bed and put her head on the pillow. "What if it doesn't work out?"

"It will, and either way, we can produce enough evidence to put him away for a long time." He caressed her hair. "Right now, he thinks he's untouchable and probably being careless."

"I hope so. Can I crawl in bed with you?"

He didn't want her near him because he had so many emotions going on right now. He didn't want to risk forcing her to make love to him. "Sure," he said weakly, "but you'd better behave yourself and stay on your side of the bed."

Peggy was under the covers so fast, it startled Jake. "Geez, Peggy, you could at least hide your enthusiasm." He covered them up with the blankets. "Let's sleep until noon."

"That's a deal."

But Jake couldn't sleep with Peggy so close. He tried to envision that they were just friends or that he had no interest in women and that it was just a platonic relationship, but the harder he tried to convince his brain of that fact, the more his flesh crawled with lust. He would get through this, he told himself, and then when they were done with their justice plan in Omaha, they would go back to Iowa, and there, in his bed, he would make love to her.

𝔙𝔙𝔙

John was watching news, but there was nothing that he wanted to hear. He went to the counter and poured himself another cup of coffee. He'd called Max the night before, and Max assured him that Jake would not have gotten in touch with him to screw him out of his money. There was a reason for it, and maybe Jake decided to do it differently so it would take longer. John hoped so, but that still didn't make the wait easier. He decided he had been spoiled in the past, and now he needed patience to see this through.

He and Nell had a good evening. She took his mind off his problem and kept it off for quite a long time. They heated the food they took from the restaurant and didn't get to bed until after midnight.

Nell did wake him up twice, saying he was talking loudly in his sleep, and after the second time, she took her pillow and blanket and went to the couch. He felt bad about it, and when he got up to make coffee, he woke her and tucked her in bed. She was sleeping soundly now as he surfed the channels for more news, but was soon frustrated and shut it off.

𝔙𝔙𝔙

Jake walked down to the lobby and brought back two steaming mugs of coffee. Peggy had finished dressing and put on her blonde wig. Next, she did her makeup and put on the tiny crow's feet.

"Coffee is here, my darling wife," Jake yelled in the room.

"Okay, my darling husband, I'm in the bathroom."

Jake stood in the doorway and watched her put on lipstick. That alone was such a sexual experience for him he had to quickly set the cups of coffee down before he spilled them.

To think of something else, he asked her, "Are you nervous?"

"Yes, very nervous. It's different today because I'm getting money, and if they suspect I'm not who I say I am, they could push that little button below the counter and I'll be arrested. I don't think even the best defense to catch a child molester would hold up in court."

"I'll drive you this time."

"I thought I could handle it and drive myself, but I'm going to take you up on your offer." She gave him a quick kiss on the lips. "I think we'd better get going before lunches start, and my teller *buddy* might be gone." Why she really wanted to leave now was because she was about to lose her nerve, but they needed the withdrawal for evidence."

If they subpoenaed Johnson's records, they would see a cash withdrawal for the exact amount of cash that Styles charged for the photo shoot today. No matter how long and hard Johnson denied the accusation, physical proof was hard to deny.

☜☞

"Hi! It's nice to see you again. What can I help you with today?" asked Brittany.

Peggy let out a sigh of relief and handed her the withdrawal slip. "Are you watching the Corn Huskers tonight?"

"Of course I am! I haven't missed a game in three years."

"We'll be watching, too." Peggy knew if everything went as planned, they would be watching the game. She only hoped things went as planned.

"I'll have to get an okay from my manager to take out this much cash." She locked her drawer. "It shouldn't be a problem, as you know your husband takes out cash all the time." She locked her computer. "I'll be right back."

Peggy was glad Joyce gave her the password on the account. It seemed like forever until Brittany came back with the money. It was all strapped, and she unstrapped it and counted it out to make sure it was all there.

After the money was strapped again and put in an envelope, she handed it to Peggy and said, "Go Big Red."

"Go Big Red," Peggy repeated, smiled, and left the bank.

She went right to the car and got in. "Let's gun it to the hotel."

Jake looked at her. "Did you hold up the bank or did you withdraw the money?"

Peggy laughed, and the tension slowly left her body. "I withdrew it."

"I was stunned when you got into the safe deposit box, but now I'm totally shocked." Jake looked out the window at the entrance to make sure no one was chasing after her. "What did you say? What did you do?"

"I said, Go Big Red."

"Imagine that!" Jake started the car. "Let's go to the hotel and put the money in our room safe, then go someplace to eat. I'm starving."

ဆင်ယ

Brad Hensley checked into the hotel by four o'clock, freshened up, and went across the street to a mom and pop restaurant. He bought the local paper on his walk over and was reading the local news when the waiter took his order. "What do you suggest?" asked Brad.

"The meatloaf is good. You get mashed potatoes with it, and green beans are the vegetable of the day."

"Perfect. Bring me a cup of coffee, too."

He browsed the paper, and when his food came, he folded it and put it on the seat next to him. He hadn't had meatloaf since his children were young. His wife made it about once a week. Since they moved out and his wife passed away last year, he didn't cook much anymore.

Brad took a sip of coffee and watched a couple being shown to their table. They were young and looked very much in love the way they held hands and walked very close to each other. They had on red T-shirts and Cornhusker hats. He'd forgotten about the loyalty Nebraskans have for their college team.

He continued eating and thought about the meeting he had later with a man he had wanted to meet for some time. Someone he thought was a great role model to the community and to mankind. Yes, he was anxious to finally meet him. He had another cup of coffee with a slice of apple pie, then went back to his room and waited.

Jake and Peggy watched the man walk out of the restaurant, not knowing he would be instrumental in the evening's activities. They were nervous, and even though they were hungry, they ordered only a bowl of soup and nothing more.

"I'm glad we got Mrs. Johnson and the children out of town last night. They don't need the disgrace of being here when it happens. I'm amazed, though, how willing she was to go."

"That was nice of you to give Mrs. Johnson all that money to help the boys and her get counseling. You have a kind heart, and I'm glad I'm a part of your life."

He didn't care if they were in public. He took off her cap and kissed her, knowing the time would be here soon when they put their justice plan to work for the first time. They kissed with a longing that ached through their whole body. When they parted, Jake said, "I love you, Peggy, and whatever happens, we have to know we at least helped the Johnson family remove themselves from Daniel. We have that to hold onto."

"I know. I just thought it would be easier, easier to bring people to justice." She put her cap back on. "But the awfulness of molesting children is beyond anything I can imagine." She felt the tears. "Let's go. I want to call Joyce to see how she's doing."

⅜⅓

Justin Styles had the van packed with his photography equipment, and had room for three children cramped on the one seat in the far back. They were scared, and the little girl was about to cry. "It's okay," said the boy next to her. "Hold my hand." And she did. He was her brother, and he always helped her through the tough situations. Her younger brother sat there and watched.

Their parents sold them and took away a big stack of cash. The children had talked about that situation many times. They could have at least exchanged the money in another room. It was hard enough to comprehend for a small child why their parents would just leave them with strangers, but they would never understand why their parents took money.

The three of them joined hands. No matter what happened, they would have each other.

The van pulled into a parking lot, and with the abrupt stop in the parking stall, the littlest boy fell on the floor. Still holding hands, the other two pulled him up, and the little girl wiped away his tears. "Hush," she whispered in hopes the man wouldn't hear.

Styles was busy unloading his equipment and setting up while the children sat in the van wondering what was going to happen next. Sooner than they hoped, he came for them. "Get in the building and I don't want to hear a peep out of you." They did what they were told.

"I'll take care of them from here," said Joyce. They looked so scared. She told them to sit down in the reception area. After Jason left, Joyce said to the children, "I will take care of you."

The littlest boy gave her a hug, but the two older ones knew she was lying. They just knew it because of all the people who said they would take care of them and didn't. This started with their own mother selling them to get rid of them.

Joyce had tears in her eyes, remembering the abuse she had taken without a word of protest when she was their age. She also knew they wouldn't believe that she was here to help them, protect them, but she would keep trying to gain their trust. Trust she knew was nonexistent in their world.

Joyce took out the envelope of money, took it back to Justin, then came back and sat at the desk.

Brad Hensley pulled into the lot and saw the big van. It looked similar to a news van, but it didn't have any lettering on the side. Finally, he thought, his vision of helping children was about to start. Only he didn't know how profoundly he himself would be helping the children.

As he approached the desk where Joyce was sitting, he saw the children, smiled, and walked to the desk. "I'm here to see Daniel Johnson."

"Oh, yes, you must be Brad Hensley. Please take a seat. Mr. Johnson isn't here yet."

CHAPTER NINETEEN

"How did you know how to pick a lock?" asked Peggy.

"Well, Arnie and I had to pick a few locks when Adeline locked herself out of the house. It was right after there was a robbery in Boone that worried Adeline, so she wanted to start locking the house, but she'd forget to take the key when she left the house. So good old Arnie showed me what to do."

"I hope no one comes back to Styles's office. I'm already scared out of my skull."

They walked into the office. When they couldn't find what they were looking for, they followed the hallway to the studio. Peggy opened closet doors while Jake opened cupboards. "I found it," shouted Peggy. They loaded what they needed in the trunk, checked in with Joyce, called the local news station, then drove to the shelter.

೮೦೮೩

Joyce took the children in back and told them to sit on the bed. She felt the little one trembling. "Don't touch them until Daniel gets here," she said to Styles. "He'll tell you what he wants."

"Don't get so snippy. It's not like they're real people."

Joyce stopped. It took all her energy not to punch him in the nose, but she resisted because soon, very soon, the bastard would be locked up. She went back to her desk.

Daniel pulled into the lot and saw the van. "Jesus Christ! What the hell?" The other car he assumed was Hensley's. *What is Styles doing here? I hope it's just a visit.* He rubbed his face. Nothing else needed to happen to him today. His wife left and decided, she said, to take a long vacation with the boys. He took a deep breath and went in.

Joyce introduced the two men, and while they were talking, she went in the back and told the children to lie down on the bed. It broke her heart to tell them that. "And you," she said, pointing at Justin, "leave your dirty hands off them." She turned around and almost ran into the camera that was set up and ready. Instead of hitting it across the room, she went back to her desk and told the men they could go back and start the tour. Once they went in back, she called the police and social services.

She hung up the phone, walked to the door, and looked into the parking lot. Jake and Peggy were finished with Johnson's car. *Okay*, she thought to herself. *Now I wait for the police.*

☙❧

The men walked in the back, and what Brad Hensley saw shocked him. "What the . . ."

Justin was unbuttoning the little boy's pajamas.

"Justin, what the hell are you doing here?" asked Johnson.

"Hey lighten up." He pulled a roll of money from his pocket. "You paid me in cash to take pictures."

Johnson panicked and felt his world crashing in on him. He knew then that the real reason his wife left was because he . . . he couldn't think of it right now. He had to get out.

Joyce went into the back and instructed the children to come with her, and they quickly followed her out front.

Hensley grabbed Johnson's arm. "I thought you were a hero, saving these kids from their abusers." He wanted to punch him, then decided he would. Johnson flew back and landed on the bed. Styles grabbed his camera and started packing his equipment.

༄༅

Peggy sat down with the children, and Jake explained to them that they would be safe. The littlest one poked Peggy's arm. "Are we really safe?" The pleading in his eyes broke Peggy's heart.

The police flew through the door, and Joyce pointed the way. The policeman heard shouting and drew his gun and slowly went back. "Okay, everyone, step away from each other," shouted the policeman. Johnson picked himself up from the bed as he rubbed his jaw. Styles stood and held up his hands. "Now what's going on?"

Hensley spoke first, "I'm Brad Hensley from Florida for a tour and found small kids on this bed." He pointed behind him. "The guy with the camera was unbuttoning the boy's pajamas. Yes, I would like to know what's going on, too."

"He paid me money to come here and shoot pictures," said Styles. "He'd done it before, so I didn't think anything of it." He shrugged his shoulders. "I'll just pack up and leave, but I'm not giving the money back."

"Let's just say your equipment is evidence and you won't be getting it back anytime soon."

"You can't do that!"

The policeman waved his gun. "Oh, yes, I can."

Backup came through the door and took the two men away in handcuffs after an explanation of what to book them on. Johnson shouted, "He hit me. Arrest him, too." Hensley didn't know what to do or say. He was dazed, utterly stunned at what he had just witnessed.

"I'll have to have you come down to headquarters and answer questions. You're free to go until then."

"I'll go now."

The policeman holstered his gun and walked to the lobby. Social services were there talking to the children. He instructed Joyce she would need to come in for questioning as well as Jake and Peggy.

He walked into the parking lot, and the two men were waiting to be transported downtown. "Whose cars are these?"

Johnson pointed to his car, and Styles pointed to his van. The officer went over to Johnson's car. The trunk was open, and he looked in. "What the hell . . ." He staggered away from the car and looked at Johnson. "I hope you're locked away for a long, long time."

"What do you mean?" asked Johnson who was becoming very confused by all that was happening.

"Take a look and then tell me you don't know what I mean." Johnson looked in his trunk and paled as he stepped back wondering where it came from. Sure he looked at it plenty of times, but why was all this child pornography in the back of his car. He was set up, and he knew it, but there was nothing he could do about it.

The officer went to Johnson and helped him in the backseat of the car. "I'm going to subpoena every computer, personal and business, and all your bank records for the shelter and your personal expenses." He slapped his hand on the back of the front seat. "Get this slime out of here."

A Newswatch photographer took pictures and went over to Jan from the news station. "Let's roll a newscast, have the cameras shoot the police car leaving the parking lot, scan the shelter, and return to the parking lot then we'll roll.

"This is Jan Wells on Newswatch 7 at ten o'clock. Daniel Johnson, the founder of Children are Safe, was arrested today for staging a photography shoot involving three minors. After Johnson was escorted out of the building, child pornography was found in his car. He was arrested along with Justin Styles, a well-known photographer in Omaha. Good night and we'll keep you posted."

Jan went without camera and mike to Peggy. "Do you have anything to add?"

"No, I'm here for Joyce. I don't know what's going on."

Joyce stepped in and said, "That's all we know. Thank you for coming. I'll give you what I can in the next few days." Joyce just wanted to go home and sleep for a week. She was exhausted and was glad it was finally over, but now she had to make a statement. She would ride with Peggy and Jake because she didn't think she could concentrate enough to drive.

The news crew packed up and drove away just as the tow truck pulled in to impound the vehicles for evidence.

80C3

Joyce, Jake, and Peggy were all questioned separately and asked the same questions. How did you know Daniel Johnson? Were you aware of what was happening? If you were aware, how long in advance did you know about it? What were you doing at the shelter?

Peggy and Jake both told the man that was asking questions that they were giving a donation and they were unaware of what was going on. The police must've been all right with their answers because they were allowed to go home.

≠ℂ⌓

"John, you want to get in here and watch this!" shouted Nell. John hurried into the kitchen, not sure what Nell wanted him to see. "They are coming back after the commercial with the story."

"What story?" John asked apprehensively.

"They mentioned the name of the guy you keep dreaming about. I knew it was just a matter of time before I would hear that name in the news in some shape or form."

John made no comment. He wished she didn't start putting the pieces together. He wasn't ready to explain anything to her. He didn't want her to think he was associated in any way to these people. But with John talking in his sleep and Nell hearing the same names on TV, it made sense that somehow John was involved.

We bring you live from Newswatch in Omaha. Today, Daniel Johnson, the founder and supporter of the Children Are Safe shelter, and Justin Styles, a well-known Omaha photographer, were arrested. The police were called when Styles set up a camera in the shelter and three small children were part of the shoot. The secretary called 911 immediately. In the meantime, Brad Hensley, a Florida businessman, was visiting Johnson because he wanted to open a shelter in Florida to protect the children there.

Hensley was stunned by the camera, children, and the pornography that was later found in Johnson's car. Hensley is heading back to Florida, saddened and dejected by the situation. But, he stated that now more than ever he wanted to keep children safe.

Bank records and computers are being confiscated. A source close to the case told us Johnson has been skimming donations and putting them into his personal accounts.

Johnson's wife could not be reached for a comment.

A slow smile spread across John's face. *It's done.* He thought. *No blood, just done.*

Nell watched him and knew there was more to the dreams and talking in his sleep than John was willing to tell her, but she would not pry.

∞⟡

Jake shut off the car radio after the broadcast and squeezed Peggy's hand. "It's done. Your justice plan worked, and there was no blood, just the invisible kind, and Johnson and Styles will have that blood on their hands for the rest of their lives."

Peggy nodded. She was still thinking about the three little ones that were so frightened. She wanted to take them home with her, where they would always be safe, but Joyce assured her social services would do a good job of placing them together in a loving home. Joyce even thought about adopting them herself and hoped that whatever happened, they would never have to worry about being abused again.

"Peggy," said Jake gently.

She looked at him with tears in her eyes. "We got justice, Jake." She put her head on his shoulder. "How far are we from Lincoln?"

"We're almost there. Are you sure you're up for a Cornhuskers game?"

"Yes, I need to cheer and scream and get a little crazy right now."

Jake wondered what that would look like. He smiled at her, pulled over to the shoulder, and held her until everything was right. They went to the game. The Cornhuskers won, and Peggy knew her cheering was not in vain.

CHAPTER TWENTY

O N THE WAY home, Jake and Peggy stopped and bought two gold chains
to put their wedding rings on and wore them under their red T-shirts.
Jake put his hand over his. "This is the most important ring of my life,
and soon I intend to be able to wear it on my finger all the time."

"I loved wearing it," said Peggy. She looked at Jake. "And how long
is soon?"

Jake laughed. "As soon as possible."

They dropped off the rent-a-car and took the bus home. They didn't
want to bother Arnie. Besides, they wanted to sleep the rest of the day,
and they knew Adeline would want them to come for dinner, but they
were surprised when they did arrive home. Adeline had the refrigerator
stocked with food, food they could put in the microwave and heat up.
"God bless Adeline Cole," said Jake.

They ate, then crawled into Jake's bed and slept for four hours. When
they were done unpacking, they took the cash that they picked up at the
specified post office box in Omaha, brought it downstairs, and added it to
the rest without counting it. The money wasn't why they wanted justice.
They wanted justice because it was the right thing to do.

They called Arnie and Adeline and invited them over for a campfire.
"I'm so glad you're back," said Arnie. "Adeline was lost without Peggy. I

think she wanted to show her a new stitch or something with the yarn." Arnie laughed. "We'll be over in a few minutes."

When they were all settled on the deck and the fire going, Jake talked about their trip, the parts they could talk about. "It's good you went to the game," said Arnie. "No one goes to Nebraska without going to a game. At least that's what my dad used to tell me." He looked at Adeline, then at Jake and Peggy. "It's so good to have you kids back home." Arnie joked about Adeline wanting to see Peggy, but he missed Jake's company as well. Arnie thought of all the times they had talked about having children, and they even thought about adoption, but that's as far as it went. Arnie mentally adopted Jake as his son, and now that they'd met Peggy, he felt Adeline had done the same with Peggy as a daughter.

"When are you heading back home?" asked Adeline, hoping the answer was never.

"I should be heading back soon. I want Jake to meet my parents, and then I'll meet Jake's parents, too."

"I want to ask Peggy's dad if I can marry his daughter."

Not quite comprehending what Jake just said, Adeline sat there a minute not saying anything. When it fully sunk in, she stood up and clapped her hands. "That's wonderful! Where will you get married? Just let us know, and we'll be there. Right, Arnie?"

"Yep, that's right."

They talked more about their trip and about going to the Cole's tomorrow for dinner. When Arnie and Adeline left, Jake and Peggy were tired, even though earlier they'd had a long nap. "I'm going to call Joyce, find out if she's all right, and find out what else has happened since we left. I'll call her in the morning."

⁃

"Hi, Peggy, I'm so glad you called," said Joyce. "They came and took the computers and bank records. I'm surprised they did it so quickly. Now I think it's a matter of time before the shelter will shut down."

Joyce played with the pen on her kitchen table, and when she spoke, her voice was shaky. "Peggy, I want to run the shelter myself. I was doing it anyway, doing all the paperwork, doing the banking, paying bills."

When there was no response, she continued, "Those three children got me thinking that I need more in my life. I want to adopt a child of my own, but I should get married first. It's not fair to only have one parent."

"That's wonderful, Joyce. Give Brad Hensley a call and I'm sure he'll help you get the shelter back in working order. He's your age, too, isn't he?"

Joyce laughed. "What else do you and Jake do besides your justice plan . . . and *matchmaking?*"

"That's it so far." Peggy hesitated a second. "Please, Joyce, keep in touch and let us know what we can do for you. Or just a visit would be wonderful, too."

"I will. You haven't heard the last from me."

Peggy relayed Joyce's information to Jake while he made sandwiches and coffee, and then they sat at the kitchen table and planned when they were heading to Minnesota.

Jake was going to call and make plane reservations, then Peggy had a better idea. "Let's buy a car and drive. I'll have to get a job so we can make payments, though."

"I think we can pay cash, Peggy." He took her hand and kissed it. "We can use the money we just received and pay in full. That way, we, you, or I, won't have to get a job."

"I feel bad spending your money."

"Ah, my darling wife, it's our money. We earned it together."

"We'll have to invite the Coles to help us pick one out, don't you think?" asked Peggy.

"They would be delighted!"

The next morning they went on a bike ride on the trails in Ledges Park. The plan was that the Coles would pick them up and go to Moffitt Ford, off Marshall Street, after Adeline got off work.

They test-drove a Ford Flex, thought it would be big enough for their justice plan in case they needed a lot of extra space. Peggy whispered to Jake, "Our Justice Mobile." Jake nodded in agreement.

They also wanted to buy a small car, one they could drive around town or on trips.

They looked at a Ford Fusion and thought 33 mpg highway miles were perfect for long road trips. They weren't sure how they would explain buying two vehicles to the Coles when they knew Peggy wasn't working.

While the finance person was writing up a contract, Jake wrote out a check for fourteen thousand for a down payment on both vehicles. After checking credit scores, they were told they needed a cosigner. Jake never had a credit card. Peggy had one, but never used it. Neither one had ever taken out a loan. Peggy's dad bought her, her car.

Jake approached Arnie and told him the problem they were having. Arnie understood and was more than willing to sign the contract with them.

The finance guy smiled wide when Arnie's credit score came in at over eight hundred. Jake drove the Flex home, and Peggy drove the Fusion. When they all arrived home, both vehicles were parked in the garage with plenty of room to spare.

Jake started a fire and they all sat on the deck. An hour later, Adeline and Peggy went inside and made barbeque sandwiches.

While they ate, they talked about their trip to meet Peggy's parents. "I hope you don't get stressed trying to figure out what car you're going to drive." Adeline hit Arnie's arm. "At least with your bikes, you just hop on and go."

"Funny," said Peggy, then giggled. "We can take the Flex and put the bikes in the back. When the traffic is too bad, we can hop on our bikes." Peggy smiled at Adeline and took a bite of her sandwich.

"Hey, how's your knitting? Have you made anything new?" asked Adeline.

"No. Do you have any ideas?"

"At my knitting circle, we just got a pattern for bears. We make the bears, send them back to the company, and they send them overseas to children. It's quite easy. Why don't you and Jake come over tomorrow and I'll show you how it's done. While you're on the road, you can make bears."

Jake looked at Peggy and Adeline and smiled. He was glad they got along so well. They had their crafts, and Jake and Arnie had their tools and projects. Without Jake's parents close, he found comfort in their friendship.

ഇ൬ഇ

Jake and Peggy started out early Friday morning. It would take around three hours to get there. Peggy's mom planned a big lunch with Penny and her new boyfriend, Ross, so she wanted Peggy to be on time.

They took turns driving their new car. They took the smaller car and didn't have room for their bikes, but with the way Peggy's mother was planning their every moment, they didn't think they'd have time anyway.

They arrived in Fridley, Minnesota, thirty minutes before lunch. There was time enough to wash up and for Peggy to introduce Jake to her family. "I'm going to have a hard time keeping all these P names straight," admitted Jake while he unpacked. "Paula is your mom, and Penny is your sister, and Peggy is you, right?"

"You won't have any problem keeping my name straight, right?"

Jake laughed. "Not unless your dad has a P name too, then I'm giving up."

"His name is Peter." Peggy giggled so hard she had to sit down on the bed. "His name is really Noah."

"You are so funny." He smiled at her and wanted to make love to her, but knew he wouldn't be doing it under those four walls. "We'd better get to the kitchen. I'm starving."

Penny's date was introduced to everyone, since he hadn't met any of Penny's family before. "I know I won't fit in with the P names, but it looks like none of the guys do," said Ross.

Jake didn't know what it was like to have siblings and so many people at a table eating a meal at the same time. He was having fun laughing and joking around. Jake noticed Noah had a great sense of humor and thought it would come in handy for later when he talked to him about Peggy.

Thinking back when they met, Jake didn't know how he got so lucky and met Peggy. He realized now his life was empty without her. As soon as possible, he would talk to her dad and then Peggy, and then they could plan their wedding.

Jake got a break after dessert. Noah walked out to the backyard and checked on his garden. His garden, Jake thought, was even better than the ones he'd seen at the homes of Peggy's client. She definitely got her talent from her dad.

The assorted colored roses were in one section on the right of the backyard. The rest of the yard were mostly flowers and slate walkways with bonsai trees. It had an oriental look to it, and Jake loved it.

Noah knelt down and pulled some weeds around the purple impatiens. Jake knelt down and helped. "I love your backyard," said Jake. "And I love your daughter." He hadn't planned to say it like that, but it was said, so he waited.

Noah stopped pulling weeds, stood up, and brushed his hands together. "Are you talking about Penny or Peggy?" Then he smiled.

"I would like your permission to marry your daughter, Peggy. I haven't known her very long, but I know I can't live without her."

"She's very young, and so are you. Are you able to provide for her?" He looked at Jake. "If you get married, will you stay in Iowa or move to Minnesota?"

"Whatever Peggy wants. Wherever she'll be happy."

"How soon will you be married?"

"Again, whenever she wants." Jake bent down and picked up the pulled weeds. "I want her to be happy, and I'll do anything so she is."

"What do you do for a living?"

He had no idea what to say. He used to just say he worked with computers, but that was a lie, and he wanted to be honest with Peggy's dad. "I don't have a job right now." Jake walked over to the waste receptacle and threw in the weeds. "But my house is paid for, so I don't have to worry about that."

"That's amazing. That helps if you don't have a job. I just need to know she'll be happy."

"I will be happy with Jake," said Peggy.

Noah turned and saw his daughter. "I worry about you getting married so young."

"We'll be fine, Dad. You worry too much."

"I can understand where your dad is coming from. I'd be nervous, too, if you were my daughter." Noah looked at Jake, and didn't think he could've said anything more sincere than what Jake had said. "I would still like to marry her, Mr. Bailey, Noah."

"Dad, you should meet Arnie and Adeline Cole. They are two of the best people. Arnie teaches Jake how to build things, do plumbing and electricity. There isn't anything Jake can't do. And Adeline taught me how to knit. I knitted four pairs of slippers, and Adeline taught me how to make bears for a charity organization." She held her dad's hand. "So you see, we have the Coles to take care of us."

"For one thing, it's hard to believe you would have an interest in knitting. And for another, you don't have a job either. You can't be sitting around knitting all day or doing nothing. You're too young for that."

"I can let Penny take over the apartment lease so I wouldn't be paying rent for that. Sounds like she and Ross are quite serious and they'll need a place to stay. With the market the way it is, she might not qualify to even rent. So if they just stayed at my place, they can make the payments until they decide to do something different. I only have seven months left on the lease."

"You'll have to get it approved with the landlord first." He looked at his daughter, then at Jake. "I must admit, when I look at you two, I can see the love in your eyes. I don't see that with your sister and Ross."

Noah let go of Peggy's hand and held it out to Jake, and they shook hands. "Yes, you can marry my daughter."

Peggy gave her dad a hug. "Thank you so much, Dad!"

"Go tell your mother. We need to celebrate. She'll know which wine to open."

Peggy ran off to tell her mother, and Jake stayed behind. "It means a lot to me, Mr. Bailey."

"Call me Noah." He put his arm around Jake's shoulders, and they walked into the house and sat at the dining room table. "I would like to come to Iowa real soon to visit and meet the Coles."

"You're welcome anytime."

The wine was poured, and congratulations were made. Food was brought out and heated up. When the wine and the food were gone, Ross went home.

Jake and Peggy stayed two more days but were anxious to get home. Peggy's mom and dad were coming on the weekend, and they wanted to get things cleaned and in order. The first night when her parents were there, they would have the Coles for dinner so they could meet each other. She was sure they would love the Coles.

CHAPTER TWENTY-ONE

Paula and Noah drove in the driveway, and Jake and Peggy were sitting by the fish pond waiting for them. "Hi, Mom and Dad." Peggy took her mom's hand and showed her the pond while Jake helped Noah carry in the overnight bags.

Before he showed him their room, he asked, "Do you want to sleep with me? Or I can sleep on the couch. Peggy gets my room, and you and Paula get the guest room."

"You can sleep on the couch. I don't know you that well to be sleeping with you."

"Yeah, I thought the same thing." Jake laughed. "Follow me. I'll show you your room." They walked to the end of the hallway. "Peggy still has her stuff in here." He picked up her backpack, clothes, and tennis shoes and moved them into his room.

They joined the ladies on the deck. "The Coles are coming over later for dinner. I hope you can behave yourself, Dad."

"You'll just have to wait and see," said Noah. "It sure is peaceful out here. I heard you and Arnie made the deck. It's a nice one." He looked at Jake. "Is it okay if we come out here after dinner and build a campfire?"

"Sure," said Jake. "The Coles like a campfire, too."

After a while, Peggy and Paula went in to make dinner and left the two men out on the deck. The birds were chirping in the trees at the edge of the woods. After several minutes, Noah broke the silence. "You sure have a nice place."

"I like it, and I think Peggy does, too."

"At first, I thought Iowa was so far away. But after driving here, it's really not that far."

"On the way, we stopped at Diamond Jo's for the buffet. They had some good food," said Jake, watching two birds flying from tree to tree. "Peggy is a good cook, too."

"She never cooked at home. I'm looking forward to tasting her cooking." Noah looked over at the garage. "That's a big garage. What all do you have in there? I hear you are really handy around the house, so you should have some tools, right? My dad never had one tool and didn't know how to fix anything, but I learned all on my own."

Jake had a feeling that Noah wanted to see the garage, so he said, "Come on and I'll show you."

"These look like brand-new cars." He opened the front door of the Flex and pulled the hood latch, then looked under the hood. "They sure pack the stuff in these cars. I remember my first car. I could see the ground." He turned his head and looked at Jake. "You get regular oil changes, don't you? That's what keeps the cars running in good shape."

"This is my first car, so I haven't had the oil changed yet, but I'll do that. How often should I get it done?"

"Every three thousand miles, or three months." Noah shut the hood and walked over to the tool bench. "You don't have that many tools."

"Arnie brings his tools over when we work on stuff."

Noah picked up each tool and set it back down. Then he walked over to the bikes. "Peggy told me about the bike you gave her. She said she really liked the basket."

"Yeah, we like the same things."

"How did you meet anyway?"

Jake thought telling him about the trial would be safe since Peggy mentioned that she went from trial to trial whenever it caught her interest. "We met at Senator Ames son's trial."

"That was something. I'm glad he was found guilty, and what about Judge Klein? Unbelievable."

Jake did not want to talk about anything pertaining to the trial. He just wanted to talk about Peggy. "We had breakfast together the first day, and we hit it off after that." He looked at Noah. "And by the way, we haven't had sex, just in case you were about to ask."

Noah laughed. "I was thinking about asking you that, but I didn't want to seem impolite."

෫඀ඁ

"Tell me, honey, do you love Jake? I know you told me, but there was a room full of people. I figure now, just you and me, you can tell me how you really feel."

"Mom, I do love Jake. I love being with him. I love being in his house. I love everything about him."

"I can tell by the way you two look at each other. He's so polite and nice, and he's very good looking, too. I just wanted to hear it from you, that you loved him."

Peggy slid the baking dish into the oven and set the timer for sixty minutes. "This is very good meatloaf. It's one of Adeline's recipes."

"By looking at your recipes, they are all from Adeline."

"Did you bring yours, Mom, like I asked? I want to copy yours, too."

"We can do that tomorrow." Paula put the finishing touches on the salad and put it in the fridge. "By the way, you don't look at those catalogs you were always looking at."

"You're right. I guess with Jake around we keep busy, and I don't need to look through them. I never bought much anyway. I turned over a lot of pages, but then just recycled the catalogs. I could probably look at them again and buy stuff for the house."

"Paula looked around. I guess the house does need a lot of decorating done to it."

"Then I'd better e-mail all the catalog companies with my new address."

"I wish you lived closer, but after we drove here, it didn't seem that long. I just can't call you and expect you to come right over and go shopping."

"I still love you, Mom." Peggy thought of the fun she had had shopping with her mom and sister. It wouldn't be the same, but she was sure Adeline would fill the void whenever necessary. "When we set a date, you can stay here and help me with all the arrangements."

"I would like that, honey." She hugged her daughter. "You'll have the wedding in Iowa?"

"I need to talk to Jake first." Peggy wasn't sure where she wanted to get married. If they went to a justice of the peace, she would be just as happy as long she could spend the rest of her life with Jake. "I really love him, Mom."

"I know you do." They sat at the table. "I can tell because you never talked to me about boys, or about anything that bothered you or made you happy. Your sister would tell me everything. I mean things I didn't want to hear, but you . . . this is the first time you've told me how you felt about anyone." Paula put her hand on her daughter's. "I love you."

The buzzer sounded and startled them. Paula took the meatloaf and baked potatoes from the oven. "It looks good, Baby."

Peggy looked out the window and saw Arnie's pickup. Peggy took out the salad. Paula cut the meatloaf, while Peggy turned on the microwave to heat the peas.

When the table was set, Peggy called out the window, "Dinner is ready."

Jake thought he'd better mention the talk about marriage and a wedding before it got casually mentioned in conversation, but first Noah said grace. "Bless this food, Lord, and bless our new friends, Jake, Arnie, and Adeline. Amen."

"Arnie and Adeline, I asked Noah if I could marry their daughter and . . ."

"And I said yes," said Noah.

Adeline was so happy tears streamed down her face. Arnie rubbed her shoulder, and his own eyes were moist. Jake was just someone Adeline talked to every day at the library. He never thought such a close bond would have been formed, but then Adeline started inviting him over for dinner, and Arnie would take him in the garage to work on projects. Arnie squeezed her shoulder then he wiped his eyes and started to eat.

Paula broke the silence. "Peggy asked me to come and stay while she's planning the wedding." She looked at Adeline. "But since I don't know where anything is around here, Adeline, you'll have to be part of the wedding planning team."

Adeline didn't remember the last time she had been so happy. In a shaky voice, she responded, "I'd be honored."

"Why don't you two knit a wedding dress?" said Jake.

"With beads all over it," said Noah, then laughed.

Little did they know Adeline had her brain going in high gear about going back to Knitted Together and asking her friend for a pattern. She wanted the date to be soon, but to get the dress knitted would take some time. She might have to ask permission to do it at the library during downtimes. Or she could just retire.

Adeline hadn't thought of retiring in a long time, but now she felt she would have a good reason. And besides, Arnie had wanted her to retire for several years already. A smile came to her face. She would tell her husband about her plan on the way home.

Adeline went to the fridge and took out her Oreo pudding dessert and dished up some for everyone. She gave Jake extra because she knew it was his favorite. Jake smiled when Adeline handed him his dessert. "You know me too well, Adeline."

"Jake, do your parents know you want to get married?"

"They don't even know I'm dating." Jake laughed. "But I guess if I tell them I want to get married, I should tell them I've been dating. I'll call them later. I know they'll want to meet Peggy before we get married." He took a bite of cookie. "The wedding might not take place for a while."

Adeline secretly said, "Yes! More time to knit!"

"How long *have* you been dating?" Noah asked.

Jake and Peggy looked at each other, and Peggy answered, "A month maybe."

"A month, *maybe*?" asked Noah.

"Yeah, that's about right," agreed Jake. "We met at the trial. We were together for around a week. Then Peggy came here, and we've been together for the last three weeks. So yeah, about a month."

"I guess when I said you could marry my daughter, I didn't have all the details." Noah grinned at Arnie. "You would know better than her mother and I if this is going to work."

"Sure it will. Adeline and I knew each other a short time, and it worked for us. Besides, those two kids were made for each other."

Noah knew it must be true if Arnie could see it. He was still a little leery of the fact they didn't know each other that long, but he wasn't going to concern himself with it. It was clear they were happy and in love.

CHAPTER TWENTY-TWO

"WELL, MAX, YOU told me my patience would pay off, and it certainly did."

"If you listen to me, pal, you won't lose so much sleep at night." He looked at John. His wildcat hair was tamer today. "What's with the hair?"

John pushed it down on top of his head, but the curls still popped up. "I got me a girl now. I thought I'd look the part."

Max laughed. "Too funny, my friend. It must be Nell."

"Yes, Nell. I think we're starting to get serious. Once I stop talking in my sleep, she might think I'm worth the commitment."

"Hopefully, now that there are no more deaths with Norman out of the picture, you'll sleep better. By the way, did you see those two people during the newscast when the camera zoomed in on the shelter?" asked Max.

"I don't think I did. I don't really remember," replied John.

"I thought maybe this Jake person was hanging around, so I was watching very closely to the newscast. There were two people wearing red, but for some reason, the camera blurred out their faces," said Max.

"Why would he hang around? It was probably two Nebraskans heading to the Cornhuskers game." John was up and pacing. "Do you really think it might be Jake?" asked John.

"I can try to get the film before the faces were blocked."

"Since I don't know what he looks like to start with, there would be nothing to compare it to. Besides, I'm pretty sure he works solo."

୫୦ଔ

"Arnie, I have good news." She slid her hand over and covered his. "I'm going to retire."

"Do you want me to have an accident? Do I need to pull over? Is there more to this story?"

"I was thinking, since Peggy and Jake are getting married and they want me to help out . . . well, it's . . ."

He squeezed her hand. "What's the real reason, Sweetie?"

With more confidence now, she said, "Jake had a good idea. I could knit Peggy's wedding dress. I've seen it done on the Internet. I just have to get Peggy's measurements and find a pattern. It will take a while. And I figured, if I retired, I could work on it all day every day until it's finished."

Arnie laughed. "My dear Adeline, I don't really care why you're retiring. I'm just so glad that you are."

Adeline crossed her arms and smiled. She would get on the Internet and look for knitted wedding dress patterns, and in the morning, she would call the knitting shop and talk to her friend. She had a plan and was anxious to get started. *I'll need to tell Peggy first.* "Arnie, do you have your cell phone on you?"

When she finished the call, Arnie asked, "What did Peggy say?"

"She's very excited about it. Her mom will take all her measurements in the morning, and they'll pick me up and head into Des Moines to the knitting shop."

"Wait a minute. You haven't retired yet. You have to work tomorrow."

"I'll make history and call in sick."

Arnie let out a peal of laughter. "I love you, Adeline."

୫୦ଔ

Adeline stopped by the library, then was heading over to Jake's. She had made a coffee cake after she printed out several patterns the night before and thought it would be perfect for breakfast.

"Sue, I've written up my resignation. I'm going to retire."

Sue was surprised, because Adeline said she would never retire, and now she was standing in front of her as happy as she'd ever seen her. Sue hugged her. "Congratulations. Are you giving a date in the future, or is it this minute you're going to retire?"

"As long as you put it that way. This minute!"

Sue hugged her again. "I'm going to throw a party for you. It will be right here at the library. You just write up a list of people you want invited, and I'll send out the invitations."

Adeline let out a nervous laugh, never thinking she'd have a party. "There are a number of people I would like to invite, but two of them are heading home in a couple of days."

"If they can stay until Monday, we'll have it Monday after the library opens. I'll take your list and call people instead of sending invitations, if that's okay with you."

"Thanks, Sue." With talk of a party, Adeline felt it was final. The party, then retirement. She thought she'd work forever. She loved working at the library and was able to socialize with her friends as they made weekly visits. She'd made new friends over the years, knew who was new to the area, and knew who was moving away. She also knew about people's families, their children, their grandchildren. *Will I miss the library so much I'll be miserable?* she asked herself. *Something I'll just have to deal with.* "I'm on my way over to talk to my friends now. I'll call you with that list."

Adeline arrived at Jake's, parked in the street, and proudly walked to the back door with her coffee cake. Peggy opened the door before Adeline had to knock. "You're too good to us, Adeline," Peggy said as she took the cake.

"It's a celebration, but if your parents can stay until Monday, I'll have the real celebration."

Peggy poured Adeline coffee and set it in front of her. "What are we celebrating?"

Adeline sat at the kitchen table and cut the cake. When she put down the knife, she announced, "I went to the library today and told Sue I retired."

"Wow!" said Jake. "That's great. Now you can help Arnie and me in the garage."

"Oh, no! No garage stuff for me. I'll be knitting." Adeline took out the patterns from her purse. "Take a look at these, Peggy and Paula, and let me know if you like them."

Peggy studied the patterns and could not believe a dress so stunning was knitted. "I like them all. Look, Mom, aren't they beautiful?"

Paula agreed with her daughter, "Look at this one. It's so striking. It will look good with your small shape,"

"Adeline, which one do you like?"

"I like them all. Why don't you choose one, Peggy, and we'll get all the stuff today. The sooner I get started, the sooner you can get married."

"Okay," said Jake, "you women better get to the store so that dress gets made."

Peggy put her arms around him and kissed him. "I agree." She looked at her mom. "Let's get moving."

The first stop was the yarn shop. Adeline spread the patterns out on the table. After much discussion and help from Adeline's friend, they decided on a pattern.

The store owner didn't have enough white yarn, the color Peggy wanted, so it was put on order. Paula insisted on buying the yarn, and Adeline said she would pay for it. Peggy was the peacekeeper and said her mom would buy the yarn, because Adeline is doing all the work.

"Good idea," said her mother. "Now I think we need to go shopping."

As they left, Dorothy, the store owner, called to Adeline. "Hey, you call me if you need anything, or just come into the store. I'll be more than happy to help."

"I'm sure you'll be hearing from me." Now that it had all happened, Adeline was very nervous. *What if I can't figure anything out? What if it takes me too long?*

Peggy sensed Adeline was nervous about her new undertaking, and before they got into the car, Peggy hugged her. "Whatever happens, you know I will be just fine with it."

"I'm so nervous. But I feel better about retiring so I can devote all my time to knitting."

"It will be fine, Adeline. I promise." Peggy helped her put the yarn in the trunk. "I think Mom wants to go shopping. Are you up to it?"

"Count me in."

Several hours had passed, and only Adeline had bought something. She bought a pair of jeans. "I told Arnie that whenever I retired, I would buy myself a pair of jeans."

"Now you have to buy tennis shoes to go with them."

"Okay, I know just the place where they sell them."

Adeline gave directions from the backseat while Peggy drove. "I think we should all get matching tennis shoes. Since we are going to be the 'get ready for the wedding' team, we need shoes and matching T-shirts, too," said Paula.

Adeline laughed. "I think it's an excellent idea." She couldn't wait to get home and show Arnie her new stuff and tell him all about her day. She could actually tell him something other than who checked out what book.

They came out of the shoe store wearing matching pink tennis shoes, but decided not to get matching shirts. "Shopping sure makes you hungry," said Paula. "Let's find a place to eat."

8003

The Coles were at Jake's most of the weekend. Adeline was knitting whenever she had a chance. The campfires at night had everyone talking about their childhoods, where they grew up, and the wedding. The women wore their tennis shoes all the time, and Adeline loved her jeans. She thought of going back and getting another pair.

"Where are you getting married?" asked Noah.

"Here. Right, Jake?" said Peggy.

"We have a lot of relatives in Minneapolis," said Paula.

"But it's not that far away. They can travel, can't they, Mom?"

"I want everyone to be happy," said Jake. "If you want to be . . ."

"No, I really want to get married here, Mom." Peggy looked away. "I feel more at home here than I do at my own place." She took Jake's hand. "I don't want to make waves, but Ledges Park would be a great place to get married. We could have the ceremony by the stone arch bridge. Of course we'd have to find out if they would allow it. We can grill at the picnic area. That would cut down costs."

Noah always wanted his daughters to be happy, and he could tell Peggy was. "I think the outdoor wedding is a good idea. Maybe I can sneak off and play golf."

"Noah!" Paula said, "You will not be sneaking off anywhere."

"Let's still have the wedding here," said Noah. "I can tell my baby is happy right here where she is."

Adeline felt like she was holding her breath forever and let out a long sigh when the wedding was to be in Iowa. She didn't mind traveling. It just seemed Jake and Peggy were a part of the Cole family now, and she was so proud of them she wanted to invite all her friends. Friends that were up in age like she and Arnie and weren't interested in traveling, especially not as far as Minnesota. She realized she dropped a stitch and had to rip out a row and start over. *You need to concentrate, Adeline, or you'll never finish this dress.*

CHAPTER TWENTY-THREE

"I'D LIKE TO just stay home tonight." Nell sensed that was not what John wanted to hear. "But you can come to my house. I'll cook dinner for you."

John's face brightened. He paid their lunch tab and kissed her on the cheek. "I love your cooking." He winked at her. "See you tonight."

Now that what he was talking about in his sleep was taken care of, thought Nell, *he was less tense and more playful. I don't know if I should try to find out what was wrong, or just let it be,* wondered Nell.

૪૦૯૩

"It sounds like something is brewing in Charleston. I have yet to get the details."

"Just take it as a rest period, John. At least until that time, you'll get a good night's sleep."

"Yeah, I can tell Nell is bothered by my fitful nights. Sometimes, I wished I never would have started this."

"Every now and then, you wish that. But you're a kindhearted guy, and you can't stop bringing justice to the world."

"It's all for my parents. I loved them very much, and they got a bad rap. I will make sure it doesn't go unnoticed." *One of these days, I need to tell Max the whole story about my parents.*

"What you are doing is better than getting revenge. Most people would be so filled with anger that innocent people would get hurt." Max walked to the door. "See you tomorrow . . . hey, a good way to not talk in your sleep in front of Nell, make sure you do something other than sleep when she's with you." A wide grin formed on his face as he walked out the door.

⁎⁎⁎

Adeline was stressing over what she would wear to her retirement party. "Arnie, does this look okay?"

"Why don't you just wear your navy blue jacket? It looks great on you, Babe." He pawed through her side of the closet. "Here it is." He held it out to her.

She held it up. "That does look good." Adeline gave her husband a peck on the cheek. "You want to dig out my navy blue pants and that white blouse you got me last year for my birthday? If it wasn't for you, I wouldn't have all these spiffy clothes to wear."

"I like my women dressed just right." He gently pulled her into him. "I'm so glad you retired. Now I get you all to myself."

She giggled. "I'll be busy with my own project. I don't do car stuff."

"You'll have plenty of time to learn."

"You better get out of here so we can get to the library on time."

"Yes, good idea since it's your party."

Adeline dressed quickly, put on earrings, and went outside where Arnie was waiting by the car. "Now don't you look good!"

"Thank you. I'm nervous, Arnie. Sue told me that a lot of people were going to come. It's nice that Peggy's parents are coming, too."

Arnie started the car and put it in gear. "I'll be right by your side the whole time, so there's nothing to worry about."

Sue just finished putting out the cake when the Coles walked through the door. "Adeline, how do you like the place?"

"It's so nice in here." Streamers were hanging from the ceiling. On the tables by each place setting were confetti and a flyer with Adeline's picture and bio. "The cake is so big."

"As soon as I told people you were retiring, they said they were all coming. So, of course, I had to order a big cake," said Sue. "Myra sure was excited about the business. I think Jake was some help in picking out your favorite colors. He even picked up the cake. Did you know Jake got himself a car? When he offered, I had to find out if his bike basket was big enough." Sue laughed. "He'll sure miss you when you're not at the library anymore."

I'll think he'll see enough of me. Maybe more than he bargained for.

"Poor fellow, he'll just have to get by without me," Adeline said.

Adeline had fun introducing all her friends to Peggy and her family. She thought of her new pink tennis shoes, and wondered when Paula would come back to town. She would make sure she found out before they left.

Adeline thought retiring from a job she'd had for over forty years, and one she loved, would be hard. She didn't look at it as retirement. She looked at it as starting a new life. A life with her friends, Jake and Peggy, Paula and Noah.

She didn't think about what she was leaving at the library. She thought about what she was gaining—a whole new family.

Sue gently touched her shoulder. "Adeline, are you all right?"

"I'm just thinking, that's all."

"I know you are officially retired now, but would you be interested in filling in once in a while?"

Okay, she thought, maybe she would miss it, and this would be a great opportunity to bring in a little money once in a while. "Sure, I'll fill in. That would be so nice."

"That's great. Thank you." Sue gave Adeline a hug. "I'll miss you, so come in and visit once in a while."

"I will do that. Thanks, Sue, for everything."

››•‹‹

"Now we have to tell your parents that we're getting married and find out when they can travel," said Peggy.

"Uh . . . Peggy, I have something . . . to tell you. I know I should've told you right away, but with everything I've already told you, I didn't want you to think I was a big loser."

"You'd better sit down. You look like you're going to pass out."

They sat at the table. "My parents do exist and I am the only child, and they do live somewhere. It's just that we . . . haven't talked since I left after high school."

"How come?" asked Peggy, worried.

"Well, they sort of moved away, too, and never told me where they were going."

"Are you serious?" Peggy was shocked. "How could they do that to you?"

"I always felt like they didn't want a child and that I was a big burden to them. I guess I was right."

"Do you know for sure that they live in Florida?"

"I made that up, too."

"She could see the hurt in his eyes. "Do you want to try and find them?"

"I thought about it, but they moved away on purpose, so they wouldn't see me again."

How awful, thought Peggy. She would love to find them just so she could shake them and let them know how inexcusable it was for parents to leave a child. What possibly could've been the rush to abandon their only child?

Peggy poured more coffee, sat down, and looked at Jake. "My parents just met you, and I know they love you already. Look at Arnie how he teaches you things, and then there's Adeline. She adores you, Jake. And I love you."

"I know. It's just hard sometimes when I think of what they did to me. Especially now that we're getting married. I would love to have them here."

"Do you have any aunts and uncles?"

"I have an uncle, my dad's brother."

"Let's call him. He might know where your parents are. I'm serious about this, Jake. You can demand some answers from them, and then you'll know it wasn't your fault. You need to put your past behind you." She took his hand. "I want you to heal, and not have anything in your past that's painful or uncomfortable."

Jake smiled. "I love you." He pulled her shoulders closer and kissed her. "Do you still have your computer here?"

"Sure, what do you have in mind?" She brought her backpack to the table, took out the computer, and plugged it in. Peggy hooked up the wireless device and slid it over to Jake. "It's all yours," she said, then slid her chair closer to his.

After several failed attempts to locate Jake's uncle, he was ready to give up and forget the idea of locating his parents. "Okay, do you have any cousins?" asked Peggy.

"Yes, my uncle had four boys."

"That's good. They'll all have the same last name."

"I was in touch with one cousin not too long ago. I went to his wife's funeral in Colorado. I never asked about my parents because it was still very painful at the time. Jake continued to research names. Peggy wrote down addresses and the phone numbers they found, then she took over the search and looked in Facebook. She thought if she could find them in Facebook, they would have a better chance of sending them a message through private e-mail.

"Peggy, I was going to make dinner, but all we've got in here is stuff to make barbeque sandwiches. I think we've had them enough, don't you?"

"Yeah, but they sure are good."

"Do you want to go for a bike ride and pick up groceries?"

CHAPTER TWENTY-FOUR

T HE SEXUAL TENSION between Jake and Peggy was getting harder and harder to ignore. They no longer took naps together and were nervous just kissing each other. Although they didn't plan to wait until they married before they made love, it just seemed like that's what was happening.

They hadn't set a date yet. Peggy wanted to see how Adeline was coming on the dress. When she called the Coles, Arnie told her Adeline had worked on the dress all day and hardly took a break. Jake still hadn't received messages back from his cousins on Facebook, and they didn't want to move forward until Jake got some answers.

Peggy wanted everyone that mattered at the wedding. She wanted Jake to have his family present. Jake decided he would wait a week. If no one answered by then, they would go ahead and set a date.

"I think we should go over and visit Adeline," said Peggy. "We probably should bring something to eat. The way Arnie talks, Adeline does nothing but knit."

They loaded up their bike baskets with leftovers and headed to the Cole's.

"Well, well, what brings you two here?" asked Arnie. "And that better be food in those containers."

They all laughed. "Let's head into the kitchen. I'll go tell Adeline you're here."

"Peggy, Jake, I'm so glad you're here." Adeline looked at Peggy putting hot dish in a bowl, then sticking it in the microwave. "Poor Arnie says I'm trying to starve him."

"I know you are busy, so I just eat soggy crackers all day." He put his hand up to his forehead. "I feel weak. I should sit down."

Adeline swatted his arm. "You should be in theater with that act."

Peggy set the table while Arnie was carrying on about losing weight. "How's the dress, Adeline?" asked Peggy.

"Yeah, can we see it?" asked Jake.

"No. The groom can't see the dress until the bride walks down the aisle with it on."

"I thought the groom couldn't see the bride before the wedding," Arnie said.

"When you think about it, my food-deprived husband, it's the same thing."

Arnie winked at her. "I can't get by with anything."

Adeline took Peggy's hand. "Let's go to my bedroom and I'll show you what I've done so far."

Peggy had never been in their bedroom before. The dresser had pictures of what Peggy thought were their parents. She recognized a picture of Sue. Peggy picked up a picture with a younger woman with a stylish hat. "Is this you?"

"That's when hats were in, and I loved wearing them. I was hoping someday before I die, they would come back in style."

The room was decorated in tan. There was gold shag carpeting on the floor which was popular in the early seventies. There was a double bed on the far side of the bedroom with a tan and gold comforter. All Peggy could see was yarn on the bottom half of the bed.

Adeline moved the yarn and held up the top of the dress. "It looks like lace." Peggy touched it. "Oh, my, Adeline, it *is* yarn. It doesn't look like it, but it feels like it."

"Do you like it so far?"

"I love it. I wish Mom was here to see it."

"The next part is what takes the most time. Since it's going to be floor length, and it's a high bodice, the skirt section will be time consuming. I make sure I knit every day, though. My friend at the knit shop said it would take a good month to finish, if not longer. So if you can wait, maybe two months for the dress, I'll have it done. Guaranteed."

"It's a lot of work. Are you sure you want to go through with it?"

"Yep. I made the commitment, so I'm going to finish it." She put the knitting back on the bed. "I thought you could come over tomorrow and knit a couple of rows, then when I see Paula again, she can knit a few rows. That way we can say we all helped."

"That's a fantastic idea, but when people ask me about my dress, I'm going to tell them you made it."

Adeline smiled. "Thanks, but let's make sure it gets done first."

There was a knock on the bedroom door. "I won't come in, but dinner is ready."

"We'll be right there," Adeline said.

"Now this is good food," said Arnie. "Peggy, you'll have to take over for Adeline. Just stay here in the guest room and make sure I get my three squares a day."

"You won't starve, Arnie," said Adeline. "You could stand to lose a few pounds."

"A few, maybe, but I lost that yesterday." Arnie put another big spoonful of hot dish in his mouth and took a drink of water. "I'm just joking with you, dear. I'm so glad you're home with me every day, that eating is optional."

₧₨

"It was nice of Peggy to let me stay in her apartment," said Penny.

"It's also paying, not just staying," reminded her mother.

"I know. I didn't think I'd ever have a steady job so I could move away from home. My job is going well, and now I only have a mile to drive to work. So life is good. I could even walk if I wanted to."

"Let's go get another load of your stuff and bring it up. I wish your sister was here to help."

"She's got it bad, doesn't she?"

Paula laughed. "She sure does."

They worked another two hours. There wasn't that much to do, but Paula started cleaning and then it seemed to her everything needed cleaning. Penny was perfectly fine with letting her clean all she wanted.

Paula's cell phone rang on the kitchen table. Penny picked it up. "Hello, Peggy!"

"Penny! How are you? How's Ross?"

"I'm great! I'm in your apartment now. Mom and I just moved in all my stuff. Ross is good, too. He's coming over for dinner tomorrow night. Mom doesn't know yet, so don't tell her. I think she thinks this is like home, and I'm not allowed to have boys over while the parents are gone."

"I won't tell her. Just don't let Dad find out or he'll ground you." They kept talking and laughing, and Paula was standing in the doorway watching her daughter. *I'm so lucky the girls get along so well.* Paula had a friend whose children weren't even talking to each other. She felt lucky.

"Let me talk to Mom, unless she's still cleaning then leave her alone." They started laughing all over again. Penny was laughing so hard she just held out the phone to her mom.

"What's going on?" asked Paula.

"Hi, Mom." She tried not to laugh. "Adeline will have my dress done in no time.

She said she made a commitment, and she was going to keep it. She's the best, Mom." Peggy and Jake decided not to tell anyone about Jake's parents, in hopes they would come to the wedding, but it was hard not to tell her mom about the situation. She always had good ideas, and maybe she could help solve this one, but Peggy didn't say anything. "Jake and I decided we should wait until spring to get married. Minnesota winters can be harsh, and I don't think anyone will want to travel in the winter."

"That's probably a very good idea. How are Iowa winters?"

"I'm afraid to ask. Nothing could be as bad as Minnesota, could it, Mom?"

Paula laughed. "I hope not."

"Say goodbye to Penny for me, and hug Dad for me."

"You take care. Love you."

Jake was on the Internet looking at his Facebook account. He waited for Peggy to get off the phone with her mom before he opened the messages.

"I'm not so sure I can deal with the answers, Peggy, if they're not positive."

She slid the computer in front of her and opened the first message. *Hi, Jake. It's been a long time, hasn't it? I didn't know your parents up and left, so unfortunately, I can't help you. Let's keep in touch.*

Peggy opened the second one. *Jake, buddy! That's tough, having your parents leave you. Must be in the genes. Dad doesn't keep in touch with me either. He's a nice guy and all, but not good on the family thing. Hope you find what you are looking for.*

"Great! Everyone has their own problems." He rubbed his hands through his hair. It was getting long, so his fingers got tangled, and he pulled them through as he felt the pain in his scalp.

"This one is from Larry. He might be able to help." *Jake, I enjoyed seeing you at my wife's funeral. You were the only family member who showed up. Guess my brothers were too busy. I've been thinking about your questions on finding your parents. Dad would probably know all the details. He was close with your dad. I put Dad's number at the bottom. He doesn't read his e-mail, so you'd have to call him. Or just show up on his doorstep. He lives in Missouri, address at the bottom, so that might be close to you. Let me know what happens. Larry.*

Jake wrote down the information. "I want to call right now before I chicken out." He walked around the house looking for his phone and found it on his bedroom dresser, came back to the table and dialed the number.

He let it ring. *I don't want to keep calling every hour to see if he'll answer his phone. If he had voice mail, I could at least leave a message.* On the tenth ring, he disconnected in frustration.

"Do you want to take a road trip?" asked Peggy.

"I don't know. It seems like a dead end. If he doesn't know, we've wasted our time, and if he does know, I'm not so sure I want to know anymore."

"I can understand why you feel that way, but let's not leave it alone until one day your uncle is no longer alive and your cousins don't really care. I think we need to move quickly on this, but I don't want to push you into anything you don't want to do."

"I need to think about it. I'll let you know in the morning."

CHAPTER TWENTY-FIVE

JAKE WAS UP early and made blueberry muffins. He couldn't sleep. The thought of talking to his uncle about his parents both excited and stressed him. All sorts of questions went through his mind. *What if my parents don't want to talk to me again? What if they are gone and no one can find them? What if I chicken out at the last minute and don't want to see them?*

He felt warmth wrapped around him and felt comfort. "Hey, Jake, you're up early."

He turned in her arms and held her. "You always show up at the right time." He snuggled his nose in her hair. "Mmmm, you smell so good."

"Not as good as those muffins you're making." Jake laughed, then kissed her, slow, meaningful, sensual. The timer startled them, and they pulled away from each other. They stared at each other, still hot with lust. The timer kept ringing. Jake acted first and turned it off, took the muffins out of the oven, and placed them on the stove. Jake turned and looked at Peggy. "I'm going to run out and make sure the fish are okay." He flew out the door and sat by the pond. His elbows were on his knees as he watched the fish swim back and forth. His eyes were glued on the fish as he wondered why he was waiting to make love to the woman he loved.

Jake kept watching back and forth, back and forth. Peggy came out with two steaming cups of coffee and sat next to him. It took him several minutes to break the trance, then he sat up and took his coffee.

"Peggy, are we going to wait until our wedding night? Because if we do, then let's get married this afternoon."

Peggy smiled at him. "It would be nice to wait, but I'm open to anything, except getting married this afternoon."

"I can respect that, but I don't like it."

"I've never seen you cranky before. What else is on your mind besides us?"

"My parents. You have such great parents, and you are close with your sister. I'm just feeling sorry for myself and embarrassed that my parents left. They *left* me. There was no one else in the family. They left *me*, Peggy. Both of them left *me!*"

Peggy let him talk and get everything out. She sipped her coffee while she listened to him.

"If we make the trip, and for whatever reason my uncle hates me too, along with my parents, that wouldn't exactly cheer me up. If he doesn't know where my parents are, then I would feel abandoned all over again. If he knows where they are but has promised not to tell me, then what? Then what am I supposed to do?"

"Take some more time to think about it."

"I think we should go as soon as possible. Then I can stop feeling sorry for myself. Stop going through all these scenarios in my head and making myself crazy." He took a sip of his coffee. "Let's eat first." He smiled at Peggy and helped her out of her chair. "All this 'what if' stuff makes me hungry."

While they were eating their muffins, they planned their trip, copying directions from the Internet. Jake made a mental note to get a printer and a GPS. They made calls to the Coles and Peggy's parents and sister. It didn't take long to pack, and they were on the road.

They decided not to make the trip in one day but to stretch it out into two. The hotel where they stayed had a swimming pool and a hot tub. Jake and Peggy spent most of the night in the pool area, in the hot tub. It wasn't until after they were ready to leave that several families came and dived in the pool. Until then, Peggy and Jake were able to plot how they would approach Jake's uncle.

Jake said he was a man that got right to the point, so that was the approach Jake would take. Knock on the door, go in, a little small talk, then find out about his parents. He hoped his parents didn't live too far away from his uncle so they didn't have to do more traveling.

Although he loved road trips with Peggy, this one made him think too much about what he had done to make his parents leave without telling him where they went, and why. He tried to remember what he was like when he was two or three, or even four years old because that might have been the deciding point for them to leave him. They couldn't potty train him, he was too fussy, he didn't walk when he was supposed to, had bad grades in school. All these things running through his mind were making him on edge, but it was a trip he needed to take. Jake just hoped Peggy was able to endure his moodiness and they remain friends after the trip was over.

They parked across the street from Jake's uncle and watched in silence for thirty minutes. They saw movement in the front room so they knew someone was there. "I'm ready to go knock on the door." He wasn't really ready but saying it, he thought, would get him out of the car.

"Do you want me to go with you?" asked Peggy.

"Of course, I want you to come with me. I couldn't do it without you."

They held hands and walked up the sidewalk to the front door. Jake knocked. Several seconds later, the door opened. "What do you want?"

"Uncle Rick? Is that you?"

Rick Farms stared at Jake and scrunched his eyes. "Jake? What are you doing here?" He stepped aside. "Come on in. Who's that lovely lady you have with you?"

"This is Peggy. Peggy this is Uncle Rick." Rick shook Peggy's hand. "Sit down, sit down. Do you want something to drink?"

Jake remembered Uncle Rick loved to drink wine. "No, we're fine. We just stopped for lunch not too long ago." They did stop for lunch, but that was five hours ago.

"I'll just pour myself some coffee then." Rick walked to the kitchen and brought back a cup of coffee. "I stopped drinking last year, the best thing I ever did." He sat in the chair across from Jake and Peggy. "What brings you back home, Jake?"

"I just wanted to visit. I haven't seen you for such a long time." Jake wasn't so sure he wanted to ask the question about his parents. It was good to see Uncle Rick, sure, but could he force himself to ask the question?

"The coffee smells so good. I think I'll have a cup," said Peggy.

Rick got up with a smile on his face, anxious to please, and walked into the kitchen. "Jake, are you okay? Are you going to ask Rick?"

"I'm so nervous, Peggy. I don't think I want to do it anymore."

Rick came in with a cup of coffee and set it on the table next to Peggy, then sat down. "I thought you might stop in someday. It just makes sense that you would come back asking about your pa and ma." He shook his head. "I don't know what they were thinking leaving a fine boy like you. And you got yourself a fine friend, too." He looked at Peggy.

With more confidence now, Jake said, "Yeah, I do want to know where they went. Do you know where they are?"

Uncle Rick took a sip of coffee and then contemplated what would be the best way to tell Jake what happened. To stall, he filled his and Peggy's cup with coffee and didn't come back from the kitchen right away. They waited five minutes before he came back and sat down.

"I remember the day clearly, Jake. Your pa came to my house and said they were leaving town and that I shouldn't tell you where they were going. I didn't think much of it at the time since you were moving out anyway.

"About six months passed, and I realized just how wrong it was, but then I didn't know where you were. I couldn't find you in the phone book or on the Internet, hell . . . you disappeared.

"Then I didn't think about it much after that, and then last month, the feeling started again, that I should've done something. I researched everywhere I could, then Larry called and said he got a message from you on . . . Facebook . . . I think.

"I felt relieved and hoped you would stop by, or at least call. I guess stopping by is better."

"What happened to Dad and Mom?"

"Your mom found out that your dad had another wife." Rick waited to see if there was any kind of a reaction. *Shock*, he thought would best describe Jake's facial expression. "Your parents sold the house because your dad had big debts to pay. Once the house was sold and his debts paid off, he said he would get a divorce from the other woman.

"But he didn't divorce her and kept living with your mom in a small apartment in a bad part of town. Your mom had two jobs and was supporting them. What she didn't know was that she was supporting another wife and child across town. When she found out, she filed for divorce, kicked him out, and was going to keep working to get enough money to buy a house. So when she contacted you, she'd live in a decent place."

"Oh my god! Mom, I feel so bad for her." Jake looked at Peggy. "We need to find her and have her come and live with us."

"Where does she live, Rick?" asked Peggy. "Does she live in Missouri?"

"Yes. Right across town." Rick took his address book off the coffee table, ripped off a piece of paper from the tablet, and jotted down her address and phone number. He looked at his watch. "She's probably working. She works at the diner down from her apartment."

"Is that the only job she has?" asked Jake.

"She does office work during the day, but it's only part-time. She's hoping to go full-time once they have an opening."

"Can you give us directions?" asked Jake.

"Sure." He put directions on the piece of paper. "You're welcome to stay here until she gets home."

"I think we'll head over there. Maybe she can take a break while we're there." Rick stood. "In case you wanted to know about your Dad, he went back to his other wife and I guess is still there." He shook his head. "I've never seen anything like it, and he's my own brother." He shook Jake's hand. "Thanks, Jake, for looking me up. I needed to tell you. Your mother will be mad at me, but I hope she can forgive me."

"She won't be mad at you. I'll make sure of that."

Peggy gave Uncle Rick a hug with tears in her eyes. "Thanks so much. Would you like to know how it turns out?"

A smile came to his face. "I *would* like to know. Thanks, Peggy."

CHAPTER TWENTY-SIX

T HE DINER WAS small and crowded. With red vinyl seats on the bar stools and Formica-topped tables, it looked like something from the fifties. Jake and Peggy sat in the corner and looked at the menu. Hamburgers and fries were the main entrée. They ordered from the guy with the white apron. They didn't see Jake's mom. Jake wasn't sure he would even remember what she looked like Peggy and Jake were talking about where his mom would stay at the house. She wouldn't have to work, and she would be able to stay home and enjoy herself and get her life back together. Then she could go to work if she wanted to.

A plate dropped, and Jake and Peggy looked toward the racket. The waitress had dropped one of the plates with a hamburger and fries. Her free hand was over her mouth to hide her shock. "Jake, is that you?" she asked in a shaky voice.

Jake jumped up and started picking up the broken plate pieces and food. Peggy took the plate she was still holding and put it on the table, then Peggy took her hand and led her to the booth. "Why don't you sit down?"

"I, I . . . I think I *will* sit down."

Jake got everything off the floor, took a rag, wiped up the rest, and brought everything into the kitchen. The distraction helped, but now that he was heading back to the booth, he wasn't sure what he was going to say. He was lucky Peggy came because she started the conversation.

"Are you okay, Mrs. Farms?" Peggy would've used her first name, but she didn't think to ask Jake what it was.

Mrs. Farms took her son's hand and held it to her cheek. "You came back. I'm so sorry we left you the way we did." She let his hand go and straightened her shoulders. "I'm sorry I left you. How did you find me?"

"Uncle Rick told us," said Jake quietly.

"I told him not to tell you what happened, or where I was."

"He told us you'd be mad at him," Peggy said.

"I thought I would be, but I'm so happy to see Jake again."

"When do you get off work?" Jake looked at the hamburger and realized he was very hungry now that the initial stress of meeting his mom was over. "I . . . we want to spend some time with you, Mom."

"I get off in an hour."

"We'll hang out here and follow you home." Before his mom could object, Jake held up his hand. "It's okay, Mom. I don't care about anything anymore but to see you."

Tears formed in her eyes. "I better get back before I get fired. I'll get you two more hamburgers. This one is cold already."

The diner was busy, and Jake watched his mom wait on tables. The patrons knew her and talked about their personal lives, and one had a joke to tell her. One lady talked about her upcoming vacation. It was good for Jake to see that her whole life didn't fall apart because of what his father did to her.

After an hour, Jake and Peggy went up to pay the bill. The owner took their check and rang it up. "I'm charging her for the two extra meals." He nodded toward Jake's mom. "She's never acted like that before. I don't know what happed, but it better not happen again."

Jake gave him a hundred dollar bill and said, "Don't charge her. Take all four meals out of here and give her the rest for a tip."

Before the owner could say anything, Jake said, "If you don't give her the tip, I'll find out and come back and make sure you do." Peggy touched his arm. Jake didn't know what came over him. He felt like he should protect his mother, and he didn't want anyone to take advantage of her anymore. If only he'd known about his father, he could've protected her. They would've gotten through it. Together.

They left the diner and waited for Jake's mom in the parking lot. In a few minutes, Mrs. Farms walked over to her son. "Are you sure you want to come over? The place isn't fancy or anything."

"I don't care where you live. I just want to talk to you." He wanted to give his mom a hug. Jake felt it was long overdue but refrained and would wait until they were in her home, where it was safe, or until he knew that if he cried, it wouldn't be in a parking lot.

Peggy drove, following Mrs. Farms. Jake's legs were shaky and he didn't dare take any chances driving. "Are you okay?" asked Peggy.

"Yes. I think I am finally okay. It's so good to see Mom again. She's much thinner than the last time I saw her."

"It's probably from working two jobs and trying to make ends meet. That can take a lot out of a person." Peggy wondered if Jake could talk her into coming to Iowa. Coming to stay where she didn't have to worry about working or trying to make ends meet. Knowing Jake, he would even buy her a house of her own. She'd just have to ask.

"By the way, what is your mom's name?"

Jake started laughing then doubled over with laughter. When he could talk, he said, "It's a P name." That got Peggy giggling. "It's Pam."

They laughed the rest of the way to the apartment. Pam led them up a flight of stairs, and down the hall. She unlocked the door, hesitated, then decided to go in anyway. There were two worn stuffed chairs, a small rickety table and chair where Pam would eat her meals when she had the money to eat.

"Sit. I'm going to change out of this uniform. It smells like grease."

They could hear the shower running, and not long afterward, it was shut off. She looked refreshed, and not as tired. Pam pulled the one folding chair over by Jake. Before she sat down, Jake stood and pulled his mother into his arms.

Tears flowed freely from both of them. "I missed you so much, Mom." He held her tight.

"Jake. Jake. I'm so glad you're here." She moved away and sat down. Jake did the same. "Now tell me all about this lovely lady," said Pam.

Jake didn't know where to start. Now that she wanted to know about Peggy, it seemed too complicated to tell the story of how they met.

"Ah, I can answer that," said Peggy. "We met in Minnesota, and after being away from each other about a week, we decided we couldn't live without each other. So I'm living with him now." Before anyone could respond, she quickly added, "We sleep in separate rooms."

Pam laughed. "I wasn't even going to ask." She wanted Jake to stay a few days, or even a week. Calling in sick in the morning to her office job would be out of the question. They would fire her, and she wouldn't be able to pay the rent. *How can I get them to stay? I never want to be separated from my son again.*

"Hey, Mom. I want you to come and live with us. You don't have to get a job if you don't want to. You'll never have to struggle to survive or pay the rent again."

The tears that were dried reappeared. "I don't know what to say. It would be wonderful, but now you have a girlfriend that lives with you." She looked at Peggy. "You don't want your future mother-in-law living with you, do you? Or, I guess I'm assuming you'll get married."

"Mom. Yes. We are getting married. We can build one of those suites in the basement for you with a kitchen and bedroom."

"I've struggled for five years now. Not much to show for it as you can see. I was left with nothing and had to work for several weeks before I could even afford a place to stay. I am tired, son, but I think living with you would be a real imposition."

It was quiet. Pam wanted to live with him, but she wanted to give him the opportunity to change his mind. Peggy walked to the front window and looked down onto the dirty street where kids were playing. A horn honked, and the kids scattered.

"Mom, I'm not going to lose you again. You are coming with us as soon as you can get ready."

The tears were back. "I should give notice at both my jobs. I can still go back to the diner and give my notice, but I'd have to go in tomorrow and let them know I'm moving."

Jake looked around. "You don't have a phone, do you, Mom?" He didn't wait for her to answer. "You can use my phone to call the diner, then you can call your other job if you want." He took out his phone and handed it to her.

"I was lying in bed last night and wishing someone would rescue me. Not that I have a bad life, I would just like to have some time to myself instead of working all the time. The dreams I had were all crushed, and I didn't think I'd ever have the opportunity to get them back."

"Call, Mom. You'll have everything you wanted."

"I don't even know where you live."

"We live in Iowa."

She laughed, truly laughed. "I've never known anyone to live in Iowa, but I've heard all the jokes."

"All lies," said Peggy. "It's a beautiful place to live, and Jake's house is so nice, you'll love it."

Pam smiled. "I know I will." She walked to the folding table and looked up the diner's phone number from her small address book, dialed, told the owner she's moving effective immediately, and to send her check. It would be forwarded to her new address. She did the same for her office job.

"It won't take me long to pack. But it's getting late, and it's almost dark. You can stay . . . or not since there is no place to sleep."

Jake could tell she was getting stressed and comforted her right away. "No problem, Mom. Let's hit the road, and if we get tired or want to stop, we'll get a hotel somewhere. Oh, but what about your apartment? Do you have a lease?"

"I pay by the month. This month is all paid. I would pay ahead in case I would ever lose one of my jobs and couldn't pay for a while. She took Jake's cell phone off the table and dialed the apartment owner. She left him a message about leaving, and not coming back. "I think I'm all set. I just have to pack."

"Do you need help?" asked Peggy.

Pam was uncomfortable with having anyone in her apartment, and then to have someone help her pack her things. She had to get over her embarrassment of her dreary existence. Most of her things were sold so she could get her husband out of debt. Had she known he would leave her anyway, she would've kicked him out and kept her son.

But he was here now, and she felt nothing could bring her down to the level she'd been. Pam would never lose touch with her son again.

"Sure, Peggy, that would be nice. I'll pack my clothes. You go into the kitchen and see if I have anything that you don't have at your place that we could use. Otherwise, we'll leave it all here." She took out a paper bag and set it on the bed. "Oh, Peggy, I do want my coffee cup. It's what got me by when I read the saying on it every morning. It might be cheesy, but once I had enough money, I was going to pursue all my dreams. All a head game, I guess."

Peggy walked to the kitchen and looked through the cupboards, but most of them were empty. She didn't see anything that Jake didn't already have in his kitchen until she opened the last cupboard. It was a small watermelon bowl like the ones that women sat around at night and made in ceramics class. She put it on the counter. She found the coffee cup by the coffeemaker. *I understand why she wanted to keep the cup.* Peggy read, "Go confidently in the direction of your dreams. Live the life you have imagined. Henry David Thoreau." *Now she can live her dreams.*

Pam came into the kitchen. "Oh, my bowl. I had forgotten about that. She carefully put the bowl and her cup on top of her clothes in the paper bag. "Sad to say, but I'm ready to go. I guess it's good I don't have more stuff. This way I can start all over again."

"Do you like to garden?" asked Peggy.

"I do . . ." She was going to say, *but I wasn't allowed to garden because my former husband didn't like the mess.* "Yes, I do like to garden."

Jake stood when the women walked to the door. He took his cell phone and his Mom's bag while she closed the door on several years of bad memories. Pam walked slowly down the stairs, not because she was dreading the move, but because she didn't want to walk too fast in case Jake's car really wasn't out in the street, and this was all a dream. Then she remembered her own car.

"Wait! My car. She looked in her purse and pulled out the title. Pam had it ready in case one day she'd have to sell it to pay the rent. "I know just who I can give this to. I'll be right back."

She knocked on her neighbor's door, and a lady in a wheelchair answered. "It's always nice to see you, Pam. Come in."

"I can't stay, Sally. My son found me, and I'm going to live with him."

Tears formed in Sally's eyes. "I'll miss you. You've done so much for me and Josie. She's at work right now, but I'll tell her when she gets home."

"I know you've wanted to buy her a car, but since I'm moving, I won't need mine anymore." She laid the title and the keys on Sally's lap.

Sally reached up, and Pam bent down and hugged her. Tears streamed down her face. "You're too good to us. She'll be so excited. You keep in touch, you hear me."

"I will," said Pam as the tears welled in her own eyes.

CHAPTER TWENTY-SEVEN

Jake decided to drive straight through. They stopped along the way for rest and food breaks. When Pam suggested they stop for ice cream, Jake remembered how much she loved it. When he was small, they would stop all the time. Her favorite flavor was strawberry, and now when they stopped, she ordered her favorite again.

"I don't remember the last time I had ice cream. This is delicious." She looked at her son. "Remember when we went to the Dairy Queen, and they started our order when we walked through the door?"

Peggy did not feel left out of the conversation, but saw it as a part of learning about Jake's life, a part he kept secret. Now he could freely open up about it and know he was *not* the reason his parents left, and Peggy could tell he was happy about that fact.

The drive didn't seem as long as it did on the way down. On the way down, they were worried about finding Jake's mom. If they did find her, would she come back with them? All sorts of questions and worries had crossed their minds.

Now they didn't worry about any of that. The ride was full of tears and laughter, and when they pulled into Jake's driveway, tears came again. It was after midnight.

Peggy quickly changed the sheets in the guest room and took her clothes and set them in Jake's room. She was tired, and wanted to go to bed. Even sleeping on the couch would feel good after being awake all night.

Pam was shown to her room. She hung up her clothes, and there was still room left in the small closet. She took her undergarments from the paper bag and put them in the dresser across from the double bed. "All I have left is my coffee cup and watermelon bowl."

"We just leave our cups on the cupboard since we drink coffee all the time." Peggy took them from Pam. "I'll put these in the kitchen, but first, I'll show you the bathroom."

₧₨

It was noon before Pam stirred in her bed. She didn't remember the last time she had a good night's sleep. She stretched and rolled over on her side. Her eyes were taking in the room. The wallpaper had narrow cream stripes with red mini flowers in the alternate rows. Not what she would picture her son as having.

The room, she noticed, was bigger than her apartment bedroom, but that wouldn't take much, she thought. Today, she decided she would have coffee in her favorite cup, check out the fish pond, and sit on the deck she saw earlier this morning. She would sit as long as she wanted, not worrying about work, paying the rent, or stressing over all that happened to her in the past.

Yes, today, she decided, would start her new life, and the best part of her new life was her son. She heard a light knock on her door. "I'm awake. Come in."

Peggy came in with Pam's cup filled with black coffee. "What would you like for lunch? We can go out, or I can cook."

"I don't think I can decide. I might just want to stay here under the covers." Pam sat up in bed. "But I'll take the coffee first." She took a sip and then took a long slow swallow. "This is good coffee."

Peggy sat on the edge of the bed. "Jake is so happy you decided to come here."

"I didn't want to at first, but then I thought of my lonely existence, saving money like crazy so we could be together again someday. I always thought by the time I saved enough money, it would be too late, and Jake wouldn't ever want to see me. Or could I even find him? I never would've thought to look in Iowa."

Peggy smiled. "Jake has a busy day planned. The first thing he wants to do is introduce you to the Coles." Peggy sipped her coffee. "Then we'll probably go to the hardware store to get you a new bike."

"A bike?"

Peggy giggled. "Before we bought cars last week, Jake went everywhere on a bicycle. When I came, he had a brand-new bike waiting for me. I figure it's only right for you to have one too."

"It's been a long time, but I'll give anything a try."

Jake peeked his head in. "How are my two favorite women this morning?"

"Just wonderful, son. I slept very well, and Peggy brought me coffee."

"You look rested, Mom."

"I hear you have a full day planned for us."

Jake grinned at her. "Just as soon as you get dressed, we'll start our day."

⊱⊰

"I checked with the media in Omaha and tried to get the film before the faces were blocked, but they said it was a privacy issue. I tried pulling strings, but they didn't care who I was. They weren't giving out the video," said Max.

"Like I mentioned before," said John, "I wouldn't know if it was him or not."

"I think I'll hang around the area next time something goes down and take my own pictures," said Max.

"Why all of a sudden are you interested in finding out who Jake is?" asked John.

"I just have an interest, that's all. Aren't you a little bit curious?"

"I was when I couldn't contact him, but I have no interest now," said John.

"Well, if I found out who he is, remind me not to tell you," Max said, laughing.

"Enough of this nonsense. I'm going to take Nell out tonight. She wants to see *The Sound of Music* at the Guthrie."

"You're getting cultured now. That's a hoot, John."

"My lovely lady wants to go, so I'm going to take her."

"To think all this started because you only wanted information from Nell to find Jake. Now you don't want to find Jake, but you want to go out with Nell."

John smiled. "Why don't you keep your riddles to yourself? I have to pick up my lady."

℠γ

Jake served breakfast, put the dishes in the dishwasher, wiped off the table and counters while Peggy and Pam watched. "Hey, ladies, don't think you'll get off this easy tomorrow."

"I love you, Jake," said Pam.

"You too, Mom. Now let's get moving."

Jake took them to the hardware store, where Pam picked out a bike. Jake put it in the back of the car. Next, they headed to the library. Jake remembered his mom loved to read. This would be a good opportunity for her to get a library card and read all she wanted.

"Jake, Peggy, what brings you here, today?"

"I wanted you to meet my mom, Pam."

"Hi, Pam." Sue shook her hand. "Have you met Adeline yet?"

"No, we are going there for dinner later."

"We sure do miss her. There is so much to do that we just took her for granted, but now that Adeline's gone, I realize just how much she did."

"She was always doing something when I was here," said Jake.

"I've been looking for help, and no one has come in to apply. I even put flyers in the hardware store."

"What are the hours," asked Pam.

"Mom?"

"Well, for now, I would like to have someone come in from ten to four, Monday through Friday. I can't pay benefits, though."

"May I apply?

"You sure can! I'll get you an application."

"Mom, what are you doing? You don't have to work anymore."

"I have to do something, and I don't want you to always pay for everything. Ah, do *you* have a job? I don't remember you mentioning anything about one."

Jake sighed when he saw Sue coming back. Pam was shown to a desk in the back to fill out the application. Peggy and Jake looked at magazines while they waited.

"I didn't want Mom to work, Peg."

"Maybe she needs to keep busy. It might be easier to have a job when she doesn't really have to work, than when she's got two jobs, struggling to pay the rent."

Pam brought the finished application and handed it to Sue. "I didn't know Jake's phone number, or his address."

"We have it on file because he has a library card. Since it's the end of the week already, can you start Monday?"

"Start?"

"Yeah, I need help as soon as possible. Adeline hasn't had time to come in and help. She's knitting the wedding dress."

"Sure, I'll be here at ten on Monday."

Once they were outside, Pam jumped up and down. "I've never gotten a job so quickly before." Her blonde hair was pulled back and showed how thin she was. But she was happy.

"Mom, you're amazing." He put his arm around her, and the three of them walked to the car. "This is cause for celebration." He looked at his watch. Two hours before dinner at the Cole's. They would have time to have some wine, make his mom's day special. "Maybe the Coles will meet us at the bar and grill down the street."

"I'll call Adeline," said Peggy. When she disconnected, Peggy announced the Coles would be there in ten minutes.

The Coles immediately liked Pam. When Pam announced that she got a job already, the Coles wondered where she would be working.

"The library!"

"You got my job! I'm glad they found someone to take my place. I said I would come and help out, but I'm too busy knitting." Adeline smiled. "Do you knit?"

"I have, but I would be rusty now. I would need lessons."

"Peggy, did you show Pam the slippers you knitted?

"No. I'll have to make you a pair."

Adeline filled Pam in on what she might be doing at the library. "You won't know you're working. It'll be so much fun." Pam needed fun in her life, and now she believed she found more than just Jake. She found a family, *and* friends. The last place she lived, she never had time to socialize outside of work, except to say hi to Sally and her daughter between jobs.

Pam didn't miss her old home, or as she called it, just a place to stay. A place to stay until she found her son again and started over. It happened many years before she thought it would. Definitely no regrets in finding Jake earlier. She sipped her wine and watched the four of them talk and joke around with each other. Yes, this is what she wanted. What she needed. What she missed out on for too many years.

"Hey, Adeline, what are you making for dinner?" asked Jake.

"It's a surprise."

"She's never made this before, so it *is* a surprise. I picked up all sorts of things at the grocery store for her. Liver, frozen grasshoppers—stuff like that," said Arnie, with a grin on his face.

"Yuck," said Peggy.

"She washed them first, so they should be all right."

Everyone laughed. They ordered more wine, and when they finished, Adeline announced they had to get going to get dinner on the table. Arnie put his arm around Adeline. "I bet those little varmints are jumping all over the house."

"Oh, Arnie!"

⁂

Adeline's surprise dinner turned out to be fabulous. She started out with wild rice soup and a salad. Lemon Greek chicken baked with red bell peppers, potatoes, onions, mushrooms, and seasonings were served next.

Everyone was full, so they decided to have dessert later. Adeline asked Peggy if she would mind if she showed Pam the dress. Peggy was thrilled to have her see it. Peggy hadn't seen it for a while, and she was anxious to look at it, too.

The three women walked down the hall to the bedroom. Adeline shut the door behind her. She didn't want Jake to get a look at the dress. She took the cloth covering off the dress on the bed and held it up. "It's beautiful," said Pam. Peggy didn't know what to say. It *was* beautiful.

Peggy felt it and held it up to her face. The dress was thigh length. Adeline took the dress, got behind Peggy, and held it so it covered her shoulders. As they looked into the mirror, it was hard to imagine what it would look like when she could see her jeans and her T-shirt peeking through. She had an idea and told the two women to wait outside the door.

Peggy took off her clothes and put on the dress. It fit perfectly, a little short, she thought, then giggled. She imagined it long, and she was holding roses walking down the aisle to meet Jake at the altar.

She was glad Jake's mom would be at the wedding. Adeline was knitting so fast that Jake and she should actually set a date. She twirled around in front of the mirror. *I just love it!* There was a knock at the door. "Can we come in?" asked Pam.

Peggy yelled, "Oh, yeah, come on in."

It is beautiful, only because Peggy being in it makes it so, thought Adeline.

My son is going to marry a lovely lady, thought Pam.

"You look great, Peggy," said Pam.

"Yes, very lovely," Adeline said.

Peggy took the dress off and covered it again. Before they joined the men in the front room, Jake had been telling Arnie about his mom, and what his dad did. Arnie didn't like anything bad to happen to people and was saddened by Jake's story. Jake had come into his life, and Arnie felt an attachment to him, like a son, or a grandson.

Arnie was happy about the end story, that Jake had found his mother and brought her home with him. A wedding was going to take place soon, and his wife had retired. He felt content with his life. So much happiness was what life was supposed to be, he believed.

They talked well into the evening. At one point, Adeline made coffee, and Pam helped serve warm cherry cobbler with vanilla ice cream. Pam was glad her son had met the Coles and that they took him under their wing and watched out for him. She had imagined many things that could've happened to him over the past years. Pam was glad none of it was true.

CHAPTER TWENTY-EIGHT

PAULA AND NOAH wanted to come back to Iowa to meet Jake's mom. They decided they would stay in the hotel next to the hardware store, and Jake and Peggy wouldn't have people all over their house. Since they both took early retirement, they could come and go as they pleased.

Peggy, Paula, and Adeline picked up Pam at the library after her shift. They headed into Des Moines, stopped at the yarn shop, and picked up another order of yarn. No, was the answer she gave her friend when asked if she brought the dress with her. Adeline would show no one else the dress until Peggy walked down the aisle in it.

Peggy helped Pam pick out yarn for her slippers, and then she wanted to get another skein of yarn so she could practice. She had some cash, and was going to pay for it, then Adeline said, "Put all the yarn on my bill."

Pam gave her a hug and thanked her. It was rare that Pam ever got a hug in the past, but now everyone gave them so freely. It touched her, so she was trying to do the same.

"Okay, Peggy, we have to make another stop at the shoe store," said Adeline from the backseat.

"For sure, that's where we're going next."

The women had their pink tennis shoes in Peggy's trunk, so when the next member of the wedding planning team came out, they would surprise her. Pam went into the store and asked for her size. "I'm not so sure I like pink, Peggy," said Pam.

"Just trust me. You will."

"I didn't think I'd like pink either," said Adeline. "I didn't own anything pink." *Oops, I hope I didn't ruin the surprise.*

Luckily, they had a size that fit perfectly. They convinced Pam to wear her new shoes home. Adeline had to check the trunk to make sure she had the correct number of skeins of yarn before they drove off and went home. Pam decided to stay in the store for a few minutes and look for a purse. She assured her new found friends that it would not match her pink tennis shoes.

When Pam walked toward the car, she saw the women leaning against the trunk with their pink tennis shoes on. Pam rushed over to them and laughed. "You brought your shoes." She looked down at everyone's shoes. "Now tell me the real story behind these shoes."

Paula talked first. "We are all part of the wedding planning team. We welcome you into the club."

Tears fell down Pam's face while they took turns giving her a hug. Right when she thought there could be nothing better to her new life, there was. Three new beautiful friends. Now she was going to help plan a wedding for her son. *I'm so happy!* She soared on the inside.

"So what do we wear riding bikes?"

They all laughed.

They walked to the restaurant across from the parking lot. People stared at them when they walked in with pink shoes. After they ordered, Adeline and Paula asked Pam questions. Where did you work before the library job? Where did you live? What do you think about Jake getting married? Jokingly, they asked what she thought of Peggy.

Pam tried to answer the questions as best she could without straying too far from the truth. One thing she would never tell was how her husband treated her, how he had two wives, and chose the younger one instead of her. Chose not to ever see his own son again. The issues with her husband were closed as far as she was concerned. If someone asked about her husband, or Jake's father, she would simply say they were divorced and she no longer knew where he lived.

The subject was changed to Peggy's wedding. With Adeline knitting so fast, they could soon have a wedding; however, with winter coming, Peggy wanted it to be warm, something she hadn't talked over with Jake yet. There'd been too much going on that Peggy and Jake hadn't had any alone time lately. That would be something that Peggy would have to change.

It was late before the four women drove into town. Peggy pulled into Jake's driveway, and the men were on the deck. They had their own evening out, but it was right there at Jake's house.

"Look at that." Arnie pointed at Pam's shoes. "They broke you, didn't they? Wore you down until you gave in and bought . . ."

"Arnie, now they don't look that bad."

"Oh, yeah, right," agreed Arnie with a hint of sarcasm.

Jake missed Peggy and went over and put his arm around her. He whispered in her ear, "I love you."

Peggy whispered back the same thing.

"I better get to bed. Seems like I'm the only one that works around here." Pam laughed, said "good night," walked into the house, got ready for bed, and crawled under the covers. She replayed the evening in her mind and smiled. In no time, she was sleeping.

Before Noah and Paula left for the hotel, Jake announced that Peggy and he were going alone on a picnic the next day. And he stressed the word *alone*.

⁐⁃⁓

They took their usual route, parked their bikes, and walked on the stone bridge. They looked down into the water and saw a fish. They watched for several minutes, then held hands and walked over to their bikes. Jake locked them together and took the backpack with lunch and a blanket.

They strolled along the trails hand in hand. The leaves had changed colors, and Jake wondered why he hadn't noticed until now. He was thinking about his life as Peggy was walking next to him. He found his mom, and now she was living with him. He would soon be married to the love of his life. What would happen next?

He hoped things would stay good, but his mind kept bringing his life now back to the life with his dad. He was trying to remember how his dad acted during his childhood. What he said to him, what he did, what behaviors did he have? Did his mom and dad ever fight?

Jake wanted to see his dad one last time. One last time to gain closure. To get answers to his questions. He also wanted to tell him off. He was angry inside that he didn't notice anything was going on when he was growing up, but Peggy kept telling him that it wasn't his fault. He had to remember that, but still he wanted to see his dad.

Mostly, he didn't want to turn out like him. He knew he would never marry two women at the same time, and wanted to make sure he didn't act like his dad, distant and mentally abusive.

"Hey, Peggy, let's go over there."

"Yeah, looks nice." They sat on the blanket and pulled out the food from the backpack—sandwiches and cherry cobbler. Peggy noticed Jake was quiet, but she didn't want to ask any questions. A lot had happened over the last several days, and she thought that's what he was thinking about, but she did want to talk about setting the wedding date.

"Jake, Adeline is half done on the dress. I think we should set a wedding date."

"Yeah, we probably should."

"With winter coming, I'd rather wait until it's warm."

"How about a spring wedding?" asked Jake.

"I'd like that. What date should we have?" She scooped up the cherry cobbler. "This won't be as good cold and without ice cream."

Distracted by her, he said, "I'd like to marry you right now."

Peggy looked at him. She could see the lust in his eyes. The very same feeling that was in her. He mechanically ate his dessert but didn't take his eyes off her. Jake wanted her. All of her. Now. His mom was at work, but Peggy's parents were at the house. He thought of his garage in the backseat of the car, or right here, right now . . . His thoughts trailed off, but he wanted the first time to be special.

There wasn't a place he could think of that they could make love. He had to get over this feeling before it literally drove him crazy.

"Peggy." When his voice was stronger, he said her name again in a husky voice. "Peggy. I want to make love to you."

Looking into his eyes, she said, "I want the same thing."

"I've gone over every possible place to do it, but nothing would work."

"My parents are leaving in the morning, and your mom will be at work."

"Tomorrow it is then." When he touched her leg, lust shot through him and gripped his thighs. "Take my hand off your leg before I break our date for tomorrow and attack you right here."

Peggy smiled and took his hand off her leg. "Feeling better now?"

"No, worse. I think we'd better race home. It might be as good as a cold shower."

He stood and quickly picked up the containers, stuffed them in the backpack. Peggy took the blanket, and they headed for their bikes. "The last one home has to make dinner."

∞ଔ

The next morning, Jake and Peggy were up early, saying goodbye to Paula and Noah with a huge breakfast of cinnamon rolls, scrambled eggs, hash browns, and leftover ham. Pam was putting coffee in to-go cups for their trip home.

Pam rode her bike to work every day and told Jake she did not want a basket on the front. Noah offered to drive her to work before they left for home, but Pam refused. She said she needed the exercise.

It didn't matter when they all left. It wasn't soon enough for Peggy and Jake. As Noah and Paula were pulling out of the driveway, Arnie and Adeline pulled in front of the house. At least twenty more minutes passed before they left. Pam came out of the house and said Sue called from the library. A water pipe broke, so they weren't sure if the library would even be open today.

With the anticipation of being alone with Peggy and the sexual tension mounting, Jake sat on the grass and laughed hysterically. Peggy knew the feeling, and tried to reassure his mother that he was fine.

"Did Sue say when they thought they would know for sure if you needed to go in?"

"No, she didn't have any idea. I told her I would come in and help clean if it was needed. I'm sure there will be water damage."

As Jake was working down to a few giggles, he got off the ground and sat on the deck. "Woman, get me my coffee." He yelled in Peggy's direction.

Pam looked worried. "He doesn't treat you like that all the time, does he?" Thinking back about Jake's father doing the same thing, Pam needed to ask.

Peggy smiled. "Only when he tries to be funny."

Jake got his own coffee, and the three of them sat on the deck all morning. It was late afternoon when Sue called Pam and told her she wasn't needed but that she would have to come in an hour early in the morning.

Jake decided not to hope for a free morning after what happened today. He started cleaning to keep his mind off what he missed out on today. He scrubbed the walls in the kitchen along with the floor. He wiped down the kitchen table and chairs, cleaned the cupboards, and cleaned out all the drawers. He decided he didn't need anything that had accumulated in the junk drawer. Now that Peggy was living there, she had organized all the recipes that usually were scattered in a drawer. Peggy organized most of the drawers, but since most of the junk was his, he threw it out.

He got the vacuum out and did all the floors. He washed all the drapes and curtains that were washable, and threw out all the outdated magazines that were on the coffee table.

While Jake kept busy, Peggy helped Pam with her knitting, while she knitted another pair of slippers. Pam was worried about her son, but Peggy knew exactly what was going on.

Every so often, Jake and Peggy would look at each other, and Jake would wink at her. She would wink back, and he would clean all the more. Peggy thought his cleaning might last into the night.

Pam made dinner, and Peggy helped Jake move the furniture, while he vacuumed underneath. When he finally took a break for dinner, he was exhausted, which is what he wanted. *Would morning ever come*, he wondered.

CHAPTER TWENTY-NINE

Jake made his mom a to-go cup of coffee and gave her keys to the car. She was late getting up, but if she drove, she would make it to work on time. Peggy and Jake were still in their pajamas when she left.

"What do you think, Peg? Should we make love or wait another day?"

Peggy jumped in his lap and showered his face with kisses. "I think we should wait."

Jake wrapped his arms around her and held her as close as possible. He kissed her on the lips, hard and sensuous. All the lust that was stored up was surfacing.

He stood up with her legs wrapped around him and walked to his bedroom. He gently set her down and lay on top of her. He kissed her passionately and wanted this moment to last forever. His love to be with him always. To have his children. To grow old with. He didn't think his life could be any better.

Jake kissed her neck, her arms, her hands. "Peggy, I love you so much."

He captured her mouth again, tasted her sweetness. He could feel the urgency in her kiss. Jake pulled off her shirt, and he marveled at how beautiful she was. Her ivory skin. Soft, silky skin. He noticed how thin she was and lightly moved his hand on her hot sweaty flesh.

Those warm brown eyes watched him in anticipation. He pulled off his clothes, then finished undressing her. She closed those sexy eyes in the sensuality of the moment, waiting, anticipating, longing for them to become one.

Once he made love to her, how could he possibly let her sleep alone at night and leave her side during the day? His breath caught, "God you're beautiful."

She smiled, and his heart melted. When their flesh was on fire from touching and could no longer bear the heat, the heat got stronger, and they moved with each other until they climaxed together.

His kiss was gentle now, slow, drugging. "I love you, Peggy." He moved off her and covered them with the sheet. Jake pulled her closer and put his arm around her and snuggled below the covers. "I'm sorry I hurt you. I didn't know it was your first time."

"I was waiting for just the right person."

Should he tell her it was his first time too? He wanted a relationship, and this woman beside him waited for him. Wanted him. Needed him. No one else.

Jake felt her warmth and easy breathing. He would do something special for her today. Pamper her all day and the next time they made love, he would be devoted to making her happy and content.

Yes, he would tell her it was his first time, too. He wasn't embarrassed by it.

"Get some sleep, my love. We'll start again when we wake up."

Peggy faced him. She was a little embarrassed as no one had ever seen her naked before. She loved Jake and knew the embarrassment wouldn't last that long.

"Peggy, I'm sorry if I hurt you. I hope you are okay."

"It did hurt, but I'm okay. Maybe next time it won't hurt so much. I guess the first time is the worst."

"It's the first time for me, too."

Peggy smiled. "I thought you had done it before. Guys usually do it more in high school. At least at my high school."

"I wasn't one of *those* guys." He stroked her hair. "I love your hair."

"I wasn't one of *those* girls."

"I'm glad." He kissed her on her cheek. "I should be tired, but all I can think about is food. And you."

"Let's get up and eat. No sense fighting it."

"Good plan." He hated to leave the warmth of her, but he knew she wasn't going anywhere. She lived with Jake now, and no matter how it happened or how it was decided upon, she was with him.

They dressed and went to the kitchen. Jake opened the fridge, and they both stood looking in. Jake was making a mental list of things he was going to do to make a special day for Peggy. Dinner at a fancy restaurant came to mind. He would call Arnie and find out what he recommended.

While they were drinking wine and eating a good meal, he would ask her to marry him. But he had to go shopping tomorrow morning and find a ring. They already had rings, but he wanted one that would complement her wedding band.

"Hey, aren't you hungry anymore?"

Jake cleared his head. He took the leftovers out. "What do we have here?"

"Looks like eggs. Who put eggs in there?"

"Probably Mom. She saved everything because she didn't have that much money. So I suppose every little bit helped."

"That's just sad."

"If Mom can eat leftover eggs, so can I. What are you having?"

"I'm making peanut butter toast. Lots of toast and lots of peanut butter." She took the toast from the toaster. "I never knew sex made people so hungry. I'll have to ride my bike more to wear off all this extra food."

"No, my dear, it's what you do *before* you eat that wears it off."

ⅎ☃

Jake and Peggy went to Des Moines in the afternoon, and Jake told her his plans for their special night out. When they left the car, they each went their own way. Peggy headed to the dress shop across the street. She never did enjoy shopping, but now that she had something to shop for, it proved to be fun. She tried on several dresses, but so far she didn't see anything she liked. She went back out on the floor and kept looking through the numerous dresses.

She pulled out a few more at random. Nothing really interested her, but she would try them on since she had a lot of time. The first one was blue, short, and revealed too much cleavage for her to feel comfortable.

The next one was red. It was too long, too bright, and too uncomfortable. She tried on the next one. Peggy looked at her reflection in the mirror and imagined she was with Jake. *I think this one will work just fine*, thought Peggy. The dress was black, long, and one shoulder was bare. She put her hair behind her and studied the dress again.

Yes. Perfect! she thought.

The salesclerk helped her pick out a gold necklace with a single black star. Peggy didn't want earrings, but when she was shown the small single-starred earrings, she couldn't resist.

"There's a shoe store down the block if you're looking for shoes." She looked at Peggy. "Spiked heels would look great, but you don't seem like the type to wear such high-heeled shoes."

"You're right. I have always worn flat shoes, and that probably won't look good with the dress."

"People are still wearing sandals. They have some rhinestone-studded ones that are really cute." The clerk rang up the purchases and carefully put a garment bag over the dress. "Good luck to you."

"Thank you for your help." Peggy walked out the door and decided to put the dress in the car. With the garment bag, Jake wouldn't see what it looked like.

At the shoe store, she found the rhinestone-studded sandals and tried on a pair. She couldn't exactly imagine what they would look like with her dress, with her jeans on, but they weren't too high, and yet they were appropriate.

Peggy walked to the car happy that she was done shopping. She put the shoes in the car and then wandered along the sidewalk, looking in all the shops. She walked to the café, bought coffee and a scone, took them outside, and sat at one of the green tables. *Why am I eating again?* Then she smiled and thought about their morning.

She thought of calling her mom and telling her they made love, but she decided it was probably something her mother did not want to hear. *Her Loss!* She decided and giggled.

"What are you laughing about?"

Peggy looked up and saw Jake. "You, and how nice it was this morning."

"Can I share that scone with you, and probably your coffee, too?"

"Sure you can have the rest." Jake scarfed down the scone and gulped the coffee. "Are you hungry?"

"Funny, but so true. Yes, I am hungry." He ate the last morsels of the scone and drank the last drop of coffee. "But now I'm getting hungry for you."

Peggy looked around. "I don't think it will work here."

He gave her an Eskimo kiss. "I love you, Peggy." He thought a minute. "I don't even know your middle name."

"It's Ann. What's your middle name?"

"It's Henry."

"Jake Henry Farms. It sounds sophisticated."

"Peggy Ann Bailey sounds like a rock star."

"Funny. What's in the bags?"

"My sophisticated outfit for tomorrow night."

"Well, my rock star outfit is in the car."

They pushed their chairs as close to each other as they could, held hands and people watched. The weather was sunny with a slight chill in the air. Peggy wondered about her dress. If it was colder than this tomorrow night, she might need a coat. When they decided to go home, Peggy told Jake to wait while she went back to the store. She would purchase a warm shawl. *Too bad there wasn't enough time to have Adeline knit one.*

Pam stayed at work an extra hour. The water damage wasn't that bad, but there were a lot of books that needed to be moved back to the shelves from the day before. Peggy and Jake took their time making supper, knowing she would be late. What they really wanted to do was make love again.

Adeline and Arnie stopped over later in the evening. Adeline talked to Pam about work, and they shared library stories. Adeline had never remembered such disarray at the library when she worked there.

Arnie told Jake he should build a hutch for Peggy's new china. "New china?" asked Jake. "Where am I going to get new china?"

"I'm sure Peggy will have nice dishes when you two get married. You'll need some place to put them."

"There will be no problem with space. Three-fourths of Jake's cupboards are empty," said Peggy.

"Wrong answer," said Adeline. "Arnie wants to put a hole in a wall, and I won't let him do it at home."

"A hole in the wall." This intrigued Jake and was willing to give it a try. "Sure, let's do it."

"Let's go in and measure a wall," said Arnie. "Then we'll go to your garage and see if you have the right tools."

Adeline moved closer to Peggy. "I'm doing well on your dress. In a few weeks, you'll have to stop by and try it on."

"Jake and I are going out tomorrow night on a date. I bought a dress today, and I want to show you two. I put it in your closet, Pam. I hope you don't mind."

"I don't mind at all. Let's go in and check it out."

They walked in Pam's room and shut the door. Peggy took the dress out of the closet, took off the garment bag, and held it up.

"It's beautiful, Peggy," said Pam.

"I agree," said Adeline. "What a nice dress."

"Oh, wait. Peggy took the shawl out of the closet. This goes with it because it might be cold out. She walked to the living room, dug through her backpack, and found the box with the earrings and necklace and handed them to Adeline. "Look at these." Adeline held up the necklace.

"These are beautiful. I think you'll have to try this on because I won't see you tomorrow when you go out."

"You and Arnie should come over for dinner, and after the two lovebirds leave, we'll eat," said Pam.

"Sounds like a wonderful idea," said Adeline.

Peggy was thinking about the dress, the shawl, the jewelry, and then thought about her hair. She wanted to curl it but didn't think to get a curling iron when they were in town. She knew Pam didn't have one. "Adeline, do you have a curling iron?"

"I do. I'll bring it with me when we come for dinner tomorrow."

છ૦૩

Jake and Arnie were sitting on the deck, waiting for Peggy to get dressed. Jake had on a dark blue suit with a red tie and black polished shoes. He looked very handsome in his suit. "You look good cleaned up. If you want to work on our project instead of going out, let me know," said Arnie.

"I want to go out. Jake pulled the ring out of his pocket. Look at this."

Arnie took the ring. "Very nice, son. Very nice."

Pam and Adeline were both involved in getting Peggy ready. Adeline helped her with her dress and jewelry, and now Pam was working on her hair. "I'm so nervous. You'd think it was a blind date."

"If I was Jake, I'd be nervous too, with you looking like that," said Pam.

"Jake is in for a big surprise," said Adeline.

"I'm still nervous."

They laughed. Peggy knew Jake bought new clothes for tonight. She'd never seen him dressed up in a suit, although he mentioned he did wear a suit before. For all Peggy knew, he bought a new pair of jeans and a pair of tennis shoes.

"You are good at this. Where did you learn how to fix hair?"

"I went to beauty school after high school. I graduated too, but after I got married, I didn't look for any jobs." She knew why too. Her husband didn't want her to work. Apparently, he only allowed one of his wives to work. *I sure made up for it in the long run. Having two jobs at a time.* "Not that my own hair reflects that I know what I'm doing."

"Everyone has hidden talent," said Adeline with a grin.

"Thanks."

"Now *girls*! I'm supposed to be the center of attention," said Peggy.

છ૦૩

Peggy's hair was in front of her shoulders in a mass of curls. Everything was perfect according to Adeline before they all left the bedroom. Pam walked outside and told Jake Peggy was ready. The two men walked in the kitchen, and Arnie and Pam joined Adeline at the table.

Jake leaned on the cupboard and waited for Peggy. He thought maybe she was having second thoughts. No one was talking, and with this group, there was always somebody talking.

Peggy put on her shawl, then took it off and draped it over her arm. She touched her hair and pushed it behind her shoulders. She didn't like the lipstick, but Pam reassured her it looked great on her. She pulled up her dress to make sure the straps were fastened on her sandals. The small fake jewels looked good.

She checked her makeup, another rarity. She thought Pam did a good job with that, too. *Okay, you can't wait forever.* She took a deep breath and exhaled, then walked into the kitchen, looking a little shy.

"Peggy, is that you?' asked Jake. He could feel the tightness in his groin. He held onto the counter for support. When he could find his voice, he whispered, "I guess we better get going."

"Goodbye, everyone," said Peggy. "Thanks for all your help."

Arnie winked at Jake. "I hope you can walk."

Jake smiled. "Funny, Arnie." He took Peggy's shawl and put it around her shoulders.

"I think we should stay in. There might be a law for going out in public looking so good, Peggy."

"Thank you. That was nice."

Jake put his arm around Peggy. "Goodbye, everyone. Don't wait up."

Jake helped Peggy into the car, shut her door, then he quickly got in the driver's side. "It will take around thirty minutes to get to the restaurant. I hope you're not too hungry."

"I'm not hungry yet." Peggy looked at Jake. "You look very handsome. I'm so glad we are getting out on our own. I know we spend a lot of time together, but this is different. It's like a date we never went on. Kind of backward. We lived together, made love, and now we are dating."

"Some would say we do things backward in Iowa." He pulled off the road and pulled her close. "Kiss me, Beautiful."

She kissed him and held on to the front of his suit. She felt warm and sensual. "We should probably head to the restaurant."

Jake put the car in gear, put on his signal, and merged into traffic. He thought to make reservations, but never got around to it. Arnie told him there should be no problem with getting seated at Johnny's Italian Steakhouse on a weeknight. He wanted the evening to be perfect, and if the restaurant was too crowded, he didn't know where else to go. He decided not to worry about it and concentrate on Peggy instead.

Jake let Peggy off at the door, parked quickly, and joined her in the lobby. He took her hand, and they sat down and waited for their name to be called.

The wooden tables and chairs reflected off the shiny wooden floor. Peggy looked around the dining room. "I think this is the best restaurant I've ever been in."

An elderly couple walked in the door, gave their name to the host, and were looking for a place to sit. Jake and Peggy stood up, and Jake gestured to their seats. The man patted Jake on the back. "I'm not as spry as I used to be. Lucy and I are celebrating our fiftieth wedding anniversary." He sat down. "I'm sure you two will celebrate your fiftieth before you know it. Right, Lucy?"

Lucy nodded her head. "That's right, Lenny."

Twenty minutes later, they called Peggy's name. When they walked to the host, Peggy told her to seat the elderly couple first. Jake and she didn't have a problem waiting. The hostess went over to the couple and said, "Lenny, your table is ready."

"Well, that was a short wait." Then he realized the young couple he was talking to was still waiting for their table, and they arrived first. "Hey, that was nice of you two."

Jake held out his hand, and Lenny shook it. "Happy anniversary."

Lucy had a wide grin on her face. She walked arm in arm with her husband to their table.

Jake and Peggy sat back down. "You sure look great," said Jake. He wasn't just saying it to make her feel good. Jake was first attracted to her in the courtroom in Minneapolis because, for one, she looked like someone he wanted to get to know, and once he did, they liked the same things.

Seeing her now, feeling her warmth next to him, he knew his instincts were right when he invited her to visit him in Iowa.

Jake was happy that his mom was staying with him, or them, but tonight he wanted to make love to Peggy, and he didn't feel comfortable with his mom in the house.

After their name was called, they followed the host to their table and were given a menu. When the waitress came they decided on steak and shrimp, and wine. Jake and Peggy had some celebrating to do. He just hoped he could figure out a way to ask her. Even though the wedding was in the planning stages, he was still nervous to ask the love of his life to marry him.

They talked about Joyce and wondered how she was doing. Peggy made a mental note to call her when they got home. They made plans to do more landscaping in the yard around the fish pond. Peggy said how happy she was that Penny was staying at her apartment. Everything fell into place nicely, which made Peggy wonder if something bad was going to happen.

"This steak is so good." He cut another piece. "How's yours, Peg?"

"Very good. We might have to take your mom here sometime. She probably likes steak." Peggy giggled. "Who doesn't like steak?"

Jake pulled out his cell phone and gestured to the waiter to take their picture. Jake sat closer to Peggy, and as the waiter was about to take the picture, Jake said, "Wait! There's something missing." Peggy looked at him and didn't understand what he meant.

He pulled out the ring from his pocket and showed Peggy. "Will you marry me?"

"Yes! I'll marry you," she said without hesitation.

Jake put the ring on her finger. It was a thin gold band with three inlaid diamonds. "I didn't think you wanted a huge diamond sticking out."

"You're right. I love this one." She kissed him. "Yes, yes, yes, I'll marry you."

Suddenly realizing that the waiter was still there, they posed for the camera. Jake held Peggy's hand to show off her ring, and they both smiled.

"Sir, I've been taking pictures since you asked the question. I hope you don't mind."

"Not at all. Thank you for doing that." The waiter handed Jake his phone, then left to wait on another table.

CHAPTER THIRTY

Peggy couldn't stop looking at her ring. It fit perfectly, and would accent the gold band she usually wore around her neck, but tonight, she'd bought jewelry for their special date tonight and took her chain and ring off.

"I think this calls for dessert," said Peggy.

"I think so, too." He gestured to the waiter and told him to box up two pieces of cheesecake and asked for the check.

Peggy wondered if they were going home to share their dessert with Pam. She would much rather eat it now so she could prolong her time alone with Jake. Jake put the money in the leather folder, and stood. He took Peggy's hand and put it under his arm, and with his other hand took the bag with the cheesecake.

Instead of going out the door, he led her through the lobby of the hotel and stopped at the desk. "I have reservations for my wife and I, Jake and Peggy Farms."

Peggy couldn't help but smile. What a lovely way to spend an evening with the man she loved. "Did you two just get back from a wedding?"

"No, we were on a date."

"How nice. Married couples don't go on dates. At least not the ones I know."

Jake smiled at her. "It's a necessity." He took the card key and escorted Peggy to their room.

"This is nice, Jake. What about your mom? Won't she be waiting for us?"

"I mentioned we might stay in town. I don't think she'll care. She likes you."

He walked to the desk where the wine was chilling, just like he asked when he called for reservations. He poured the wine into two long-stemmed glasses sitting by the ice bucket. Peggy hung up her shawl.

"Hey, what do we use for pajamas?" She took a sip of her wine.

"I never thought of that. I guess we don't wear any."

They sat in the two comfortable chairs and put their glasses on the table between them. "Now would be a good time to pick our wedding date," said Jake.

"Let's get married in March. Hopefully, winter will be over, and spring will have started. Do you have a date picked out?"

"Nope. I'll pick the same day as you do, my dear."

"Okay then, let's get married on March thirtieth. I was thinking about that date, so I know it's on a Saturday."

"Now that we have that figured out, we should get ready for bed, don't you think?" asked Jake.

Jake stood and took off his jacket. He loosened his tie and lifted it over his head. He started unbuttoning his shirt when Peggy stood in front of him and slowly unbuttoned it for him. She rubbed her hands on his bare chest until his nipples swelled on his firm chest. She unzipped his trousers and let them fall to the floor. Her hands went inside his briefs, and his senses went wild.

Jake put his face in her hair and took in her scent. Her hands were doing things to him that made him weak. He reached behind her and unzipped her dress. He slid it off her shoulder and moved it down her body. He was surprised when she wore nothing underneath.

"You're driving me crazy, Babe."

"My goal in life."

He took off his briefs, shoes and socks, while she stepped out of her dress and took off her sandals. Jake pulled her close to him and kissed her lips, her shoulders, her breasts, her navel, and went lower but realized the lust was so overpowering he had to have her. Now!

He moved her back, and they fell on the bed. He was kissing her all over her body with an urgency that was driving him wild. They embraced and rolled over so Jake could get on top of her.

She let out a groan. The more he immersed himself into her, the harder it was to hold out. Her back arched. She held Jake's hands, and he nuzzled into her body. Several more drives, and they orgasmed together.

Hot sweet fluid was exchanged between them. Jake was breathing so heavily he had to move off Peggy and just breathe, get the air back into his lungs. He put his arm around her, and he waited until his breathing was normal again so he could tell Peggy how much he loved her.

With much trouble, Jake said, "You leave me breathless, Babe." He turned on his side and kissed her cheek. "I love you so much, Peggy."

"I love you, too, Jake." She put her arm around him and held him close to her. "I think we should get back on the bed."

"I thought we were in bed." Jake smile at her. "You wild thing."

After several attempts, they got up and crawled into bed. "Everything aches," said Peggy. "But it's a good ache."

"I hope you didn't get hurt falling off the bed." She did, but she didn't want to say anything, but decided telling the truth was better.

"I think I did." She smiled at him. "It's my arm, but I think it will be better in the morning." Peggy felt the warmth from his body and was content just lying there. "Do we need to get back tonight? Or can we stay until morning?"

"Mom can take the car to the library in the morning, or her bike. She knows how to make breakfast, and she's old enough to spend the night by herself." He rubbed his chin. "So I would say no, we don't have to go home tonight."

"Ah! Wonderful." Jake was massaging her arm. "That feels good, but it's the wrong arm."

They lay on their back and laughed. When the laughing was over, Jake was on top of her, kissing her face. "Again, my love."

They made love again. This time staying on the bed. It was slow and sensual, not as urgent as before. Jake loved Peggy so much. He had hoped he could tell their children that their parents went on a blind date and had such a good time they started dating and fell in love. Instead, if he told the truth, he would tell them they met at a rape trial after their dad witnessed a judge getting shot and didn't do anything about it.

Jake would change that this week. He would take care of it so he could stop thinking about it and move on with his life with Peggy.

He smiled in the dark and realized it didn't matter how they met. It didn't matter about anything right at that moment. It only mattered that they were together and that he would never get enough of her. Of her conversation, her company, her humor, her body. He would never tire of her.

Sleep came, and when dark changed to light, they didn't notice the difference. Back at Jake's house, Pam was finishing breakfast, wondered where the kids were, and hoped they were having fun. She could figure out what they were doing, but she chose to think they were just having a good time in the city. She got ready for work, and since the sun was already shining, she decided to take her bike. *Maybe Jake will call me at the library since there is no phone at home,* she thought.

Jake woke up next to Peggy. Her eyes were open. "Good morning, Peggy."

"Good morning, Jake."

"Let's get dressed and go down for breakfast."

"I love that idea," said Peggy.

CHAPTER THIRTY-ONE

P AM *WAS* WORRIED, although deep down she knew they were okay and just wanted to get away by themselves. She was nervous staying at the house by herself. Lots of flashbacks from her husband came into her thoughts. She thought he was coming after her, and every little noise made her jump.

She looked around for a fan, and when she found one in the basement, she set it up in her room and turned it on. It masked most of the noises, and she was able to fall asleep. The only thing she remembered was the alarm going off in the morning.

She rode her bike that morning because the weather was supposed to be nice and sunny. After lunch it started to pour down rain, and she hoped she didn't have to bike home in the storm. The afternoon was busy for Pam with putting returns back on the shelf, and finishing up several projects that Sue had her doing.

Four o'clock came quickly, and Pam dreaded the ride home. It was raining in spurts now. She went in the back, got her backpack from her locker, put it on, and reluctantly walked outside. Luckily, the rain had briefly stopped.

Pam unlocked her bike from the rack, and when someone touched her on the shoulder, she jumped. "Mom, I'll give you a ride home."

"Jake!" She gave him a hug. "It's so good to see you." They heard thunder in the distance.

"We saw the other car in the garage and decided to come and pick you up. Come on, let's get your bike in the car."

"Peggy has dinner all made. She made Adeline's meatloaf."

"Oh, Adeline came to the library today. She wanted to know how your date went last night." Pam watched while Jake lifted her bike into the back of the car. "I didn't know what to tell her, so I said she'd have to come over later tonight and find out for herself. I hope you'd be home by then."

Jake put his arm around his mom. "I know I should've called you, Mom. But we just got caught up in the moment, and it seemed like nothing else mattered. We'll have to get you a cell phone."

"You love Peggy, don't you?"

"Yes, I do, very much."

"You didn't date in high school. I wondered if you'd find someone." The rain started. "We'd better get in the car."

Peggy had the table set and was just putting the hot food on the table when Jake and Pam walked through the door. "Talk about service," said Pam. "Let me wash up first and I'll be ready to eat."

Pam said grace before they ate. "It's nice to get home from work and eat. What's even nicer is getting home from work and not having to go to work again."

"Those days are over, Mom. You really didn't have to get a job at all, you know."

"I feel like I'm contributing something. I'll pay you rent every month. I know your house is paid off, but you can use it for utilities."

Jake looked at Peggy, then back at his mom. "Mom, no, I won't take your money. You spent all your money on me for eighteen years. Now it's my turn to help you out."

"That argument would fly, except you don't have a job and neither does Peggy. You just bought two new cars that Arnie and Adeline had to sign for. I'm not sure how you'll be making payments, but that's where I'll be helping."

He had to accept her money or tell her how they made *their* money. She might just accept what Peggy and he were doing now, but he wasn't willing to tell her right now.

"Okay, Mom. We'll work something out."

Pam smiled. "I hoped you'd see things my way. It's probably a first." She laughed and Jake gave her shoulder a squeeze. "Now tell me about your date."

Peggy spoke first. "Your son asked me to marry him." She held out her hand so Pam could see her ring.

Pam took her hand and touched the band of gold. "It's beautiful, Peggy." She let go of her hand and looked at Jake. "You picked out a beautiful ring. I didn't know you had such good taste."

Peggy looked at her ring and loved the way it looked on her finger. She was anxious to have the other gold band right next to it. "Oh, we have set a date. It's going to be March thirtieth."

"I'm happy for you both." Her son couldn't have found her at a better time, a time when he found a woman he loved so deeply that he was going to marry her. She was lucky, she decided, *so lucky* not to have missed a major event in her son's life.

Adeline and Arnie came over an hour later. They all sat around the kitchen table and ate Adeline's Oreo pudding dessert while Jake told them about their date. Peggy showed Adeline her ring, and when she showed Arnie, he said he'd already seen it.

Adeline slapped Arnie on the arm. "Why didn't you let me see it, too?"

Arnie shrugged. "It's a guy thing. Only guys get to see the ring before it's presented."

"I never heard of such a thing before," said Adeline.

They stayed for another hour. Adeline was relieved she had some time before the dress needed to be ready. She'd read on the Internet where she could sew beads on the dress. If there was enough time, she would start her bead project.

Pam went to bed that night without worry, content that her son was home.

CHAPTER THIRTY-TWO

JAKE COULDN'T SLEEP. He didn't want to wake Peggy or his mother by walking around the house, so he quietly went outside to the deck with his blanket. He wrapped the blanket around him and sat on one of the deck chairs. He rocked while contemplating what he would do next.

Peggy was going to marry him. They set a date. He found his mother, loved his future in-laws, and had Arnie and Adeline as good friends. Why was he restless? But he knew why. It was because so much good had happened in his life that he now had to straighten out his past. It had to be done before the wedding.

He formed a plan in his mind, and with the conviction that he would set his past right starting in the morning, Jake fell asleep, content for the first time in a long time.

80C3

Jake and Peggy flew to Minneapolis. The one thing they *did* count on was Jake getting arrested. He would give his testimony. He had written down what had happened on the plane ride home on that disturbing day in Minneapolis. He was thorough and didn't leave out any details to his knowledge.

They checked in to the Whitney Hotel, and in the morning, they would both walk to the Minneapolis police station on Fifth Street. There was a phone number to call the tip line about a crime, and Peggy thought Jake should do that first, but Jake thought he was being a coward long enough. He needed to face it head-on and hoped the guilt that was eating away at him would subside once he confessed.

That night, they ordered room service. While they ate dinner, Jake read the notes he had written of the incident. As he read the account, he envisioned himself there with the judge. Jake didn't change anything. He read it through several more times.

Peggy was afraid he would get locked up and never get to go back home again. She knew he needed to do this for his own peace of mind, but wasn't sure if they arrested him how peaceful he would then feel. She remembered her grandmother telling her to pray if she couldn't do anything about an incident, then Peggy bowed her head for a few moments.

Jake had a fitful night's sleep. The second time he was up pacing the room, he walked outside and walked around the hotel a few times. He had no idea if it was safe in Minneapolis during the middle of the night, and he didn't care.

The alarm went off at six, and Jake was already in the shower. Peggy wasn't aware Jake had been up most of the night. The bathroom door opened.

"Hey, Babe." He was dressed and didn't feel well. "I'm going to skip breakfast."

Peggy went to him and put her arms around him. "When do you want to go?"

"As soon as you're ready. I hate not knowing what's going to happen."

"I'll hurry." Peggy took her clothes out of her suitcase and went to the bathroom to take a quick shower.

༄༅

"I would like to talk to someone about being a witness."

Hearing this before, the officer asked the usual question, "A witness to what?"

"Judge Klein's shooting."

For the first time, the officer looked up. "Judge *Howard* Klein?"

"Yes."

"Okay, sit over there and someone will be with you right away." Before they got a chance to sit down, the officer was on the phone. "Yeah, hurry. I think you'll be interested in what just walked in." He hung up the phone.

An officer walked into the waiting area. "I need to check your backpacks. It's routine."

Peggy and Jake let him go through them, and when he was satisfied, he headed back to the desk.

&OCR3

"I won't say anything unless my friend can stay with me," said Jake.

"Is she also a witness?"

"No, but she's staying."

"That's fine as long as she doesn't interfere with your testimony."

"She won't." Jake took his backpack. "I need my notes." Jake took out his notes and set them on the rickety table. "What do you want me to do now?"

"Just tell me what you know, and trust me, you don't want to be wasting my time. There are certain things about a case that are not released to the public, so I'll know if you're lying."

There were seconds of silence, then Jake started reading. The officer could hardly control his excitement as Jake read through his notes. There were answers to questions in his testimony that baffled the department when the shooting occurred. He wanted to stop Jake and ask questions, but he let him continue until he was done. There were times when Jake stopped reading, took Peggy's hand for support, then continued.

"That's all I have. Now what happens?" He knew it would be a matter of minutes before the handcuffs were put on and he'd be led to a cell. The scenario had gone through his mind a hundred times before he'd come back to Minneapolis. Was he ready though to be locked up for a crime he didn't commit? Would he be considered an accessory?

"Sit tight. I'll be right back." The officer took the recorder, left the room, and walked down the hall. "Hey, Joe, remember when we thought the shooter brought in the phone and laid it next to Judge Klein? You need to hear this." He turned on the recorder, and his partner listened intently.

The recorder stopped. "Well, crap, Roy. That clears up all our questions. Do you think he did the shooting?" asked Joe.

"Watching him, his body language while he read his notes, holding his girlfriend's hand, his nervousness, I don't think he did the shooting. But what do we do with him?"

"I want to question him. Did you ask him any questions?"

"No," said Roy. "As soon as he was done reading his notes, I brought the recorder in here."

"Okay, this is how we'll play it." They discussed how they were going to question him, but the girlfriend had to watch from the observation room. They wanted him alone.

‘’

"Why can't Peggy be here with me?"

"She's in the next room and not going anywhere. All our questions are for you right now," said Joe. He watched Jake, his eyes, his hands, his body language.

"You will *not* be asking Peggy any questions. She's here to support *me* and wasn't there with me at the judge's house."

"We'll see about that. Now answer my questions. Why were you at the judge's house again?" asked Joe.

"To interview him about Luke Ames' trial because I heard he might possibly get Ames off."

"Why would that concern you?"

"Because . . ." *This was going to be harder than I thought.* "Ah, because he seemed to be covering for people who were guilty, and I wanted to find out his reasoning."

"If that were the case, do you think he would've told you if he was shady and who he was protecting?"

"Not openly." Jake shifted in his chair. "I was hoping as arrogant as he is, he would've said something indirectly to prove my point."

"Why didn't you call the police and stay at the house if you weren't guilty?"

"I was scared. I was afraid I would get accused of the attempted murder and be locked up."

"And you're not afraid of being locked up months later?"

"Yes, I am afraid of that, but I needed to come in and confess."

Roy gestured to Joe. "Let's step out a minute."

⍋⍡

"We need fingerprints. The shooter touched the door frame when he came in the house. We weren't able to match them in the database. There was dirt on the judge's front yard. He was reseeding. We got . . ."

"Oh, yeah," said Joe. "I forgot about the shoe impression. So we need an outline of his shoe. Even though it might not be the shoes he was wearing that day, we can tell what shoe size he wears and if the size matches."

"What if he won't let us get fingerprints and a shoe impression?" asked Roy.

"Then in my book," said Joe, "he's guilty, and he wasted his time coming back here if he thought he'd be let go."

"Let's send in Judy to get the prints and the shoe impression." Roy looked toward the observation room. "What about the girlfriend? She seems broken up by his testimony. I wonder if she's the shooter, and he's trying to protect her."

Joe was good at what he did. He was an honest cop and could question people without them thinking he was forcing them to confess if they were innocent. If this woman had a role in the attempt to kill Judge Klein, then Joe would find out by asking the right questions.

"Well, it's either both Jake and his girlfriend who attempted murder on the judge, or there truly was someone else. Let's let Jake sit and stew. While you question the girl, I'll tell Julie what we need," said Roy.

೮೦೧೮

Before Julie attempted to get Jake's fingerprints and shoe impression, she took Peggy to another room where she could be questioned.

Joe walked into the room and looked at her with cop's eyes, observing her leg bouncing under the table, while she was rubbing her right hand. He noticed one thing for sure. She held eye contact with him from the second he walked into the room.

He sat across from her. "I'm going to record this with your permission."

"You have my permission."

Joe noticed her voice was firm and confident. She stopped rubbing her hand, and from the stillness of the floor, she'd stopped bouncing her leg in nervous movements.

Joe asked her what she was doing the afternoon of the shooting, and she answered without hesitation. "I did landscaping for people. On that day of the week, I was at the Jeffries' home putting in a pond for them. I had my radio on outside, and there was a newscast interruption about Judge Klein being shot."

"How did you get messed up with this Jake guy? If you were gardening, how did you get hooked up with the guy that was at the scene of the crime?"

"First, let me say, I did not have anything to do with the judge. I've gone to trials and sat in on them before. After I heard the newscast, I wondered if Luke Ames was going to be tried, or wait until Judge Klein recovered, if he did recover."

"That still doesn't explain how you met up with Jake."

"Once you allow me to finish, you'll see just how it explains it."

"Okay, keep going."

"There was this guy in the courtroom. I sat in the row ahead of him, and when there was a break for lunch, we talked and decided to eat lunch together. We've been together ever since."

"Did he tell you why he was at the trial?"

"No. Not at first."

"What did you do when he did tell you?"

"I was shocked, and wanted him to confess about being a witness. I knew he was struggling with it, and scared, so I didn't pressure him. But now we're here so he can tell you what he knows."

Joe turned off the recorder. "I'll take this to Roy so he can listen to it, and he might have some more questions."

"Where's Jake? I told him I wouldn't leave his side when we came here. I want to be with him now."

"Wait here. I'll see what I can do."

Joe walked out of the room with mixed emotions. He was certain the girlfriend didn't have anything to do with it, and if she didn't, then they weren't any closer to closing the case, unless Jake did it, but Joe was becoming very doubtful these two could shoot someone.

ॐ

Julie sent the fingerprints and shoe impressions to be processed. She noticed how willing Jake was when she explained to him what she needed. He looked like a good clean-cut kid. He was probably just at the wrong place at the wrong time and wanted to tell his side of the story.

Julie had seen many criminals come and go through the station, and she could usually pick them out, but Jake didn't look like a criminal. Luckily though, they had to go through the due process of the law, because she knew her opinion didn't count.

CHAPTER THIRTY-THREE

J AKE AND PEGGY were separated for another two hours. The results of the fingerprints and shoe impressions weren't back yet. Joe wanted to make sure that if they did match, they hadn't let them leave the station. He wanted this case closed, but had to be careful he wasn't accusing innocent people just to get his name in the paper. And it wasn't about being the hero in closing the case, it was about justice, and to put innocent people behind bars was not justice in his book.

"Joe, the lab wants you to come down," said Julie.

"Okay," he said hesitantly. "I don't know what to hope for anymore. I just want this case closed. Call Roy and tell him I want him in the lab with me."

Joe got up from his desk and slowly walked down the stairs while he was going over Jake's testimony in his head. If he wasn't the shooter . . . *how did I miss it?* He would wait for the results, then he would have more questions for Jake.

Joe's phone rang. "Joe, Roy is on his way down," said Julie.

He heard footsteps running down the stairs. "Don't start without me."

"Geez, Roy. Do you have to be such a show-off?" Roy laughed.

Joe didn't feel like laughing. His bones were weary, and he felt if he fell asleep, he could sleep for days.

"I ran this guy's fingerprints," said the lab tech. "They don't match any of the prints we got from the judge's house. The shoe impression is too big. The guy's shoe at the house is two sizes smaller. I would have my doubts if Jake's foot was smaller, he could always wear bigger shoes, but his feet are too big to start with." The lab tech switched to another set of results. "This we can't use, but Julie gave me the water glass the woman used."

"You can't do that." Joe wanted everything to be above board so if they found the shooter, they wouldn't get let go on a technicality. "I don't want to know what you found."

"Hey, wait a minute. I already know we can't use it. Her results don't match either. You'll want to ask her for her prints so we can clear her the legal way."

Joe let out a sigh. "I'll tell Julie to get her prints." He looked at Roy. "I need to talk to you upstairs." He thanked the lab tech and walked back up the stairs with Roy.

"Remember when Jake was reading his testimony and he mentioned this guy named Norman? I'd forgotten all about him, and was just assuming Jake was the guilty one. I need more information on Norman. Do we allow his girlfriend back in with him?"

"It wouldn't hurt. She didn't distract him at all the first time. I think we've kept them apart long enough."

∞∞

"I need to know more about Norman."

Jake took Peggy's hand, then told Joe and Roy everything he knew about Norman. The cities Norman was in, and the names of the people Norman killed. Roy was writing as fast as he could. Even though it was all being recorded, he slipped out of the room and told Julie to research the names on the list. Then he went back in the interview room.

"Why were you in the same cities as Norman?"

"We were after the same criminal. Only I had no interest in killing them, just stopping them."

Thirty minutes later, there was a knock on the door. Julie handed Roy printouts, then shut the door. He sat down and looked through them.

While he studied them, there was silence in the room. Several minutes passed.

"He's telling the truth, Joe." He looked at Jake. "The names match up with every city."

"Which could mean a few things: You were in on the killings because you set them up for Norman. I can't really see why you'd be in the same city at the same time, not once, but five or six times."

Jake wondered if he should reveal his contact. Then they would know he wasn't acting on his own. He was in these cities trying to get justice, but how much would they believe him. He wanted to find out. If he told the truth, he thought he'd be better off than leaving something out.

"I wanted to help people. All those names, from reading articles after their murders, you know they were doing something they weren't supposed to be doing. They were causing harm to others, in some cases, both physically and mentally. I did research before I went to these cities, tried to find out who the victims were, and tried to help them.

"You can contact the victims in all the crimes that the murdered people were a part of and find out that I helped them. I have a list, but it's at home." He shifted in his chair to try and get comfortable. "I wanted to help them, so I did."

Peggy sensed Jake was tired. They hadn't eaten all day, and now it was early evening. There were dark circles under his bloodshot eyes, and the hand Peggy was holding was cold.

"Could we get some hot coffee?" asked Peggy. "It would be nice to eat something, too."

"Yeah, I guess you've been here awhile." Roy walked to the door. "I'll tell Julie to order sandwiches. I'll be right back."

"I'm going to do some research on the information you gave us and be back when dinner arrives." Joe walked out of the room and made sure he shut and locked it. Then decided to unlock the door.

"Jake, how are you holding up?"

"I'm tired and hungry. I'm freezing, too."

Peggy pulled out a sweatshirt from her backpack and handed it to Jake. He put it on and rubbed his arms so he'd warm up. Julie brought in two cups of hot coffee with cream and sugar on a tray.

"The sandwiches should be here soon. Is there anything else I can get for you?"

"We need a bathroom break."

Since they seemed harmless, and Julie felt they weren't guilty of any crime, she took a chance and let them go down the hall and use the restrooms. She did stay close though to make sure they didn't make a break for it. She'd be in trouble if that happened. She hoped Roy and Joe would let them go, but she knew there was a process they had to follow.

Once they were finished, Julie escorted them back into the room and shut the door behind her. She looked for Joe in his office, and he was behind his computer deep in thought.

"When are you going to let them go?"

"I don't know yet."

"You know they're not guilty. Just let them go."

"How do you know they're not guilty?"

"Because the prints don't match and the shoe print doesn't match. So that means someone else was there. Probably this Norman guy. Sure, he gave you all the important information, but he helped the victims, and he looks like a guy who helps people, not hurts them."

"I know."

"What! If you know, why are you holding them?"

"I have a few more questions."

She threw up her hands and went back to her desk and waited for the food delivery.

෨෬

Julie brought in the food and bottled water. They looked tired. They were holding hands, and Peggy had her head on Jake's shoulder. She wasn't sure what other questions Joe could ask of them, but she wished he would hurry up and ask so they could leave and get some well-deserved rest.

"Is there anything you'd like to drink besides water?"

"Water is fine," answered Jake.

"If you need anything, knock on the door. I guess Joe has a few more questions for you."

When Julie left, Jake said, "I've thought about what else they could possibly ask us, but haven't come up with anything."

"Unless they want more about Norman."

When they were done with their sandwiches, a man came in and introduced himself. "My name is Clark." He had a sketching pad and several pencils. "I want you to describe to me the person you saw with the gun."

Joe came in the room. "Peggy, you'll have to come with me."

Peggy did not argue or complain. She was just plain tired and wanted to leave, but didn't want to make it harder for Jake. So she followed Joe to the lounge.

Back in the interview room, Jake got his notes back out of his backpack. He read the description through that he had first and then gave Clark small parts of the information so he could sketch an image of Norman.

Clark asked a lot of questions that proved to be helpful in getting some identifiable marks that Jake remembered when prompted, but didn't remember at the time.

The air outside was cooling, and darkness was descending upon Minneapolis. The traffic lessened, but was more prominent toward the Nicollet Mall, with Orchestra Hall, the Orpheum Theater, and First Avenue.

Peggy sat in the lounge and drank a cup of coffee. She hoped Jake was doing okay. She thought of what it would be like if he went to jail, and felt an emptiness. Jake, she thought, was probably feeling more pain since he would be the one locked up.

Peggy tried not to think about that and thought about the good times they'd already had. She walked over to the couch and lay down. It would be for a few minutes, just enough to ease the stinging in her eyes. Two hours later, Julie woke her and told her she could join Jake.

ՖՈՋ

"Peggy." Jake got up when she walked in the room and wrapped his arms around her. "You look rested. I hope you got some sleep." He kissed her briefly, not knowing if they were being observed. "I feel good about the sketch. It took a while, but I feel the picture that resulted is a good one of Norman."

"Are they going to let you go?"

"I don't know, Peg. I didn't think to ask. I would think they'd either have to arrest me or let me go. I'm hoping they let me go"

There was a knock, and Joe walked in. "We are going to get the sketch out to the areas you mentioned where Norman was to see if anyone recognizes him. It's late. You must be tired. I'm going to let you go for now. You get back here in the morning because overnight, I'll probably think of more questions that I didn't ask you. If you show up on your own, I won't have to look for you and arrest you. You've been a great help so far. We just need to see this to the end."

"I can go?"

"Yes, but tell Julie before you leave where you're staying, and your phone number. We also need your home address. She'll ask you all sorts of questions. Just make sure you answer them before you leave."

⟡⟡⟡

"Joe, get in here." Roy waited until he came into his office.

"Hey, I want to go home. It's been a long night."

"So do I, but there's eight messages on my phone."

"Didn't we put your phone number on the flyers and newscast?"

"Yep. Now people are calling in to say they recognize this Norman guy."

Joe sat down. "Okay, play them *all* back."

Joe wrote notes during each of the messages and didn't say anything until the last one played back. "Go back and play the third message."

"I knew you would say that. I had to listen to it several times myself."

Once it had played back three times, Joe stood. "I have a few phone calls to make. So much for going home."

"You can't make calls this time of night."

"Yes, I can. She wouldn't have left that message if she didn't want to be called back."

"Okay, but I'm listening in while you make the call."

They went to Joe's desk, and Joe punched in the numbers from the log Roy printed of the calls. Joe waited patiently while the phone rang. "Hello, is this the police?"

"Yes, it's Lieutenant Stacey, call me Joe."

"I saw the guy in the sketch. I've seen him before."

"Can my partner and I come over and get your statement?"

"Now?"

"Yes, now."

"I guess the sooner, the better." Gladys gave the lieutenant her address, then put on a pot of coffee.

𝕏𝕏𝕏

"Sit down, Joe, and who's with you?"

"This is Roy." She shook hands with Roy.

"I'll bring out some coffee then we can get started."

"Ma'am, I need your permission to tape your account of the situation."

"No problem." She continued to the kitchen.

Joe and Roy sat on a worn brown velvet couch. The red rug underneath the coffee table looked brand new, but with no foot traffic, it would stay that way. There were two plush brown plaid chairs on the other side of the couch in the quaint living room. There was a big chest between the chairs.

Joe set up the recorder on the coffee table on top of one of the many books.

"She must like romance novels," said Roy to no one in particular.

Gladys came out with three cups of coffee on a tray with a pitcher of cream and a sugar bowl. When the coffee was handed out and made how they liked it, Joe started with the questions.

"Tell us when you saw this person," said Joe as he tapped the picture on the coffee table.

"It was the day Judge Klein was shot." She looked back at the picture. "I was outside sitting on the front step, thinking about Mrs. Klein. She put up with so much. There were times when the judge would yell at her in the front yard . . . oh I'd better stick to the story."

"Yes, stick to the story, and when you are done, if you have to add anything, we'll talk about it then."

"I was sitting outside, and I saw this guy walking down the block. He parked two houses down, walked to the judge's house, and knocked. The judge opened the door right away. They said a few words, then they shook hands. The judge stood back from the door and let this guy in.

"The guy had a pad of paper with him. He wore jeans and a blue shirt. I remember stuff like that."

"What happened next?" asked Roy.

"Thirty minutes later, a guy in a suit, carrying a briefcase, came walking down the sidewalk very confident looking. I thought it was strange when he knocked on the door. The judge never gets any company. This guy leans on the door and looks in the peephole of the door. Not that he could see anything anyways, so I thought it was strange he did that."

"Show me how he leaned on the door."

Gladys got up and walked to the door. She put her right hand on the door and leaned into it. "Just like this."

"Good. Sit down and explain what you just did so we can record it."

Gladys explained again, then went on with her story. "When the judge came to the door this time, the porch light went on. It was getting dark, and he didn't step aside to let him in. He backed away from the entrance, and this guy went in and slammed the door.

"I decided to go in the house in case there was trouble. As I walked into my house, I heard the gun shot, then I quickly got in and locked the door behind me." She looked again at the picture. "I looked out the window when he left, and he walked back down the street the way he came. I don't know where he parked his car. The other guy's car was parked down the block, and that was the only car on the street.

"We usually don't park on the street around here. We all have three-car garages."

"The guy that left is the guy in the picture, right?"

"That's right."

"Roy, do you have a field kit?"

"In my trunk."

"Get it out and head over to the judge's house. Dust the front door for prints. They may have dusted them before, but make sure you dust the whole damn door."

Roy left. "When did the other guy leave?"

"I'm not really sure. I was wondering what I should do, should I call the police. Then before I could make a decision, I heard the sirens. I looked down the block and the other guy's car was gone."

"Why didn't you give the police the information you gave me?"

"Because I don't like the judge, and I was kind of glad he got shot."

Joe didn't bother telling her that obstruction of justice was a crime. "Gladys, you've been very helpful." He shut off the recorder. "If I have any more questions, I'll call you."

"And if I think of something, I'll call you."

CHAPTER THIRTY-FOUR

I T WAS A hard winter that year. The snow was never ending. There were over forty inches, and there was a week where the temperatures never got above zero degrees. Normally, without a car, Jake never had to worry about shoveling his driveway. He'd shovel his sidewalk out to the street when Arnie would come and pick him up for dinner.

Now Peggy was a real trooper shoveling the driveway in time for Pam to go to work in the morning. Jake tried to do it, but she loved being outside doing the work. Jake checked his answering service and was happy there was no work.

Jake and Peggy, when it was bad weather, stayed in their pajamas all day, drank coffee, and made love. Occasionally, they would meet Pam for lunch and Adeline would join them. Pam's working at the library was good for Adeline so she could keep up on all the changes and what was happening with the patrons.

They were also glad that the trip to Minneapolis was behind them, but Jake and Peggy still wondered about what happened after they left Minneapolis. They showed up that next morning, and after they were asked a few more questions about Norman, they were able to go home.

Paula and Noah came as often as they could when the weather was decent. Minnesota was having bad weather of its own. When it wasn't snowing there, it would be in Iowa. So when they did make it to visit their daughter, they stayed for two weeks at a time. Besides, they had a wedding to plan.

The pink tennis shoes were still worn whenever they went into the city for wedding planning. Most times though, they just wore them at Jake's house when they were making lists, making invitations, and eating wedding planning snacks, as they called them.

೮೮೮

"Max, something came in this morning. It's in Charleston. Our source has targeted a couple who is selling anything and everything, real, or not. All bad of course. Bad real estate, bad investments. There is a big convention where they are to get an award."

"You want these people stopped?" asked Max.

"I'm hoping Jake will have a plan like last time." He stood and paced around the office. "The people who are the victims are getting hit hard, especially in this economy. A single mom had all her savings taken, had to sell her house, and move her three kids to a bad part of town." He sat down and shook his head. "That's not right. This family is now poor, all because the mom wanted to get ahead to provide for her children. Because of all these bad investments, this couple is living high off the hog, living as if nothing is wrong with what they're doing."

"What do you want to happen during this convention?"

"I want it to happen before the convention if possible, so the award doesn't get presented."

"When is this convention?"

"March thirtieth."

Max pointed to the TV John had in his office. "News from Minneapolis."

"Incredible," said John after the newscast.

೮೮೮

"Jake, look at this. Come here and read this."

Jake walked over to Peggy sitting behind the computer.

Breaking news in the Judge Klein case. An anonymous witness testified against a mysterious man who shot Judge Klein. Then was confirmed by a second witness. Norman Williams was identified and arrested in his home at six p.m. today. Newspaper articles were found of other killings where Williams was sighted by witnesses when police searched his home.

Williams has pleaded guilty to all killings and was quite smug about it . . .

Jake sat down. Relieved that justice was finally done. "Peg, I feel like a weight has been lifted."

૦૩૦૩

The weather improved the first part of March. The snow had melted with temperatures in the thirties, and the roads were cleared of snow. No more trying to see over the high snow banks at intersections to avoid being hit by a car. Luckily, neither Jake nor anyone else in the family had such accidents.

"Peggy, a call came in."

"It's not going to interfere with the wedding, is it?"

Jake explained to her what was happening, and then told Peggy the date of the award ceremony.

"Then we have to stop the ceremony before our wedding." Peggy went into the living room where Jake had set up her computer in a permanent space where she didn't have to put it away after each use.

"What are you looking for?" asked Jake.

"I want to check out where this couple lives and what their business name is. Many businesses have endorsements listed on their site. If this couple does, I'm going to call every one of them and tell them that they don't want to be associated with this couple, and why. Then we find out this poor woman's name, where she is living now and ask her some questions. It would be nice if we could get all her money back for her.

"We'll be traveling before the wedding, maybe even the week of the wedding."

"I know. I don't know what we would tell our parents. Why we had the sudden urge to travel again so close to our wedding," said Peggy, contemplating.

"Yeah, the honeymoon is after the wedding, not before. Although, I'm sure no one would mind."

"I'd hate to leave all the last-minute arrangements for my parents while we are traveling on the East Coast," said Peggy. "We couldn't even tell them what we were doing."

"I know, Babe." He took her hand. "I can leave the contact a message saying we aren't taking this one."

"I thought of that, but I wouldn't be able to sleep thinking about that mom and her three children. It's not fair, and who knows how the crooks have damaged other lives with their fast-talking schemes. No, we are taking it."

"Okay, then we figure things out and make sure it works. We can always call Joyce in on this. She said she'd be willing to help out with anything."

"Do you think she really meant *anything*?" asked Peggy.

"I hope so."

 ⌘

Adeline had the wedding dress all done two weeks before the wedding. The way she was making progress right from the start, she thought she'd be done long ago. What she didn't take into consideration was that the dress was fuller as she knitted down to where the hem was going to be.

Now she started her bead project. She had tiny pearl beads to sew on the bodice. Paula thought it was a great idea and offered to help if Adeline needed any.

Peggy was researching day and night. She would print out articles, names, and places and glue them into a scrapbook. Jake would write down what they needed to do first: the interviews they would conduct, what Joyce's role would be in this, and how to eventually get the couple locked up for a long time.

Jake wrote down the amount he wanted to pay the mother with three children. He would wait and see how many others lost their money and were forced into poverty. He hoped he would also get money from the couple to pay most of these people back. If not all of their money, at least some of it.

It couldn't have come at a worse time, thought Jake. Peggy and everyone are doing so much planning for the wedding, and Peggy won't be able to enjoy it right up to the big day. He just hoped she wouldn't regret it later. He wanted her to be happy, and so far, she was.

The scrapbook was full of research. Jake had lots of notes. Now they had to design a plan. First, they would call Joyce and find out if she was available. The hardest part was getting away and finding the right thing to say to everyone as to why they were leaving. The *why* could be very tricky.

After several more days, Jake explained what they were going to do. "Joyce will fly into Iowa and meet us at the airport. Then we'll fly to Charleston together. Joyce will be staying until the convention. If we do this right, we can bring them down right there at the convention."

"We?" asked Peggy.

"No, we have a wedding, but what we do before will bring them down at the convention."

"Okay," said Peggy. "I trust you. I just don't want them to affect any more lives."

CHAPTER THIRTY-FIVE

UNCLE RICK TRAVELED from Missouri with his son Larry. Penny and Ross, along with relatives and friends from Minnesota, stayed at the Baymont Inn and Suites next to the Ace Hardware store. Penny, Ross, and Larry spent most of their time in the pool.

Chicken, mashed potatoes, corn, salad, buns, pickles, and olives, the standard Legion Club food was served at the groom's dinner. Peggy enjoyed introducing Jake to her friends and relatives. Jake introduced Peggy to his friends and Adeline's friends from Iowa.

Jake wore khaki pants and a tan silk shirt. Peggy wore a long black skirt with a white blouse and star earrings from her date with Jake. Jake held Peggy's hand, except when he was being introduced and doing handshakes. He wanted to keep her close and knew that there was a lot weighing on their minds.

They'd done the work. The only thing left was to wait for the call from Joyce tomorrow. The wedding was at three. The convention started at one.

"Jake, I guess you're sleeping at our house tonight," said Arnie. "Adeline thinks it's bad luck for you to see Peggy before she walks down the aisle."

"Do you think it's bad luck, Arnie?"

"Only because it would be bad luck for me if I didn't talk you into staying with us."

"No problem," said Jake. "I'll go home from here after the party, pack, and head over."

Peggy hugged his arm. "No, I won't let him go."

"Then I'm in the doghouse," said Arnie. "Adeline won't cook for a month, and I'll starve to death."

Jake laughed, knowing Adeline would never do that, at least not for that long. He turned to Peggy and mouthed, "Love you!"

Now Peggy laughed. "Okay, I'll let him go."

The party was over early. The travelers that arrived that day were ready to head back to the hotel, unpack, and relax. Jake had never had a party in his honor before. There were no birthday parties for him as a kid, and when he got older, his mom would make him a cake and give him his present. It seemed, now that he was thinking about it, his dad was never there and was supposedly working, but Jake knew better now.

Everyone wished Jake and Peggy well. Mostly everyone didn't know Jake was dating, let alone getting married. Peggy got the same reaction from her relatives and friends.

What was frequently on their mind was Charleston. They had arrived back home just yesterday. Jake's mom had kept calling to make sure they would get home in time for their own wedding. They assured her they would.

Peggy's parents just didn't understand why they had to travel, travel to someplace where they didn't know anyone, and it was days before their wedding. Paula refused to call Peggy while she was away. If there was a decision to be made, Paula made it and would deal with the consequences when Peggy came back home. Luckily, the decisions that were made were small, and Peggy agreed with them.

Peggy didn't want to get into an argument with her mom before the wedding. She wanted everything to run smoothly. The wedding planning team was the best as far as getting things done, and between all of them, nothing was forgotten.

Adeline thought they could become a team that helped other brides, so their pink tennis shoes would get more use. After all, Adeline thought they still looked good, even though they trudged through the snow with them most of the winter.

Adeline was proud of the work she'd done on Peggy's dress, but now that the day was here, she was a little nervous about it. When she saw Peggy in it, it fit perfectly. The beadwork turned out the way Adeline wanted it, and the rest of the team liked it, too. Once Arnie told her her work was beautiful, and she didn't have anything to worry about, she let it go.

Myra who owned the bakery in town would deliver doughnuts in the morning to Jake's and the Cole's house. She told Arnie that Jake was so good to her that it was the least she could do on his special day.

Jake and Arnie sat in the living room talking about marriage. Arnie did ask Jake, even though Adeline told him it was none of his business, how he was supporting himself without a job. If he needed anything, Arnie would be happy to loan him and Peggy money. Jake assured him that he was fine and didn't need or want anything. He also assured Arnie that he was able to make the car payments so he didn't have to worry about that, either.

"I was hoping you'd default on your payments on that Ford Flex. I sure like that car. If at any time you want to hand that over, I'll be more than happy to take it off your hands."

"Nope. That's the one we like, too." Jake grinned. "But you can always borrow it when you are taking Adeline out for a date. It's got a big backseat."

Arnie laughed and told Jake about the big cars they had when he was growing up. "Then they just kept getting smaller and smaller."

Jake's phone rang. It was his mom. "Jake, I wish you were here. I'd like to talk to you before your big day."

"Hey, Mom. Why don't you wait outside and I'll come and pick you up. I'd like to talk to you, too."

"Okay, I'll head outside."

&)(&

Jake and his mom sat in the restaurant and ordered wine when the waiter came to their table. "Would you like anything to eat?"

"What do you have for dessert?"

"It's late, and we only have one piece of lemon cake left."

"Yeah, bring that."

The waiter left. "I wanted to tell you how proud I am of you, Jake. You are marrying a lovely lady, and I'm sure she'll be a beautiful wife. You two complement each other."

"I think so, too."

"I'm very worried, though, on how you can support her. You aren't working, and you have two new cars and a house to take care of." The waiter poured their wine and left to get their dessert. "Or what am I missing?"

"I would love to tell you, Mom, what's going on, but right now, I just can't. Someday though, Peggy and I will sit down with you and explain everything." He took her hand.

"I will love you no matter what. You know that, don't you?"

"Yeah, I know."

"I figure if you can forgive me for leaving you, I can forgive you for whatever you've done." She looked into her wineglass. "Your father told me we were going on a vacation and that you didn't need to be told. I thought we'd be back in a week or two, so we'd just get in touch with you then.

"We did go to a hotel, and that's where he told me everything. I was glad you were gone so you didn't have to hear how he betrayed us. I was trying to protect you by not trying to find you. Then your father left me for his other wife. I don't even know if we were really married. I don't really care anymore. I'm so sorry how it all happened. I should've just left him and tried to find you."

"Look at it this way. If you found me, I wouldn't have found Peggy, and you wouldn't be living in *Iowa*," Jake said with a grin. "It may have just turned out to be the best solution."

"I think you're right, Jake."

They shared the lemon cake and had another glass of wine. The conversation changed to when both of them went to the zoo in the wintertime and Jake held a big snake. "I was so scared," said Pam. "But you weren't scared at all. When you begged me on the way home to get a snake as a pet, I had to turn you down. I'm scared now just thinking about it."

"I thought it was so cool, but after a week, I didn't want a snake anymore."

"I was so glad when you stopped asking, and I wasn't going to ask you why either." Pam laughed, then turned serious. "I'm so glad you found me, Jake. I love my new life, my new friends." She covered his hand. "Thank you, son."

Jake's eyes were wet. "I'm glad, too, Mom."

"We'd better go. You need your rest. Hey, does Adeline have room for one more guest? I'd like to be there in the morning with you. I know it sounds silly, but I'd like to make up for all the time I wasted listening to your father tell me what's best for me, for us . . ."

Jake took out his phone and called the Coles. Adeline answered. "Adeline, do you have a bed for my mom to sleep in tonight?"

"I sure do," said Adeline, without hesitation.

"Okay, we'll be there soon."

When they arrived at Jake's, he walked Pam to the door in hopes to see Peggy. He asked Paula where she was, and was told she was sleeping. Jake didn't think it was that late, but it was after ten. *Asking to look at her while she was sleeping would've been useless*, he thought.

CHAPTER THIRTY-SIX

P EGGY HAD HER dress in Jake's closet. She was going to use his room to get ready for her wedding. She never once had second thoughts about marrying Jake. She loved him, and was glad this day was finally here.

She'd already showered and was waiting for her hair to dry while she walked around the house in a white terry cloth robe. She answered the door when Myra knocked, and let her put the big box of pastries on the table. Peggy invited her to stay for coffee, but she was headed over to the Cole's with their pastries.

Myra gave Peggy a hug and wished her well. "Jake's a good guy. He'll make you happy." She walked to the door. "I'll see you at the wedding."

"Eat your breakfast and I'll start on your hair," said Paula.

"When's Penny coming?"

"Ah, you know her. Your sister loves sleeping in, and I don't think your wedding will change anything."

Peggy pouted. "I thought she would make an exception today."

To appease her daughter, she said, "You never know. She might be here early."

Noah wandered into the kitchen, took a plate from the cupboard, piled on two pastries, poured himself some coffee and went out on the deck. It was cold, but he needed fresh air. His daughter was getting married, and he wasn't sure he could handle it.

Peggy never really dated in school, and now she meets someone, never tells her dad about it, and the boyfriend comes to the house and asks her dad if it's okay if he marries her. *Too fast, as far as I'm concerned.* He wasn't sure why his wife was okay with it. Even though he gave his blessing, he had this feeling inside that he couldn't explain.

If he looked on the bright side, he would gain a son. He was still amazed at the hole Arnie and Jake put in the wall and built his daughter a beautiful hutch. It had etched glass on the door and was able to hold a twelve-piece setting of dinnerware.

Ah, Noah thought. *I can buy her some dishes.* Next week, he would ask her if she wanted to go shopping. He didn't think they were going on a honeymoon because they took a trip before the wedding. It didn't matter. He had an idea and hoped his daughter wanted to go shopping for dishes.

Another thought that crossed Noah's mind was that neither one of them was working, and yet, Noah was indifferent to it because it appeared to him, no one was breaking down Jake's door to collect on bills not paid. He even, as embarrassed as he was doing it, checked Jake's mail when he offered to bring it in for him. No bill collectors sending late notices. Actually, he'd never seen a bill. Mostly he got advertisements from Moffitt Ford.

He would have to ask after the wedding how they were paying their bills. He wondered if it was really any of his business if bills were getting paid, or if his daughter was happy. *No*, he decided, *it's none my business.*

 ∓∞∓

Adeline wanted to see Peggy in her dress and was trying to think of an excuse to head over to Jake's. Then she decided she didn't need an excuse. Pam and Arnie were there to keep Jake company, so why did they need her, was her reasoning.

"Arnie, I'm headed over to see Peggy." She put on her coat and decided an hour visit would be just right for her to get back home and dress for the wedding and make it to the church on time. "Jake, do you want me to give Peggy any messages?"

"Tell her I love her and can't wait to be her husband."

"Mush!" said Arnie. "She won't want to hear that mush."

"She sure will," said Pam. Adeline nodded in agreement.

"I'm off." She took her purse off the hook and headed out the door.

"Jake, pass me another pastry. With Adeline gone, I can eat two more of these without getting into trouble."

Jake laughed. "I wonder if Peggy would have anything to say to me if I ate four of them."

ഇരുൽ

Penny did wake early and arrived at Jake's before Peggy was out of her robe. Ross hung out with Noah on the deck. Penny took her dress into Jake's room and hung it next to Peggy's dress.

Penny's was wine colored, one of Peggy's favorite colors, and since there was only one bridesmaid, Penny was able to pick out the dress she wanted as long as it was the right color. She chose floor length and strapless which accented her thin frame. The back was low and had a bow at waist level.

She bought low shoes. Penny was like her sister and didn't like her shoes high or her neckline low. Probably something their father told them to avoid if they wanted to be considered ladies.

Penny couldn't believe her sister was getting married. Peggy never dated that much. Penny was dating all the time and never felt like she wanted to marry any of them until Ross came along. But her sister met someone and right away decided she would marry him. It didn't matter to Penny. She was just happy her sister was so happy. And even better was that Penny was able to live in her sister's apartment and she could have her car, too.

Penny had already drunk too much coffee. She put her cup in the dishwasher and wandered back to see if her sister needed any help with anything.

"Penny, how do you like Peggy's hair?"

It was swept up into a French twist. Paula cut bangs and feathered them so they looked elegant with Peggy's new style.

"It's great, Mom! How do you like it?" she asked Peggy.

"I like it a lot. Now what's next?" Peggy looked at the clock. "Are we going to have time for anything else?"

"Makeup is next, but let's get your dress on first," said Paula.

There was a knock at the door. From the deck, Noah told her to just walk in. "Yoo-hoo, is anyone home?" called Adeline when she walked in.

"Come on back," yelled Peggy.

Adeline hurried back in hopes she didn't miss anything. "Oh my, Peggy, you look lovely, and you're not even dressed yet. I was hoping you didn't have your dress on yet."

"We were just starting to do that," said Paula.

Adeline sat on the bed while Paula and Penny helped Peggy with her wedding dress. "It's beautiful, Adeline," said Penny. "What are you doing next year? Maybe you can knit me a dress."

Adeline let out a nervous giggle. She didn't think she would ever knit another dress. But for Peggy's sister, she would. "Let me know and I'll buy the yarn."

The dress was carefully pulled over Peggy's hair and pulled down until everything fit. The beaded bodice gave the dress a feminine look, and with the long flowing skirt, it was stunning. The white color against Peggy's dark hair and features was striking. Adeline couldn't take her eyes off her. "When I was knitting, it was just a dress. With you wearing it, it's more than just a dress. It's . . ."

"Totally awesome," said Penny.

"Yes, what you said," said Adeline, and laughed.

"I'd better get ready," said Penny. "Then you all can help me with my dress."

Adeline took a camera out of her purse and took pictures of Peggy, then of Paula putting on Peggy's makeup. She waited for Penny to get dressed and took some more pictures, then she rushed off to get herself dressed.

ൠ

Jake did not see the bride before the wedding. Pam kept telling herself how lucky she was to be here for her son's wedding. She vowed never to leave Jake again. She saw Uncle Rick in the entrance of the church and went over to say hi. He was nervous when he saw Pam approaching, sure he was going to get reprimanded for telling on her, but there was no need to worry.

"Rick, how are you?"

"I'm fine," Rick said, apprehensively.

She touched his arm. "I just wanted to let you know how happy I am that you told Jake where I worked. I'm living in Iowa now, at his house, and it just so happened that he was going to get married." Her hand fell to her side. "I'm glad you could make it."

"I wouldn't have missed it. I'm not real happy with that brother of mine. What he did is unforgiveable. If I ever see him again, the only thing that would need doing is slapping him around." He noticed the sadness in Pam's eyes and quickly changed the subject. "Can I sit with you?"

"Sure, but I'm walking Jake down the aisle. The ushers can seat you up front." She looked at her watch. "I'd better get going. She looked into his eyes. "It's so good to see you."

Arnie was the best man, and he was hanging out waiting for his turn to go down the aisle. He felt like his own son was getting married, and he was very happy that Jake spent the night at his house. Jake was somewhat distracted, but it was only natural on his wedding day. But Arnie sensed it was something else. He just couldn't pinpoint what it was.

The minister walked to the front of the church and stood looking out over the congregation. Arnie and Penny were waiting at the back for the minister to nod to start the ceremony. "You look nice, Penny. You probably get told this a lot, but you and Peggy could be twins."

"Yeah, I do hear that, and I just say I'm the better looking one."

Arnie laughed. They got the nod from the minister. "You ready, kid, to get this show started?"

Penny answered, "I sure am," and she wrapped her arm around his.

They walked slowly down the aisle. Arnie was proud to have such a good-looking woman on his arm. When they passed Adeline, he gave her a nod and a wink. She smiled at him with tears in her eyes.

Jake and his mother were next to walk down the aisle. When they got to the front, Jake gave her a hug. "I love you, Mom." Tears came to her eyes. She left him at the altar, turned, and joined Uncle Rick in the front pew.

The minister and Jake were now waiting for the bride to meet them at the front. Jake didn't see anyone standing at the end of the aisle. He hoped Peggy didn't get cold feet, but he wasn't concerned about it because he knew she loved him as much as he loved her.

The organist started to play. They were going to get married by the justice of the peace at Ledges Park, but with the flooding, they decided the ceremony in a church would be better, and their families were happy about their decision, too.

He saw Peggy and her parents. The minister gave them a nod, and Noah, Paula, and Peggy walked arm in arm down the aisle.

Jake felt warmth flow through his body. Peggy was so beautiful. He would never have guessed that her dress was knitted, it was so beautiful. He thought of his knitted slippers and almost laughed.

The dress flowed around her body when she walked. She was wearing a teardrop pearl necklace she borrowed from her mother, with earrings to match. The closer they came to where Jake stood, the closer Noah's tears came spilling over.

Jake, finally we'll be husband and wife. I can't wait!

Once at the front, Noah hugged his daughter, then it was Paula's turn.

The minister said, "Who gives the bride away?"

Noah responded, "Her mother and I." Noah helped Paula in the pew, then they sat down.

"Jake and Peggy, are you ready for your big day?"

Jake and Peggy both said yes. The minister was talking to just the two of them, but the congregation could hear. "You haven't known each other long, but when you two came into my office, I knew you were in love. It's been a pleasure talking with you in our sessions. I wish you all the best. It's not just the two of you, although it will be most of the time. You'll have friends and family cheering you on, and when you run into hard times, you'll have the same friends and family to help you through. Never hesitate to ask for help.

"Jake, do you have the rings?"

"Yes." He pulled them out of his pocket, handed Peggy his, and kept hers.

"Jake and Peggy prepared their own ring ceremony," said the minister. "So I will let them take over from here."

Peggy went first. "Jake, this ring signifies my love for you. It's round, so it never ends, and you'll know that my love will never run out." She put the ring on his finger. "Every day my love will get stronger, and I'll be an ever-faithful wife to you." Tears streamed down her face.

"Peggy, I love you with all my heart. This ring complements mine, and we complement each other. We share the same love, the same passion for each other. The ring is gold. Gold is the highest-quality metal, and my love for you will always be the best I have to give." He put Peggy's ring on her finger. "I will always be by your side, loving you, caring for you." He looked at her two rings. "These two rings signify the two of us, never parted. Peggy, I love you."

They turned toward the minister. He was smiling as he said, "I now pronounce you husband and wife."

Peggy and Jake turned around and the organist started playing. "You may kiss the bride."

Jake took her face in his hands and kissed her with a tenderness that brought tears to her eyes. He wiped away one stray tear and took her hand. They walked down the aisle smiling at the congregation.

When they were in the gathering space, Jake's phone vibrated. He looked, and it was Joyce. He looked at his watch. He whispered to Peggy, "I told her to call only if something went wrong."

"Hello, Joyce. Are you okay?"

Adeline's Oreo Cookie Dessert

- 1 - 18 oz pkg Oreo Cookies, Crushed - save 3/4 cup
- 3/4 C melted butter
- 2 - 8 oz Cool whip Containers
- 8 oz Cream Cheese
- 1/4 C powdered sugar
- 1 - 3 1/2 oz box instant Choc pudding mix
- 2 Cups milk
- 1 - 14 oz sweetened Condensed milk

★ Jake likes extra Cookies ★ Arnie likes Vanilla pudding

Directions

Put Crushed Cookies in 9x13 pan
Pour melted butter over Cookies
Mix Cream Cheese, 8 oz Cool whip, &
powdered sugar, spread on top
Mix pudding with milk and
sweetened Condensed milk
     - beat until THICK, spread on top
Spread on 8 oz Cool whip
Sprinkle with saved Cookies

Refrigerate over night for best
     results.
     ↑

Hard to do with unexpected guests